Devil
of Delphi

Books by Jeffrey Siger

Chief Inspector Andreas Kaldis Mysteries
Murder in Mykonos
Assassins of Athens
Target: Tinos
Prey on Patmos: An Aegean Prophecy
Mykonos After Midnight
Sons of Sparta
Devil of Delphi

Devil
of Delphi

A Chief Inspector Andreas Kaldis Mystery

Jeffrey Siger

Poisoned Pen Press

Library of Congress Catalog Card Number: 2014958047

ISBN: 9781464204302   Hardcover
       9781464204326   Trade Paperback

Poisoned Pen Press
6962 E. First Ave., Ste. 103
Scottsdale, AZ 85251
www.poisonedpenpress.com
info@poisonedpenpress.com

Printed in the United States of America

A dedication all her own to my one and only,
Barbara Zilly.

Acknowledgments

Loukas Andritsos; Roz and Mihalis Apostolou; Stellios Boutaris; Antonio Cacace; Beth Deveny; Andreas, Aleca, Nikos, Mihalis, and Anna Fiorentinos; Panagiotis Iordanopoulos; Flora and Yanni Katsaounis; Panos Kelaidis; Lila Lalaounis; Ilias Macropoulos Lalaounis; Joshua Latner; Eleni Liakopoulou; Linda Marshall; Terrence McLaughlin, Karen Siger-McLaughlin, and Rachel Ida McLaughlin; Asteria Papakonstantinoy; Barbara G. Peters and Robert Rosenwald; Frederick and Petros Rakas; Christos Roumeliotis; Alan and Pat Siger; Jonathan, Jennifer, Azriel, and Gavriella Siger; Ed Stackler; Vassilis Tsiligiris; Christos Vlachos; Miranda Xafa; Barbara Zilly; Pete Zrioka.

And, of course, Aikaterini Lalaouni.

"*There are two roads, most distant from each other: the one leading to the honorable house of freedom, the other the house of slavery, which mortals must shun. It is possible to travel the one through manliness and lovely accord; so lead your people to this path. The other they reach through hateful strife and cowardly destruction; so shun it most of all.*"
—Pronouncement of Delphic Oracle to Lycurgus of Sparta, according to Plutarch (46-120 CE)

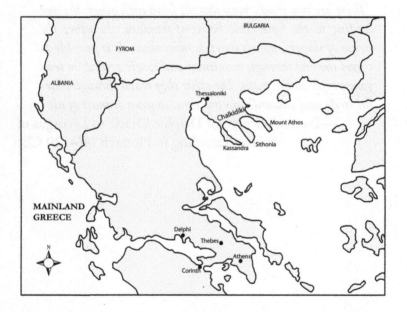

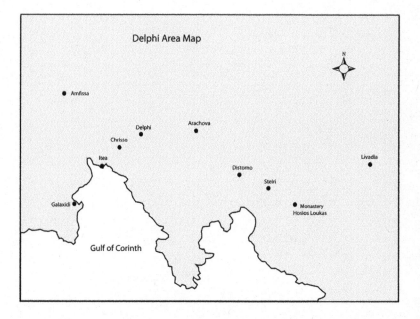

Chapter One

He was born precisely one year after his mother's death. At least that's what the birth certificate read. His father wasn't around to notice the mistake, having vanished immediately after his fateful one-night stand. Nor did the orphanage pick up on the error; they simply treated him as the child of an unidentified itinerant mother, born on the day she died giving birth in one of Athens' worst public clinics.

He learned of the mistake a dozen years ago, slightly shy of what he believed to be his fourteenth birthday. The surprise came in the form of a copy of his birth certificate shown to him just before his lawyer presented it to a court along with a citation to provisions of the Greek Criminal Code absolving a minor under thirteen from any criminal responsibility for his acts. He stood expressionless as a visibly angry judge ranted on and on before ordering him to spend his next five years in programs alongside other minors deemed in need of reformative measures.

But he never spent a moment in confinement for the murders.

◇◇◇

"I don't usually pick up hitchhikers, but I figured anyone out here in the middle of nowhere carrying a puppy in his arms must be local. Sorry, you probably don't understand a word I'm saying."

"I live in the next village."

"You understand English?" said the driver. "Wonderful. I'm new to this part of the world. Just passing through."

The passenger nodded.

"I'm headed back to Athens. Been down to Galaxidi on the Gulf of Corinth for a couple of days. Beautiful harbor, beautiful town, beautiful sea. I think I'll do a quick stop in Delphi. Mythology stuff isn't my thing, but at least I'll be able to tell my friends I saw the place. Ever been there? Of course you have. You live right next to it."

Again the passenger nodded.

"Gorgeous place, Greece, especially now in June. Maybe you can answer a question for me. Everywhere I go I see wide-open countryside. Makes me wonder why with so much beautiful, available space, almost half the country chooses to live jammed together in Athens?"

The passenger stroked the puppy. "I wouldn't know. I haven't been to Athens. Matter of fact, I haven't been much farther away from my home than the place where you picked me up."

"Really? A nice looking, well-built young man like you stuck here in the middle of nothing but olive groves all your life? Someone ought to take you to Athens and show you a good time. After all, it's only a couple of hours away." The driver shot a quick glance at the passenger.

The passenger nodded and smiled.

The man touched his right hand to the passenger's left thigh. "I'm from Georgia."

The passenger took no notice of the touch. "I wouldn't have taken you for a former Soviet."

The driver paused for a moment, laughed. "No, not *that* Georgia, the one in the United States." He rested his hand on his passenger's leg.

"Oh yes, the place of the United States Olympics."

"Atlanta, 1996. But you couldn't be old enough to remember that."

He tugged at the puppy's ears. "A bomb went off. People died, many injured. The hero who saved a lot of lives was accused of being a terrorist."

The driver stared at his passenger. "His name was Richard Jewell. The government apologized and he was cleared."

"Hard to get back your reputation once the media tells the whole world you're guilty."

"The world's not perfect."

"He had to sue to get apologies from the press and died trying."

"As we say down Georgia way, 'Shit happens.'"

The passenger nodded.

The driver gave his passenger's thigh a squeeze. "You're a pretty interesting fella. How do you know all this stuff living all the way out here?"

The passenger shrugged and looked out the side window. "Television keeps us middle-of-nowhere folk in touch with the world."

The driver laughed. "Touché." He squeezed harder.

Without turning from the window the passenger asked, "What's your name?"

"Michael."

"Michael is a nice name. In Greek it would be Mihalis."

"My mother was Greek."

"It's good you know who your mother was." He turned and looked at the driver. "You look about my age."

The driver pulled in his belly. "Maybe a few years older. And your name?"

"Kharon."

"Did you say 'Karen?' That doesn't sound like a Greek man's name."

He smiled. "It is. Believe me, it is."

"Okay."

Kharon fixed his eyes on Michael's.

Michael bobbed his head in glances between Kharon and the road. "What are you staring at?"

"Would you like to have sex with me?" Kharon smiled.

"What?"

"Do I have to ask twice, Michael?"

"Where do I pull off?"

"The next left. It's not far. Just keep driving into the olives until I tell you to stop."

"I really do like your country."

Kharon smiled and stroked the puppy. "I'm sure."

◇◇◇

They drove between two rows of hundred-year-old olive trees toward the base of a gray limestone mountain splotched in myrtle and gorse a half mile or so off the highway. Kharon told him to stop by a pair of cypress trees and led him to a grassy spot enclosed on three sides by soaring cliffs. A private place. He pointed for Michael to lie down. Michael hesitated. Kharon slowly undressed, then lay naked on his back, glancing up at a light blue sky and stray cotton clouds before gesturing for Michael to come to him. Michael grinned as he dropped down.

By the time Kharon finished, Michael lay smiling from ear to ear—directly across his throat. Kharon had slowly stripped the American naked before killing him. No reason to bloody the clothes. He might be able to use them. At least give them away to someone who could. Waste not, want not.

He hadn't planned on killing him. Things just evolved that way. It was hard enough getting strangers to pick up hitchhikers in the backcountry, even with the borrowed puppy routine. Word of something like this getting around would make it even tougher. He decided to bury the man and take his car. He'd return the puppy and drive the car to Athens, so the city would be blamed for the disappearance of—he pulled a driver's license out of the dead man's wallet—Michael C. Dillman. The money in the wallet would pay for a rental car to get him back to Delphi. He wouldn't stay long in Athens. Too many bad memories there.

He'd lied about not knowing Athens. He'd lied about other things too. But, for sure, so had the dead guy. Too bad Dillman wasn't up on his Greek mythology. Had the Georgian known of the mythical ferryman of Hades who transported souls from the land of the living to the land of the dead across the rivers Styx and Acheron, he might not have been so quick to go off with a stranger bearing the ferryman's name.

Kharon had always tried giving a choice to the people he killed. It just seemed the right thing to do. He'd even given a choice to the two older boys in his orphanage who liked raping the young ones. He told them to stop. They hadn't.

The ministry in charge of the orphanage thought widespread rape within a government institution would trigger a bigger scandal than an isolated murder incident, so it portrayed the killings as the unprovoked mutilation murder of two fine, upstanding young men. He would still be in prison if it weren't for his lawyer's last-minute gambit.

The Justice Ministry, as angry as the judge at the unexpected turn, encouraged the press to vilify the boy mercilessly. Yes, he knew firsthand what the media could do to a reputation. He'd become a household word for "injustice," and in the process, a celebrity among his aspiring criminal peers.

Once released from supervision and on his own, he couldn't find work. Everyone knew his name. Two years in the military taught him other skills, but when he returned to civilian life he again faced the same closed minds each time he sought work in his own name. That's when he went to work for his former associates, doing jobs consistent with his reputation.

Now he lived without a name. Except when they called him. And when they did, they called him Kharon.

Chapter Two

"Yianni, what are you doing?"

Detective Yianni Kouros kept lining up the contents of two cases of liquor bottles across the top of his boss' desk. "Introducing you to my world."

Chief Inspector Andreas Kaldis, head of the Greek Police's Special Crimes Division, leaned back in his chair and watched as his chief assistant turned his office in Greece's central police headquarters building, better known as GADA, into a bar. They'd worked together long enough for him to know there had to be a method to Kouros' madness.

"So, how do you like it?" Kouros stepped back to admire his handiwork.

"The vodka on the rocks, the scotch neat, and the tequila with a bit of lemon."

Kouros jerked his head straight up in the Greek gesture for *no*. "I don't think you'd like this crap."

"What do you mean? They're all top brands."

"Yes. And all counterfeit."

Andreas leaned in to take a closer look at the bottles. "*Bomba?*" He'd used the street name for the worst kind of counterfeit liquor, the adulterated stuff named for the bomb you thought went off in your brain after drinking it.

Kouros nodded. "And the packaging is perfect."

"That's not good news."

"Yep, the counterfeit booze trade has taken off. And it's not just liquor. Wine, too."

"What about beer?"

"Not there yet. Not enough profit. But there's a lot to be made in spirits and wine. They're about the only expensive consumables selling big-time in Greece. That and cigarettes. The bump up in tourism has booze sales through the roof."

"And brought in opportunists, clearly."

Kouros nodded. "It's one thing dealing with the fashion knockoffs from China sold at every beach and town square in Greece, but this stuff is dangerous. The labeling makes it all look legit, but some of what's in it can really hurt you."

"Where did you find it?"

"Petro and I went to a club in Gazi last night for a drink and the bartender served us some of this garbage. I choked on my favorite tequila, and Petro spit his vodka all over the guy."

"That must have gotten his attention." Andreas smiled. "A six-foot, six-inch gorilla with a badge spitting booze at him."

"He didn't know we were cops until later."

"How much later?"

"Time sort of stood still, but I'd say about five minutes or so after the bartender and two bouncers came at us with lead pipes."

"Don't tell me…?"

Kouros nodded. "Don't worry, they'll be out of the hospital by tomorrow."

"Sounds like you had fun."

"The real fun came after we'd 'calmed down' the bartender and his buddies," Kouros used finger quotes for emphasis. "A half-dozen cops came storming in, guns drawn. Apparently their commander had an interest in the place."

Andreas smiled. "The best protection money can buy."

"That's what the owner thought when he told us we were about to learn what happened to 'assholes' like us who 'messed with the Greek police.'"

Andreas laughed. "And?"

"The sergeant asked for our identity cards. So we showed him our police IDs. Never saw guns go back into holsters so quickly."

"What did the owner do?"

"Not the right thing. He offered to 'pay' us for our 'trouble.' I thought the sergeant was going to have a heart attack. We let him explain to the owner that we were part of the police unit charged with investigating official corruption and he'd just committed a very big no-no."

"Sounds like a fun time was had by all."

"We had the sergeant and his cops confiscate every bottle in the place and escort the owner and the bottles back to GADA."

"Did the owner have anything else to say?"

"Only that he was as surprised as we were about the *bomba*. He said he'd been defrauded by his supplier, but he couldn't remember the guy's name."

"Guess he decided a fine for selling counterfeit booze was a lot less permanent than what would happen to him if he named his suppliers."

Kouros nodded. "Mobsters in this racket don't take kindly to snitches. Best way to find who's making this stuff is get a line on someone selling it and follow him back up the chain to the top."

"Good luck at that. Besides, we already know where it's going to end up. With some Balkan mob connection."

Kouros looked thoughtful. "Maybe, but something about this stuff seems different. I know what *bomba* looks like and this stuff isn't like any of that. It's a much higher-level operation than what we're used to seeing. Someone's put some real money into making counterfeit look legit. But it's not perfect. Within identical counterfeit bottles bearing identical counterfeit labels, the stuff inside isn't always the same. Some of it's not bad and some, like what Petro got a taste of at the bar, could blind you."

"So we've got counterfeiters with great packaging but poor product-quality control."

"Whatever the explanation, I sense it could be big."

"I assume the kid agrees with you about all this?" Andreas spread his arms as if embracing the bottles lined up on his desk.

Kouros nodded. "Some kid. Petro could lift both of us over his head. One in each hand."

"Not me," said Andreas patting his belly. "I've gained a few kilos."

Kouros reached for a bottle of scotch and slid it toward Andreas. "Here, try this new miracle weight-loss drug. One swig will have you puking your guts out for a week."

Andreas spun the whiskey bottle around and looked at the label. "Thanks, but for that sort of experience, I prefer our cafeteria." He pushed the bottle back at Kouros.

"Which reminds me…" Andreas stood from his desk. "Time for lunch."

◇◇◇

GADA sat near the heart of central Athens, across from the stadium of one of the country's most popular soccer teams and close by Greece's Supreme Court. The neighborhood offered many places to eat, but convenience made GADA's cafeteria the most popular venue for those working in the building. Like every office eatery, it had its share of legendary items to avoid. On some days that meant the entire menu.

From the crowd inside, this did not look to be one of those days.

Andreas chose his food as wisely as he could, knowing he'd be cross-examined by Lila when he got home. His wife's last words that morning were, "Forget the potatoes." He'd only gained five pounds since their son was born and that was four years ago. Okay, ten pounds.

He went with the salad and a piece of broiled fish. At least it looked like fish.

"Chief, over here," shouted a sturdy, red-haired woman waving from a table shared with Petro.

Kouros followed Andreas to Maggie Sikestis' table.

"What's the matter? You don't see enough of your boss upstairs?" said Kouros.

"Watch your tongue, young man, or I'll boot you off my favorites list."

Petro smiled.

No one wanted that fate. Maggie was GADA's mother superior, keeper of its secrets, and master of its support staff intrigues. She also was Andreas' secretary and had been since his return to head up Special Crimes after a brief stint as police chief for the Aegean Cycladic island of Mykonos. On Mykonos he'd first met Kouros, who was then a rookie cop.

"Ease up on him, Maggie," said Andreas sliding onto a chair next to her. "He's been hitting the booze this morning."

"So I noticed. He had Petro lugging cartons of liquor into his office."

Andreas looked at Kouros. "You mean there's more of what you dumped on my desk in your office?"

Kouros picked up a french fry with his fingers, waved it in front of Andreas, and popped it into his mouth. "Yep, eight more cases."

"Stop teasing him with french fries," Maggie snapped, "or I'll tell Lila."

Kouros jerked back in mock fear.

Andreas picked up his fork and took a tentative taste of the fish. "Not bad." He forked up another bite. "Why'd you put them all in your office?"

"Because if I left them in the property room some asshole down there would likely drink it. Or sell it."

"Might do the force a service," smiled Petro across a tray laden with just about one of everything on the menu.

"Glad to hear you share my high regard for many of our brethren," said Kouros.

"Why shouldn't I? If the chief hadn't brought me into the unit, those assholes would still have me standing in front of GADA directing tourists to the nearest toilet."

"That's the price you chose to pay when you refused the vice boys' kind offer of participating in their share-the-wealth outreach program to local businessmen," said Kouros.

"I never quite heard it put that way before," said Maggie.

Andreas raised his hands. "Are you guys done, or would you prefer I put this conversation on loudspeaker so that every cop in this room who doesn't already hate us has a chance to reconsider?"

"Seriously, though…" Petro dropped his deep voice almost to a whisper. "I don't think this counterfeit booze business could be as big as it is without police protection."

"You could say that about most things in this country," said Kouros.

Andreas took a bite of the salad. "Gentlemen…" He finished chewing. "Illegal booze is not a problem unique to Greece, and it's not one that exists solely because of official corruption. What drives it is a very simple concept—greed. Taxes on spirits have gone up a hundred and fifty percent in three years. We're at the point where sixty percent of the price of every legitimate bottle of spirits in this country goes to taxes. That means those who can smuggle in untaxed liquor from the Balkans or the Turkish part of Cyprus through Rhodes, or wherever else they find it, will do so. Or they'll buy it from those who can."

"But that's the real thing smuggled in to avoid taxes," said Kouros. "What I'm talking about are counterfeiters who make their own stuff and pass it off as real, using whatever they can find to make it work."

Petro nodded. "Some of them don't care if it's antifreeze, nail polish, rubbing alcohol, bleach, or whatever else makes the color look right. They target those who can't afford to pay much and couldn't care less about a brand, just about getting high."

"Yes, that's all true," said Andreas. "But the big international liquor companies have done a pretty good job of protecting their own brands. Some even compete directly with the *bomba* boys by selling their own low-end booze under labels they don't advertise publicly."

Kouros tapped his index finger on the tabletop. "And I'm willing to bet a month's pay that as we sit around this table talking about it, someone's out there rebottling those cheap brands as their much more expensive cousins."

Petro paused a *keftedes* on a fork six inches from his mouth. "The question is who?" The meatball disappeared.

"For which we have no answer," said Kouros, "and won't, unless we start looking for one. Counterfeit booze is a mega, worldwide problem. The Russians seized a quarter of a million bottles of phony vodka in just one raid. The British shut down an international organized crime ring operating in the middle of the English countryside, producing one hundred sixty-five thousand bottles of fake vodka labeled as a popular brand but spiked with bleach and methanol. And in Kazakhstan, over a two-year period, more than two million liters of the shit were seized."

"Vodka's always drawn a lot of counterfeiters. Mainly Russian." Andreas took a sip of water from his glass. "I can see you're wound up over this, Yianni."

"Me, too," said Petro.

Andreas held the glass in one hand as he spread his arms. "Fine, you're both wound up. But we're up to our eyeballs in serious, ongoing corruption investigations, and let's face it, counterfeiting is a plague upon virtually everything in our life that's expensive, from pharmaceuticals to industrial ball bearings. We're talking about a worldwide counterfeit market amounting to hundreds of billions of euros a year in lost tax revenues and legitimate sales. How can we expect to make a meaningful dent in that global problem with our limited resources?"

"I'm not talking about changing the world," said Kouros. "But everyone knows there's a huge tourist market for alcohol in Greece and that sort of money attracts a lot of serious opportunists. Those are the bad guys I want to go after."

Maggie shook her head. "I never knew that my grandfather cooking up his homemade batches of *tsipouro* was part of such a big thing."

Kouros pointed a french fry at Maggie. "I know you're joking, but that's precisely the sort of attitude that gets counterfeiters off the hook. No one realizes how extensive the problem is. They think of them as guys like your uncle—romantic characters churning out homemade *grappa*, or whatever, as they merrily evade the tax boys—not as organized crime, willing to blind, maim, and kill to make a profit. And the global financial crisis has made things even worse."

"Everybody wants things cheaper," said Petro.

"Even if it means going blind?" said Maggie.

Petro nodded. "A lot of kids go for *bomba*. They think nothing can harm them and all it will cost them is a worse headache than if they drank the real thing. I see it all the time."

"Some very bad characters must be involved in the *bomba* business if they're willing to blind children," said Maggie.

"They rank right up there with the drug trade," said Kouros. "Big profits mean big risks."

Maggie looked at Andreas. "There must be something you can do about this."

Andreas pointed at his chest. "Me? No, I think you're talking to those two." He pointed at Kouros and Petro. "They're the hotshots all pumped up to get out there and kick *bomba* butt."

Petro looked at Kouros. "Does that mean we have the okay to go after them?"

Andreas answered for Kouros. "Yes, it does. I know when to surrender to superior numbers massed against me. Just be careful, because with all the big money to be made there's no telling who's involved. You can't trust anyone. And keep in mind that bad guys in this line of business are used to leaving bodies in their wake. Understand?"

Both men nodded as Maggie smiled and patted Andreas on the arm.

"Good." Andreas raised his glass. "To bye-bye, *bomba*."

Chapter Three

Finding a place to ditch the car was easy. Kharon parked it in one of Athens' worst neighborhoods. It would be gone by morning, even if he hadn't left the keys in it. By the time the rental car company or its insurance carrier got around to chasing whoever rented it, the car and any link to Kharon would have long faded away into the opaque Athens air.

He took the Metro and got off at the stop closest to Exarchia Square, Athens' central gathering place for revolutionaries of all persuasions. He wasn't a revolutionary and couldn't care less who ran the government as long as whoever did stayed away from him. And in Exarchia Square the cops stayed away from everybody. They weren't welcome there and knew it.

That's what attracted many of his old buddies to the neighborhood; that and the living they made feeding off the children of the rich who came there to repent for their families' wealth by showing solidarity with the "cause of the people." At least until it was their turn to sit atop society's pyramid.

He walked east along Stournari Street, past the National Technical University and along the northern edge of wedge-shaped Exarchia Square. Banners and placards proclaiming all sorts of grievances and threats seemed to hang on the square's every available bit of fence and tree.

He headed for a taverna directly across from its northeast corner. Inside he chose a table with a clear view of the entrance and ordered chicken *souvlaki* on a bed of rice, Greek salad, and Alpha beer.

A group of six college-age men, all sporting beards in the Spartan warrior fashion of the day, sat at the next table huddled in conversation.

The waiter brought him a small plate, a glass, silverware, paper napkins, and a basket filled with bread. He placed a napkin on his lap, carefully arranged the silverware to position the fork to his left and the spoon and knife to his right, moved the glass to his right just beyond the spoon and knife, and slid the bread plate to the left of his fork.

He sat quietly waiting for his food, alert to the six men studying him from the next table. The waiter placed the *souvlaki* neatly between the silverware, and the salad and beer to his right.

Kharon moved the salad to his left and poured the beer into the glass. He picked up the fork with his left hand, the knife with his right, and began carefully separating the chicken from its wooden skewer.

He took a bite of the chicken, chewed it slowly, swallowed, put down his utensils, picked up the beer, and took a sip. He put down the beer, picked up his fork and carefully transferred a few pieces of cucumber and tomato onto his bread plate. Using the knife, he cut each piece of cucumber and tomato into quarters before slowly eating them one piece at a time.

The men at the next table now openly stared at him. Kharon waved for the waiter.

"Yes, sir?"

"May I have a sharper knife for the chicken?"

"Certainly."

The waiter left and returned quickly with a steak knife.

Kharon used it to cut a piece of chicken. Two men in their early twenties got up from the next table and stood directly across from Kharon. They were tall, but not as tall as Kharon.

Kharon kept on eating, as if oblivious to their presence. Two other men got up from the table and stood behind him.

One of the men in front of him, wearing a Che Guevara tee-shirt, said, "What are you doing here?"

Kharon ignored him and reached for a piece of cucumber with his fork.

The man stepped forward, leaned in across the table, and growled, "I'm talking to you."

Kharon lifted the cucumber to the man's mouth. The man swatted it away with his hand.

"Would you prefer the chicken?" asked Kharon.

The man reached across the table and grabbed the front of Kharon's shirt. "*Malaka*, you're fucking with the wrong people."

Kharon didn't move or say a word. He waited until the man let go of his shirt, took his fork and knife, picked up another piece of chicken with the fork, put it to his mouth, stared at the man, and said, "I think not."

The man paused and looked at the two men still sitting at the next table.

"Who are you?" said the older looking of the two at the table.

"A customer."

"I think you're a cop."

"I think you're a fool."

The older one glared and said to his colleagues. "Bust the asshole's head."

As the words left the man's mouth, Kharon drove the steak knife into the thigh of the man behind him and to his right. At the same time he rammed the table forward into the knees of the two in front of him, pivoted out of the chair to his right, and in a single swift, fluid stroke drew the blade out of the screaming man's thigh and sliced it through the older man's beard until the tip of the blade pressed hard against his throat.

"As I said, you're a fool. The question is, do you want to be a dead fool?"

The man stammered his answer. Kharon leaned harder on the blade.

"No, no!"

Kharon looked from the man to his hesitant buddies. "Then I think you know what to say."

"Get out of here. Everybody. *Now!*"

Five men hurried toward the entrance, one limping badly, and out onto the street. Kharon kept the blade pressed to the sixth man's throat.

"Someone has to pay for my ruined meal and I'm sure you don't want this poor workingman to suffer because of your bad manners."

The man fumbled his right hand through his pants pocket and came out with a thick wad of euros.

"I see the revolution pays well." Kharon plucked a hundred-euro note from the man's hand. "That should cover my meal and provide a generous tip."

He drew the knife away from the man's throat. "I suggest you leave here and not consider coming back until I've left." He looked straight into the frightened man's eyes. "Understand?"

The man rubbed his throat and glanced at the blade. "Yes."

"Good, consider yourself, and anyone you might think of sending in here, warned."

The man backed away from the table and ran out the door.

Kharon waved to the waiter who was peeking out from the safety of the kitchen. "Sorry about the mess. This is for you," holding out the hundred euros. "Could you please bring me a coffee?"

The waiter nodded and hurried back into the kitchen.

Five minutes later, as Kharon sipped his coffee, a swarthy, bearded fellow, almost as tall as he was wide, waddled into the taverna, headed straight to Kharon's table, and sat down. "I heard you were in the neighborhood."

"How'd you hear that?"

"From the six you ran out of here. They came to my place, raging about what they were going to do to this asshole that dared violate their turf. When I heard what happened I figured it must be you."

"From the knife work?"

"No, from the way they talked about how you ate. The same as you've always done since we left the orphanage."

Kharon shrugged. "It's my way of paying respect to the plentiful food I now have to eat. I never forget that we didn't always have it that way, back in our orphanage days."

The man smiled and rubbed his belly. "I remember by eating as much as I can every chance I get."

Kharon smiled. "Are they coming back?"

"I told them only if they were interested in committing suicide."

"Thanks, Jacobi."

"So, why are you here, and not in my place?"

"I planned on coming to see you later, but the food is better here."

Jacobi laughed. "What's up, my friend?"

"I was in town for a few hours and thought I'd check in with you to see if there's any work out there you thought might interest me."

"Nothing requiring your sophisticated talents. These days it's rather rough and direct. The fiscal crisis makes subtlety less of a concern to folks in need of attitude-adjustment specialists."

"Interesting euphemism, but there's no need for one. I can be rough and direct if necessary."

"I'm sure the waiter will attest to that."

Kharon smiled again. "You're the only one who ever makes me smile for real."

"I'll remember that. And I'll keep you in mind if I hear anything. Can I reach you at the same number?"

"Yes, I'll be heading back later tonight, tomorrow morning at the latest."

"Want to crash at my place?"

Kharon gestured no. "I think I best leave this neighborhood for now, just in case those new customers I sent you rally up some courage off your booze."

"Don't worry, I only serve assholes like that the stuff that'll blind them."

Kharon smiled. The men shook hands and left.

◇◇◇

To learn about *bomba*, find a bar notorious for the wild life. A place where most patrons come for the action and hardly notice what they're drinking as long as it brings on a buzz.

During the summer, the place for Athens area nightlife action lay southeast of the city in the western seacoast towns along the road to the Temple of Poseidon at Sounion. Big-time night-spots in the center of Athens generally closed for the summer or followed their clientele out to the islands. Some of Athens' chicest neighborhoods lay out this way, as did its most popular summer clubs.

That's why Kouros and Petro were in Vouliagmeni, knocking on the door of a club owned by a Greek-Cypriot Petro knew from his time as a bouncer in Athens nightclubs. A lot of cops did that sort of work. It was one of the honest ways to supplement their meager paychecks.

"What makes you think he'll talk to us?" said Kouros.

"He owes me favors. Besides, I told him we're not going to bust him for what he tells us." Petro looked at Kouros with concern. "That was okay to say, right?"

Kouros nodded. "As long as he isn't a bootlegger or selling stuff that can kill his customers."

"I don't think he'd do that. But he's cagey, so I'm sure he's selling counterfeit to beat taxes."

Petro pounded on the door. "Aleko, open up. It's Petro. I know you're in there."

They heard the sound of chair legs screeching against a wooden floor. "Just a minute."

Two locks clicked and the door swung in. A gaunt, unshaven bald figure in his mid-thirties leaned against the doorframe. He was shoeless and darkly tanned, and his runny red eyes made him the perfect poster child for a rehab program.

He fixed his eyes on Petro. "Hey, man, what are you doing here?"

"I called you a couple of hours ago and told you I'd be over with a friend to talk to you about something we needed your help with."

"You did?"

"Yeah, I did. By the way, your zipper's down."

Petro didn't wait to be invited inside. He stepped through the doorway and headed straight for the bar area. It smelled of disinfectant almost strong enough to cover the stale beer and cigarette smells. A dark-haired woman barely out of her teens stood off by the bar. She looked afraid.

"Are you okay, miss?" said Kouros.

She looked at Aleko then back at Kouros. "Yes."

"Who's she?" asked Petro.

"I don't know," said Aleko looking at the floor. "She came in here about an hour ago looking for a job. I was interviewing her when you started banging on the door."

The girl also looked at the floor.

"Why don't you run along, miss? I'm sure you have the job," said Kouros. He looked at Aleko. "Isn't that right?"

Aleko shrugged. "Yeah, sure. She starts tonight."

Kouros saw her out, not bothering to tell her to fix the misaligned buttons on the front of her dress. She was embarrassed enough already.

"Hard finding good help?" said Kouros.

Aleko shrugged again. "Did you guys come here to bust my balls?"

"No," said Petro. "We came to talk about *bomba*."

"*Bomba*? I never touch the stuff. It's illegal."

Petro put a big paw on Aleko's shoulder. "Don't worry, man. We're not after you. I've come to you as a friend for a little background on the industry." He gave Aleko's shoulder a painful squeeze. "I don't know who you think you're kidding by playing dumb. All you're doing is embarrassing me in front of my buddy. I told him you're the man in the know."

Aleko winced and twisted away from the squeeze. "Sorry, but I can't help you."

Kouros shrugged. "No problem. We'll just take a look behind the bar and see what we can find that might refresh your memory." He headed toward the bar.

"Hey!" Aleko said weakly. "You have no right to be in my place."

"Of course we do," said Kouros without stopping. "We heard a young girl screaming…really sounded more like screeching… and came in to find you forcing yourself upon an innocent young woman who'd come to you seeking employment. Trust me, Aleko, talking to us about *bomba* on a strictly anonymous basis will be a lot less risky to you than facing a female prosecutor on the charges I'll get that girl to bring against you."

Kouros reached down behind the bar and pulled out five bottles of identically labeled, expensive vodka.

Aleko said nothing.

"Interesting bottles here, Aleko. I've seen the sort before. And the tax stamps look even more interesting."

"Okay, okay. What do you want to know? You're not going to tell anyone it's me who told you, right?"

Petro nodded and pushed him toward the bar. "Right."

Aleko plopped onto a stool, shook his head, and let out a deep breath.

"What can I tell you that you don't already know?"

"Let's start with this stuff behind the bar."

"It's from a new supplier. And it's all good stuff. I only buy the good stuff. The other shit out there could poison you."

"And how's the cost of this 'good stuff' compare to the price of the vodka it's supposed to be?" said Kouros.

"If I normally paid twenty a bottle, then that stuff would cost me from five to seven, depending on how many cases I buy."

"So, if you get twenty-two shots out of a liter bottle, at two euros a shot you're making roughly six to nine times your money," said Petro.

"Yes, but for big spenders who want the high-end brands that cost me about same as what I'm using for shots, we can easily make thirty times our cost. And I'm talking just on the price of the booze. They have to pay extra if they want a table to sit at."

"So how do you connect with a *bomba* supplier?" asked Kouros.

"They come in to see me, many sell it right out of whatever they're driving. Up to now it's been a pretty competitive business. Sometimes things got a bit nasty when I played one competitor off against another, but it kept the prices in line."

"What do you mean, 'up to now'?" said Kouros.

"Like I said, that stuff you pulled out from behind the bar comes from a new supplier. My other guys haven't been around for a while. And I'm not too happy about that."

"Why?"

"No competition means the price to me is bound to go up."

"Has it?" said Petro.

"Not yet, but any day now I expect to get that message."

"From whom?"

"The new guy."

"When's he due here next?" said Kouros.

"Thursday, in time for the weekend."

"What's he look like?" said Petro.

Aleko put his elbows on the bar, ran his fingers through his hair, and looked up at Petro. "I don't know. A normal liquor salesman. Late thirties, dark hair, paunchy. Like any number of us trying to get by in these troubled times."

"Does Mr. Just-Like-Us have a name?" said Kouros.

"He says it's George, but who knows if it's real? All I want is the booze to be real."

"Real *bomba*," said Kouros.

"Yeah, but the good stuff."

Kouros nodded, took a knife from behind the bar and began opening the five vodka bottles.

"Hey, what are you doing to my stock?"

"Don't worry, I just want to make sure this shit isn't poison."

"I told you, I only go for the good stuff."

Kouros nodded, poured a shot from the first glass, smelled it, tasted a bit with his tongue, and said, "It ain't great, but it's vodka."

"See, I told you. Only the good stuff for my place."

Kouros did the same thing with the second bottle. Same result.

He tasted the third shot without smelling it and immediately spit it out. "Bingo." He spit a half dozen more times. "I don't know what's in there, but it isn't just vodka." He held up the bottle to the light and saw white sediment on the bottom. "It's been diluted with tap water." He smelled the bottle. "And probably nail polish. Maybe even bleach." He spit some more.

"That can't be," said Aleko getting off the stool and grabbing the bottle from the bar. He smelled it and looked at Kouros. "You're right, the son of a bitch cheated me."

Kouros smiled. "Like you do your customers?"

"Hey, my customers have a great time. I run a well-known place here. Sure, the booze may be watered down a bit and sometimes I serve cheaper stuff than what the customers think they're getting, but I'm not poisoning them. If word of that got around it would kill my business. No way I'm going to destroy this place just to make a little more selling poison. Besides, two shots of this shit and you're out of it. I make my money selling booze, not quick highs." Aleko looked away from the bottle and sniffled. "No way I'd ever sell this stuff."

"Then I suggest you check out every bottle you bought from your new supplier."

"Damn straight, I will, and I'm gonna shove every one of them up his ass on Thursday."

Kouros gestured no. "Not this Thursday, you won't. Maybe the next one."

"Why?"

"Because we want to follow him."

"So I'm supposed to do what? Buy more of his shit?"

Kouros shrugged.

"But I don't want to buy any more of his poison."

"Then don't."

"But he'll be suspicious."

"Then do."

Aleko looked to be considering his options.

Kouros put his hands on the bar and leaned in toward Aleko. "I want this poison out of here today. But on Thursday you're going to act normal and put in your regular order. Consider it a fine for all the shit you have in here. You're getting off light. We could shut you down and you know it. I doubt you'll have to worry about that salesman after Thursday, but when we stop back to say hello and, trust me, we will, if we find that same sort of shit in here, all bets are off on what will happen to you and your place."

"Believe me, that stuff will be gone by tonight. I run a reputable place."

"Which reminds me. That girl you hired to start working tonight."

Aleko stared at Kouros. "Yeah?"

"When we come back, be sure she's still working here." Kouros patted Aleko on the arm. "After that interview you put her through, I don't want to find out that you broke your promise to hire her."

Aleko looked at Petro. "Are we through now?"

"I think so."

Kouros nodded.

"Good. Glad I could help the police. But do me a favor, would you? If either of you ever calls me again for help and I happen to say, 'yes,' believe me, it means either I'm too fucked up to think straight or someone has a gun to my head."

Petro smiled, shook his head, and joined Kouros in heading toward the door. "Frankly, old friend, from where your life appears headed, I'm sad to say it's most likely to be both."

Chapter Four

Kharon always thought of the two-hour drive northwest from the heart of commercial, modern Athens to the ancient world's pastoral center of the earth at Delphi as a surrealistic passage through sharply contrasting value systems. His journey always began the same way, enduring traffic-clogged, graffiti-laden, gritty neighborhoods on the way to National Road A-1 and the fifty-mile highway run to his exit.

The six- and at times eight-lane highway skirted Athens' affluent northern suburbs. It ran a gauntlet of businesses serving the desires of Greater Athens before passing through a mix of corporate headquarters and light industry. Just beyond an Army base where Kharon had once served, the road rose up through a steep pass lined with pines, gorse, and myrtle growing nearly to the crest of gray limestone hilltops. From there, the highway gradually dropped down onto broad plains dotted with facilities catering more to the needs of modern agriculture than the wants of urban life.

Ten miles before his exit it narrowed down to four lanes and the land turned decidedly to farmland. But modern times had made their way here, too, in huge pond-like patches amid fields close by the road, and in barcode-style brandings of once virginal hillsides. A new type of farming had sprouted up in distinctive air force-blue and shiny silver: photovoltaic solar panels, a far less demanding and more profitable cash crop for many than any gained by toiling upon the land.

At the exit marked Thiva, Kharon headed south for four miles before turning west for the final fifty-five miles to Delphi. Here the road turned to two lanes and passed through fields of planted cotton, olives in silvered shades of green, and more silver and blue panels—all leading off toward mountains dressed in shades of brown soil, deep-green treetops, and gray stone peaks.

Kharon wondered whether farmland lost to solar power-production sapped more from those used to working the land than they could ever hope to earn for abandoning their traditional life. Farming meant creating life, and made one self-sufficient, with success dependent solely upon your own hard work—and the fickle will of the weather gods.

Kharon couldn't imagine giving up the freedom he'd found in farm work—laboring in Delphi's mountains, valleys, and boundless olive groves amid an omnipresent spiritual essence far greater than himself. He'd first felt its influence on a rare public school trip away from his hassled life in poorest urban Athens. That memory of Delphi is what drew him back there when he sought to establish a life far away from his city past.

Nor could he imagine how anyone who truly loved the land could be party to its systematic aesthetic mutilation. To him, solar panels tore the spirit from the natural beauty of the land, much as their siblings—turbine windmills haunting random mountaintops—destroyed the sense of peace a soul drew from gazing at an endless, undisturbed horizon. He hated those who'd wreaked such thoughtless havoc on the land. But then he'd pass through a town of architectural disasters and be reminded that aesthetic planning in modern Greece far too rarely was entrusted to descendants of the creators of the Parthenon.

Halfway to Delphi he stopped in Livadia, the capital city of a mountainous farming region known for its *souvlaki* and grilled meats. It served as a must-stop place for hungry skiers on visits to the nearby mountain village of Arachova, Greece's evergreen-draped wintertime equivalent of America's aspen, and a first-class example of how Greeks could preserve great beauty when they tried.

Kharon sat alone at a table facing the front door with his back to the wall. He ate only at this place in Livadia. He didn't have to order; the waitress brought him "the usual." As a rule, he avoided routine, for routine meant predictability and predictability too often proved deadly for someone in his line of work. But no one in Livadia knew his name or where he lived, much less when he'd stop for a meal. The only thing this restaurant knew was his preference for a beer and pork *souvlaki* with tomato, onion, *tzaziki*, and paprika all wrapped up in a pita. Hold the french fries.

The town never appealed to him; it was aesthetically neutral, but he sensed the hard moral edge and dedicated commitment required of those who struggled to survive on the land, principles lacking in those who saw the pursuit of quick money as the be-all and end-all of life.

Nothing in excess ran through his mind. He smiled. His Delphic state of mind must be returning, for that phrase stood along with two others—"Know thyself" and "Make a pledge and mischief is nigh"—carved upon Delphi's most celebrated site: the Temple of Apollo. A venerated place, dedicated to its patron God of Light, son of Zeus and Leto, twin brother to Artemis, and home to the Delphic Oracle and its prophetic visions.

From what Kharon knew of the gods' carryings on, it seemed unlikely that Apollo or any other god had much to do with those carvings.

In the time of the gods, the Delphic Oracle was presided over by the goddess Themis—a bride of Zeus, divine instructor of mankind in the laws of justice and morality, and mother of the Fates. Delphi's more modern origins dated back to Neolithic times, and though the Oracle held importance in pre-classical Greece—certainly as the nearby Gulf of Corinth grew in commercial importance—it was after the rededication of the Temple to Apollo in the fourth century BCE that the Oracle attained true prominence in the classical Greek world and beyond. The temple was ultimately destroyed and its Oracle silenced in 390 CE, but Kharon doubted whether an educated soul in the world had not heard of Delphi or its Oracle.

Many myths surrounded Apollo and Delphi, but they all flowed from the same premise: ancient Delphi represented the navel of the mother of Earth, personified in the god Gaia. Apollo had slain Python, the son of Gaia, while standing guard over his mother's navel.

The version Kharon liked best had Apollo killing Python for trying to rape Apollo's mother while he and his sister lay in their mother's womb. The slain Python then fell into a fissure, and vapors released from his decomposing body found their way into the sanctuary of Apollo, intoxicating Pythia—the name given the priestess attending the Oracle—thereby allowing Apollo to convey his prophesies through her.

Kharon preferred that story because he saw the killing as a righteous deed, plus in the years of penance that Apollo was forced to serve for that act by an angry Gaia, Kharon saw a parallel to his own life.

Now Kharon, as Apollo once had, called Delphi home. But unlike Apollo's majestic temple on the Sacred Way—standing high along the southwest slope of Mount Parnassos and overlooking the Pleistos River Valley's seemingly endless olives, myrtle, pines, almonds, and thyme—Kharon made his home a bit west, on the outskirts of modern Delphi, living as anonymously as possible among two thousand, non-godlike souls struggling to survive very different times.

There, Kharon lived a simple life of *nothing in excess* and was content. Not that he'd ever had a chance at a grander life, or expected to, for he took great care to avoid secular temptations, preferring to entrust his fortune to the Fates.

◇◇◇

Andreas was away from his office when Kouros and Petro arrived at work the next morning, and by the time they got around to briefing him on their meeting with Aleko it was midafternoon.

When they'd finished, Andreas asked, "So tell me, what parts of his story did you actually believe?"

"That he makes his money selling booze, not blinding his customers with *bomba*," said Kouros. "But he's definitely passing off counterfeit as real. Didn't even try to hide it."

Petro nodded. "He'd be wasting his time telling me he didn't fool around with his booze. Back when we worked together, he was the only bartender in the place, and I caught him adding water to liquor bottles. I'm sure that wasn't the only time because he offered to cut me in on his action if I gave him a pass on telling the boss."

"His action?" said Andreas. "How was he making money watering the booze if he wasn't the owner?"

"Owners estimate receipts based upon a fixed number of drinks per bottle. By adding water, bartenders get to pour extra drinks out of a bottle and pocket the cash by never running the extra sales through the register."

"Sort of like running your own bar on the owner's inventory," said Andreas. "Fair-minded guys, bartenders like that. They cheat the customers and owners equally."

"That's why owners like those new plastic pourer inserts Greek law requires in every liquor bottle," said Petro. "You can't add water through the insert unless you break it. It eliminates one way for bar staff to rob their owners. But guys like Aleko still steal from their customers by buying counterfeit booze in bottles that come with inserts, or if they tend their own bars, by ripping them out."

Andreas chuckled. "I'm sure someone will find a way to get around the pourers and stick it to the owners. You almost have to admire the ingenuity of thieves. They always find a way. Sort of like salmon driven to swim upstream, overcoming one obstacle after another."

"The customer still gets screwed," said Petro.

"Always has, always will," said Kouros.

"But it's not our job to buy into that," said Andreas. "Look at it this way. If Aleko's supplier shows up on Thursday and you follow him around for a week, even if you never get any farther up the supply chain than the guy you're following, you'll still end up with a list of places dealing in untaxed liquor to pass on to the tax boys."

"Yippee," said Kouros.

"Hey, be happy with whatever little fishes you catch. You could starve waiting for a big one to bite."

Kouros gave Andreas a puzzled look. "What's with you and all these fish references?"

"Like I said, Lila has me on a diet. So I'm thinking fish. Would you prefer, 'A bird in the hand is worth more than trampling through a field full of bullshit chasing ghosts'?"

Petro wrinkled his brow. "Am I missing something?"

Kouros nodded. "Yeah, a twisted sense of humor. But don't worry there's no known vaccine against it for cops. It will come to you, too, in time."

"Why don't you guys come over for dinner tonight? Lila would love to have you."

"What's the matter, you hoping if we come to dinner Lila might relent and let you eat *our* kind of food?" said Kouros.

"Hope springs eternal, but I doubt she'd fall for that. I just thought it would be nice to introduce Petro to Lila and Tassaki."

"Thank you, Chief, I'd love to come," said Petro.

Kouros turned and stared at Petro. "I'm going to have to teach you how to handle these situations. Rule one. Don't rush in. We could have held out for the right to bring our own chocolate cake. Now we're at diet man's mercy."

"Out of here, both of you." Kouros and Petro headed for the door. "And no chocolate cake. You've got to be subtle if you want any chance at getting by the pastry-detector. Go with chocolate chip cookies. See you at nine."

◇◇◇

Petro craned his neck up and out the car window. "The chief lives here?"

"Yep." Kouros eased the police car over a curb onto the cobblestones separating the roadway from the sidewalk running alongside the National Gardens toward the old Olympic Stadium at the end of the street. "That's why I drove a blue and white. We couldn't park here otherwise. With November 17-like terrorist crazies back in business, internal security won't let just anyone park so close to the Presidential Palace."

"Close? He lives right next door."

"At 30 Irodou Atikou, to be precise."

It was arguably the most exclusive street in Athens. Only a few blocks long and filled with money.

"Wow."

"I had the same reaction the first time I came here. Chief's wife comes from one of Greece's oldest, most prominent families."

"Isn't her last name Vardi? I didn't know that was a big-time Greek family name."

"It isn't. That was her late husband's name. He made his money in shipping."

Petro shook his head. "The rich always seem to marry the rich."

Kouros smiled. "Though some do manage to marry a second-generation cop and find true happiness."

"I guess there's hope for us working class stiffs."

"Not here, my friend. I already asked. She has no sisters." Kouros opened the car door. "Don't forget the cookies. You carry them. Lila doesn't know you, and she's too much of a lady to tear you a new asshole for bringing them. But if I brought them..." Kouros waved his hand in the air as he got out of the car. "Don't worry, man. She's not what you might expect."

They walked across the street into the immaculately maintained lobby of a six-story, pre-World War II Athens apartment building. The doorman directed them to an elevator, and the operator took them to the sixth floor.

The elevator opened directly into a large entry foyer. Kouros stepped out and led the way toward a pair of French doors at the far end. He pointed, "There's a bell to the right."

Before either had the chance to press the bell, the doors opened and a young woman dressed in a black maid's uniform and starched white apron stood smiling at them. "Good evening, Detective Kouros. The doorman said you were on your way up."

"Hi, Marietta. How are you?"

"Fine, thank you."

"This is Officer Petro. He works with us."

"A pleasure to meet you, Officer." She pointed at the box in Petro's hand. "I'll take that, thank you."

"No need to," said Kouros.

Marietta smiled. "Missus Vardi told me to tell you that under no circumstances was I to allow you, or whoever you were with, to smuggle pastries into the house."

"She actually said that?"

"She also said to tell you, 'Nice try.'"

Kouros looked at Petro. "Like I said, not what you might expect. It's all right. Turn over the cookies."

Marietta led them through a series of rooms filled with antiques and paintings. Andreas and Lila stood in a room lined with windows offering an unobstructed view of the Acropolis lit up at night.

Petro stared out the windows as Kouros kissed Lila on both cheeks and turned to introduce him.

"Petro, this is Lila."

Lila stepped toward Petro and put out her hand. "I know how you feel. I can't believe this view is real either, and I see it every day."

Petro blushed. "Pleased to meet you, Mrs. Vardi."

"Please, call me Lila." She stood about a head shorter than her six-foot, two-inch husband and wore her dark hair simply, at shoulder length.

"Sorry about the cookies."

She smiled, "Cookies? I'd have thought Yianni would have gone for a chocolate cake. I suspect there was a broader conspiracy at play than I imagined." She glanced at Andreas.

He shrugged. "I know nothing about any chocolate chip cookies."

Lila rolled her eyes. "Then how did you know the cookies were choco—"

At that instant a brown and white puppy came racing into the room followed by a charging four-year-old.

"Perfectly timed entrance, my son," said Andreas scooping the boy up from his pursuit of the puppy. "You know how to rescue your daddy."

The boy twisted about in his father's arms trying to free himself. "Easy, Tassaki, I want to introduce you to a friend of mine." The boy stopped fidgeting as Andreas carried him over to Petro.

"Tassaki, this is Officer Petro."

Tassaki held out his hand, "Pleased to meet you, Officer Petro."

Petro shook Tassaki's hand. "And a pleasure to meet you."

Andreas pointed at Kouros.

"Nice to see you again, Detective Yianni."

Kouros smiled and waved. "You, too, Tassaki."

Andreas kissed Tassaki's cheek. "Well done, son," and put him back down on the floor to resume the chase.

"What a well-mannered kid," said Petro.

Andreas nodded toward Lila. "It's all his mother's doing."

Lila smiled. "But he gets his puppy-chasing nature from his father. Would you like something to drink? Wine, beer, whiskey."

"Wine please," said Petro.

"Red or white?"

"Red."

"And you, Yianni?"

"Whatever."

Andreas walked over and patted him on the back. "Just as long as it isn't *bomba*."

"*Bomba*?" said Lila.

"Counterfeit alcohol," said Kouros.

"I can't believe it. I was just talking about that very thing today with Alexandra."

"*Bomba*?" said Andreas.

"Counterfeiters. Her husband is a wine producer and he was complaining to her about wine counterfeiters jeopardizing his business. I assumed she was trying to get me to raise it with you."

Andreas nodded. "One of the perks of being the wife of a cop. Friends asking you to get your husband to fix their tickets."

Lila gestured at her husband. "Especially when he's a notorious super cop."

"Did she say how big a problem it was for his business?" asked Kouros.

"No, but according to his wife, Greek wines are gaining exponentially in popularity outside of Greece and someone is counterfeiting top Greek wine labels for EU markets. The stuff in the bottles is bad, but the counterfeit packaging's so good, he's worried new customers who have a bad experience with the phony stuff will give up on Greek wines entirely. He thinks it's a serious threat to the country's fragile foothold in world markets."

Andreas looked at Kouros. "Sound familiar?"

"It's starting to sound like this counterfeit operation is a lot bigger than we suspected. Or we have a mega-coincidence."

"I'm not big on coincidences," said Andreas.

"Who is Alexandra?" said Petro.

"She's a friend and the sister of a Greek government minister," said Lila.

"Do you think she called you before or after she called her brother?" said Andreas.

"After, would be my guess."

"Then I'm surprised she didn't ask her brother to call Spiros to get me involved." Spiros was Greece's minister of public order and Andreas' boss.

"Probably because her brother told her you were more likely to listen to Lila than to Spiros," chuckled Kouros.

Lila smiled.

Andreas waved his hand in the air. "No matter. I'll call Alexandra's husband tomorrow and see what he has to say. If it's as big as it sounds, we'll likely have to take it to the next level."

"Europol?" said Kouros.

"At least. If it's a multi-country operation we'll have to involve the foreign ministry. Hard to fight this sort of thing effectively without international cooperation."

"And if China's involved, forget about it," said Lila.

"We'll have to find a common motivation strong enough to overcome all the cross-border corruption and bribery that goes along with this sort of thing," said Kouros.

"That's a bridge we'll cross once we know who's on the other side."

"Nice," Kouros told Andreas. "At least you're off the fish analogies."

"Sorry I raised the subject, gentlemen," said Lila. "I should have stuck to a less controversial one, like what's for dinner?" She pointed toward a doorway leading into the dining room.

"Dare I ask?" said Andreas.

Lila took his arm and led him toward the dining room. "Fish, salad, and vegetables."

Andreas' face showed no joy.

"And chocolate chip cookies."

His face lit up.

"But only one for you."

Chapter Five

Kharon always loved his days in the olive covered hills and valleys surrounding Delphi caring for the trees and holiday cottages of wealthy Athenians. His court-ordered education had given him great skills in agriculture and the building trades, and he practiced them with devotion that drew praise from his clients and provided him with all that he needed to maintain his simple life.

But he was a child of hard times and knew they could return, as they had for so many in his country. Even the gods only helped those who helped themselves, and so he took the other work. He tucked that money safely away, but not in bank accounts in his name. A sizable bank account in a small village for someone doing his kind of manual labor spawned rumors. The type of rumors that attracted police attention. His first encounter with local police scrutiny led Kharon to ensure he would never again be the target of such suspicions.

Burglaries were the accepted price one paid for the privilege of owning a vacation home in Greece, and break-ins brought knee-jerk police attention to those who cared for the victims' homes. Attention that inevitably led to interrogations, background checks, and bank account analyses.

One of Kharon's clients, a well-known Athens jeweler, arrived one morning to find his home in the village of Chrisso plundered of a fortune. The police immediately accused Kharon. The owner said that was not possible as Kharon had been with him in Athens doing work on the jeweler's primary residence. Having lost that suspect, the police claimed they knew the local ring of thieves who'd likely done it, but could not prove it. The jeweler would simply have to accept his loss.

Two days later, all the stolen jewelry miraculously reappeared in a suitcase at the jeweler's front door. The police had no explanation. Nor could they explain what they later called the "coincidental disappearance" of the alleged leader of the ring, as well as a local police sergeant, neither heard from again. From that day on, none of Kharon's clients ever saw so much as an olive stolen from a tree.

Bzzzzz, bzzzzzz, bzzzzz. Kharon felt the vibration of the phone in his pocket. He put down the rake and reached for the phone. He recognized the number. It was the secure landline Kharon insisted Jacobi use to reach him.

"Hello?"

"It's me," said Jacobi.

"You're up early."

"Not been to bed yet."

Kharon smiled. "What's up?"

"I think I have a project for you."

"You mean a job?"

"No, a project. Something with long term possibilities."

"You know I like what I do. I'm not looking for full-time employment."

"My friend, I don't know what sort of arrangements you can work out with the people involved here, but I don't think this is the sort of thing you should just walk away from before knowing what it is. This could set you for life."

Kharon thought to say "I already am," but Jacobi wouldn't understand. And his friend was right. *Don't turn down a job you haven't been offered* was good advice. "So, tell me about it."

"All I know is that someone from up north stopped in my place last night to tell me that a big-time international operation is in need of a specialist to assure that all aspects of its business follow company rules."

To Kharon, "up north" meant the Balkans, and some very nasty work if their local bad guys couldn't handle it themselves. "And you recommended me?"

"Never had the chance. He already knew about you. Said you were the perfect guy. Freaked me out when he said that he knew you did your business through me. He said to tell you if you're interested to stop by my place tonight and he'd make it worth your while. All I know is that the job interview includes an all-expenses-paid round-trip to Rome."

Kharon had a lot of work to do here, but he could get people to cover for him. His clients wouldn't be back until the weekend. "Okay, I'll be there tonight."

"Great. And don't forget your toothbrush and a change of underwear."

"Why?"

"He said if you agree to the interview it'll be tomorrow morning."

"In Rome?"

"Yep, the guy has a private jet. This is a whole different sort of folk than you're used to, my friend."

Kharon stared at the cloudless sky above Delphi. *As I undoubtedly shall be to them.*

◇◇◇

Andreas thought about telling Kouros to make the call to the government minister's brother-in-law in the wine business. After all, the counterfeit booze investigation was Kouros' case, but Greek sensibilities being what they were, it would likely subject Kouros to an unnecessary barrage of questions over why he, not his boss, had called. It might even lead to unpleasant words between Lila and her friend Alexandra as to why, after she'd impressed upon Lila the urgency of the matter, Andreas had been too busy to personally call her husband. So, he placed the call himself.

The phone rang twice. "Hello," answered a brusque voice.

"Theo? Hi, it's Andreas."

"Andreas?"

"Kaldis. Lila Vardi's husband."

"Of course, Andreas. Sorry about that, I wasn't thinking."

The voice had warmed up immediately. *A true salesman* thought Andreas. "No problem, I'm used to it. That's what comes with having such a well-known wife."

Theo laughed. "You're pretty well known yourself. How can I help you?"

"Last night Lila mentioned to me that your wife said you're having trouble with counterfeiters."

There was a decided sigh on the other end of the phone. "Trouble is an understatement. They're threatening to destroy my business. It costs the bastards about a euro per bottle to copy my packaging perfectly—that's for the cork, bottle, label, capsule, and cardboard—and then they sell the wine as if they're my distributors for fifty percent cheaper than the real thing. They even sell it door to door as 'overstock.'"

Andreas tapped the eraser end of a pencil on his desk. "Have you tried stopping them through the courts?"

Theo laughed. "In Greece? Fat chance. I've asked my real distributors to warn their customers of the problem, and they all say they will, but I doubt they do. Or at least not in any effective way."

"Why wouldn't they?"

"They're afraid their customers might go looking for the cheaper stuff."

"Even if they knew it's counterfeit?"

"I hate to say this, but there are a lot of booze sellers out there who think, 'I'm selling to tourists, I'll never see them again, so who's to know or care?' A hell of a lot of them are already selling cheap Bulgarian and Italian wines packaged under Greek names in five- and ten-liter boxes as their 'Greek' house wines."

"Ouch."

"For sure. But my real concern is in markets beyond Greece, places where my labels are just getting known."

Andreas heard a clinking over the line. "What's that?"

"Some bottles I want to show you."

Damn, thought Andreas. Now he'll be coming over here for show and tell.

"How about if you come over to my place and I show you the operation? We have a terrific wine-tasting room."

So much for thinking he'd be pushy enough to insist on coming over here. "Thanks, Theo, but I can't possibly get away."

"It's really important." The tone straddled pleading and commanding.

"Sorry, I just can't."

Pause.

"How about if we do a Skype call? I'd really like to show you what I'm up against."

Now the sigh was on Andreas' end of the phone. "Sure, give me a minute to have my secretary set it up."

Andreas put Theo on hold and buzzed Maggie.

"Yes."

"I need to set up a Skype call with the person I'm talking to. Do you know how to do that?"

"I take that to mean you don't."

"Maggie…"

"Don't worry, it will all be up and running soon. Just sit there and wait. I'll take care of everything."

Andreas put down the phone and waited. *Someday I'll have to learn how to do these techno things for myself.*

Maggie swept into his office came behind his desk and began to fiddle with his computer. A minute later he was staring into the screen at a pudgy faced, middle-aged man in an open neck blue dress shirt, sporting a thick gold chain and a broad smile.

"Andreas, you're much better looking on this screen than on television."

Andreas smiled. "Flattery will get you everywhere. So what did you want to show me?"

Theo held up two bottles of wine. "One is mine, one is counterfeit." He turned them slowly in synch with each other. "I defy you to tell me which is real and which is phony."

"Hold them up closer to the camera." Andreas leaned forward and studied the screen. "They look identical to me."

"That's the problem. The phony is a perfect knockoff of my labels, bottles, everything but the wine. This is what's poisoning my reputation before I can build it. The same bogus packaging was introduced in three different EU countries. Counterfeiters are claiming they represent me there, and are selling their crap as my wine in legitimate distribution networks."

"How do they get it through customs?"

Theo put down the bottles. "They don't. They produce it in the countries where they're selling it. Or smuggle it in through loose borders."

"How do you know that?"

"I started getting complaints from buyers in countries where I don't do business. One leading restaurateur called me screaming about how ashamed I should be for the garbage I sell as Greek wine."

Andreas shook his head. "Ouch again."

"I hired lawyers and investigators and they traced it back to organized crime."

Andreas focused on Theo's eyes. "Organized crime?"

"Yes. That's who's distributing it in every country. And not just my wines. Other Greek and non-Greek winemakers' labels and counterfeit liquor, too."

"Who's making it for them?"

"Apparently every illegal producer they can find. They supply the producers with packaging, transportation, distribution, and pay better prices for the counterfeit than the bootleggers could make selling the stuff themselves."

Andreas shook his head. "Sounds like they've cornered the market."

"Or close to it. They're buying up every last drop they can find."

"Let me guess. Of low quality wine to substitute for the real thing?"

"If you can use the word 'quality' in connection with any of that shit, I'd say mostly yes."

Theo rubbed at his forehead with the fingers of both hands and spoke with his eyes looking down from the camera. "At the high end, they do what's called 'stretching' the wine by blending inferior wines in with the good stuff. They've gotten so good at it that some of the big name French and American producers are embedding computer chips beneath their labels so buyers can verify before purchasing whether the bottle's legitimate. Others try holograms, or fancier gimmicks, but the counterfeiters keep improvising right along with them."

He dropped his hands and stared into the camera. "At the bottom end, they add in poisons that can kill but taste sweet."

"What kind of poisons?"

"All sorts of stuff." He held a can and a bottle up to the camera. "Here's lead acetate and wood alcohol. That goes in the mix. But they also use diethylene glycol, which goes into things like brake fluid and wallpaper strippers."

"Sound like real nice guys."

"Yeah, right," said Theo, putting the can and bottle down. "And it's a big operation. Best I can tell, it's one group looking to monopolize the counterfeit alcohol beverage trade. And not just in Greece, but across the EU."

"That sounds like a pretty tough thing to do."

"Not if you're organized. Like Coca-Cola."

"You're not suggesting…"

Theo laughed and waved his hand across the front of his face. "No, of course not, but if you have the capital and proper management it could be done."

Andreas shook his head. "Hard to imagine 'managing' organized crime types. The ones I know don't go in for board meetings."

Theo pointed at the screen. "All I can tell you, Andreas, is that in three different countries my wines are being counterfeited and distributed by seemingly independent organized crime operations using identical packaging and marketing practices."

"What about the police?"

Theo smirked. "They claim it's a civil matter, one for my lawyers to pursue. Or the EU collectively. In other words, the bad guys have more juice with the police than I do. It's enough to make you want to take the law into your own hands."

Andreas raised his hand. "I understand how you feel, but I don't recommend it. Those types play a lot harder than you ever will."

Theo nodded. "So I've been warned."

"By whom?"

"By everyone."

"Did your lawyers and investigators find out who's behind it?"

"At the very top?" Theo gestured no. "No idea. We could only trace it back as far as the top guy in each country."

"Do you have names?"

"I'll get them for you."

"Good."

"I hope you can do something. It's tough enough running any business in Greece these days, but with taxes being what they are, and counterfeiters not paying taxes, there's no way I can compete with them."

"I hear you. I can't promise anything, but I'll do what I can."

Theo smiled. "That's all I can ask for. Thanks."

"Don't thank me, thank your wife."

Theo laughed. "I always do. And if I forget, she reminds me. It's the secret to a happy marriage."

"I'll remember that."

"Plus gold jewelry on birthdays, name days, and anniversaries."

Andreas laughed. "Bye." He watched as Theo disappeared from the screen. *Not a bad guy, just worried. Can't blame him.*

Andreas turned his head and stared out the window of his fourth-floor office. There wasn't much of a view. Just other buildings.

"Maggie," he shouted. They'd found yelling to be far more effective than the intercom.

The door swung open and Maggie's head popped through the doorway. "Yes, Chief?"

"Is my old friend still in charge of organized crime at GADA these days?"

"Which old friend?"

"We always called him Rolex."

Maggie gestured no. "He was too honest."

"Cute. You do know you're a cynic."

"Born out of a lot of years in this place."

"Well, see if you can find out where he landed. I'd like to talk to him."

"Will do."

Andreas nodded. "And what about Tassos? Where's he these days?"

"You mean your poor, loyal friend who thinks you've abandoned him?"

"Gimme a break. Phones work both ways."

"He's on Syros enjoying the weather."

"Working?"

"The day he quits is the day he'll die."

Tassos Stamatos reigned as Chief Homicide Investigator for the Cycladic Islands. They'd been friends since Andreas' days as police chief on Mykonos, and Tassos and Maggie had been an item since the moment Andreas unknowingly rekindled an old romance between his widower friend and never-married Maggie.

"When do you think he'll be passing through Athens?"

"Tomorrow morning, probably."

"Good, set up a meeting here tomorrow around noon with Tassos, Yianni, Petro, and me."

"And the subject?"

"Counterfeit booze and mobsters gone corporate."

◇◇◇

Kharon stood in the shadows across from Jacobi's taverna. He'd been there for twenty minutes. Watching. Not for anything in particular, just anything out of the ordinary. Ordinary for this neighborhood meant weird. That's why he'd fixed on the big man dressed all in black sitting at the bar with his back to the broad, open front door of the taverna. He'd not turned around once, but from the movement of the man's head Kharon could tell he was watching everything behind him in the mirror spanning the back of the bar. Just what he'd expect of a professional.

He doubted a man with a private jet would have walked here from the Metro or come alone. He could have come by taxi, but then he'd have to find one willing to pick him up in this neighborhood. Several motorbikes sat by the taverna. One could be his. But where are the others who must be with him? Probably parked away from the taverna so not to draw attention from the neighborhood locals. Or Kharon.

Kharon had been careful in his work, but there were those who knew of his role in many unhappy incidents, making all who possessed such knowledge potential betrayers to someone willing to bribe or threaten for what they knew about him.

Kharon did a slow walk around the square. No one bothered him. Tonight he looked as if he belonged there. Twenty more minutes passed before he returned to his place across from the taverna. The man at the bar now sat sideways on a stool, looking out into the street. He waved across the room to Jacobi and said something Kharon could not hear. Jacobi shrugged. The man looked at his watch.

That was the sort of irritated behavior Kharon expected from someone waiting for a latecomer to show up for a meeting. Quite different from the patience required of a professional prepared to execute a hit.

Kharon crossed the street and strolled into the taverna. Jacobi saw him the instant he entered, caught his eye, and gave a quick jerk of his head toward the man at the bar.

The big man at the bar studied Kharon as he walked toward him. "Mr. Kharon?"

Kharon nodded.

The big man extended his hand. "Glad you decided to come. My name is Panos."

Kharon shook his hand. "You're not Greek."

Panos smiled. "And that's not my real name."

Kharon sat on the bar stool next to Panos but looked in the mirror as he talked. "So, how can I be of service to you?"

Panos swung around and met Kharon's eyes in the mirror. "You have quite a reputation for so young a man."

"Not so young. We're about the same age."

"Still, it's quite a record you've amassed."

"I started young."

"So I've read."

"Then what's there left for me to tell you?"

"Me? Nothing. I'm just a messenger. My duty is to arrange transport for you to a meeting with my superior."

"You're ex-military?"

He nodded. "Not so sure I'd call it ex."

"I still haven't heard what you want with me."

"Not my call. As I said, I just arrange transport."

"Rides with strangers can be dangerous."

"We have no reason to want to harm you. If we did we could have done it anytime." The man paused. "Up where you live in Delphi."

Kharon smiled. "Why is it that bad guys in the movies always say, 'If we wanted to get you we could?' It's not difficult to find me if someone really wants to, but I can assure you, it's much harder to kill me."

"I'm sure that's a reason you're so attractive to my superior."

"Tell me about your superior."

"I'm not authorized. But I can offer you something as a sign of good faith. If you agree to the interview you'll receive fifty-thousand euros whether or not you take the job."

"Nice promise, but they're only words."

Panos waved to the bartender. "Hand me my bag, please."

The bartender lifted a small backpack from behind the bar and handed it to Panos, who handed it to Kharon. "This is yours."

Kharon opened the bag and looked inside. "Nice, very nice." He reached in and pulled out some one hundred and a fifty-euro notes. He turned them over, rubbed them between his fingers, and held them up to a light above the bar.

"I'm not so sure you want to be flashing that kind of cash around this neighborhood."

"Why not? It's mine to do with as I wish, isn't it? I mean assuming I go for the interview."

Panos looked around the room. "Yeah, but I still think you should be careful."

"I agree." Kharon swung off the bar stool and carried the bag over to a table where Jacobi stood talking to a customer. "Jacobi, I need your professional opinion." He dumped the contents of the bag onto the table, sending the customer leaping out of his chair.

"Sorry, sir," said Kharon to the customer, who now stared wide-eyed at the cash-covered tabletop. "Tell me, Jacobi, do you think this stuff is real?"

The customer hurried out of the taverna as Panos ran over to the table. "Are you crazy? The whole neighborhood will be in here in a minute."

Kharon ignored him. "Well, is it or isn't it?"

Jacobi studied one, then another bill. He pulled a pen out of his pocket and rubbed it across a different bill. "Very good, but fake."

"You guys don't know what you're talking about," said Panos.

Kharon said, "I suggest you pack up your cash and leave before the 'whole neighborhood' shows up looking to take it from you. Even counterfeit has value."

Panos bit his lower lip and started stuffing the counterfeit cash back into the backpack. "You still need to come with me."

"I think not."

"I'll give you the real money."

"Too late. You've lost your credibility with me."

"This isn't going to play well for you."

Kharon took Panos' chin in his hand and pried his attention away from stuffing the bag. "Far worse for you." He let go of Panos' chin. "I'd like to hear how you're going to explain to your superior why you couldn't get a poor young kid like me to show up for a meeting in exchange for fifty-thousand euros. My guess is curiosity will lead your superior to making inquiries, and inevitably to learning that I was offered counterfeit cash. If your superior gave you counterfeit, then all's fine with your world." Kharon shook his head. "But if not, and your superior begins to wonder how counterfeit got into that backpack, I think you'll have some explaining to do."

Panic broke out across Panos' face. "Don't worry. I'll give you the real stuff. I didn't feel safe carrying all that cash in this neighborhood."

Kouros shrugged. "How safe are you feeling right now?"

Panos looked desperate, as though he might cry at any moment.

"Kharon, hey, maybe you should cut the guy some slack?"

Kharon turned to Jacobi. "What do you mean? He tried to cheat me."

Jacobi nodded. "Yeah, I know. But maybe he can make it up to you."

"He's right," Panos said quickly. "I definitely can."

Kharon shook his head. "I don't know…"

"Give him a chance. I'm sure he can get you your money, and probably even a little more for your trouble."

"Yeah, sure I can."

"Say, like a hundred thousand of the real stuff," said Jacobi.

"That's crazy!" Panos looked back and forth between them. "Where can I get that sort of money?"

Jacobi shrugged. "Hey, I'm trying to help you out here. If you can't, you can't."

Panos ran the fingers of both hands through his hair. "Okay, okay, a hundred thousand."

"And your superior comes to Athens for our meeting," said Kharon.

"I can't make that happen."

"After this double cross you really don't expect me to get on a private plane with you? I'm not willing to risk having to suddenly sprout wings."

The man shook his head. "I really can't, I don't call the shots at all."

Kharon put his hand on Panos' shoulder. "Tell your boss anything you want, and your boss can even pick the spot for us to meet in Athens. But that's my final offer. Take it, or leave me alone."

"No need to rush your decision," said Jacobi. "Take until tomorrow morning to make up your mind. But if it's a go, show up here with the cash."

Panos nodded. "By tomorrow."

"Morning," said Jacobi.

"Okay, okay. I'll get back to you by tomorrow morning." Panos reached for the backpack.

"Uh-uh," said Jacobi, putting his hand on the bag, "my commission for negotiating the settlement. Besides, we wouldn't want you getting mugged in this neighborhood."

Panos glared at Jacobi, but drew his hand back from the bag. He pulled a mobile phone out of his pocket, pressed a speed dial button, and muttered something in a language not Greek. He finished his call. "Fine, tomorrow morning here."

A black Chevrolet Suburban appeared at the curb, Panos jumped into the front passenger seat, and the SUV sped away.

Jacobi put his arm around Kharon's waist. "Just like the old days. Mr. Good Cop and Mr. Bad Cop out-hustling delivery-men hustlers."

"Stealing from orphans…It sounded so easy until they tried it."

"Yeah, but in those days, it was spoiled milk and threadbare clothes they tried passing off as the real stuff. Now it's this." Jacobi pointed at the bag of cash.

"Some things never change," said Kharon. "It's the same shitty people, just doing different things."

"But with bigger paydays. Which I'll take as a definite improvement." Jacobi reached into the bag and pulled out a fistful of phony euro notes. "I can fence this paper tonight for enough real stuff to get you a killer BMW bike by tomorrow."

Kharon shrugged. "Not interested. You keep it."

"Are you nuts?" Jacobi picked the backpack off the table and headed toward the kitchen. "Never mind," he called over his back. "I already know the answer to that question."

"Like I said," Kharon said quietly, "some things never change."

Chapter Six

Kharon spent the night in a nondescript hotel just off Omonia Square. He preferred staying in that part of Athens. It was once Athens' most prominent square, filled with fine hotels, restaurants, and residences. Not anymore. Today it served as home to an around-the-clock drug and hooker trade, with Greek not the primary language of its residents. Most people living there possessed the good sense to mind their own business. Kharon liked that. It lent him anonymity, invaluable in his line of work.

His mobile rang. It could only be one person, but he wasn't calling from the secure landline. Kharon answered and waited to hear the voice on the other end.

"Kharon?"

"Did he show?"

"Yes, and with all the money."

Silence.

"Kharon, did you hear me? He showed with a hundred thousand euros!"

"Yes, I heard. So did all the world by now."

"Come on, this isn't the United States, no one's listening in on calls from my shitty little taverna in Athens."

"Where is the meeting?"

"You're to be at the foot of the Acropolis at two. At the start of the path up to the top."

"Who am I looking for?"

"He said they'd initiate contact."

"Bye."

"Wait a minute. What about all this money?"

"Hang on to it for me."

"Until when?"

"Until I ask for it."

"You definitely are nuts."

Kharon hung up. Jacobi was too cavalier about surveillance. These days everybody listened in on mobile phone calls. The only privacy you could hope to find was in the wilderness. Assuming no satellite or drone happened to be watching you.

With his friend broadcasting one hundred thousand euros to the Exarchia world, he'd better be ready for uninvited guests showing up at the meeting. That kind of money made Kharon a kidnapping target, a rising business among enterprising bad guys in Greece. He looked at the clock on the nightstand. The Acropolis was only a couple of Metro stops away from his hotel, but he needed to get moving. He had a lot to do before two.

Hoping for the best was fine, as long as you prepared for the worst.

◇◇◇

"What's this?" said Andreas staring at the large box Tassos had dropped on his desk. It bore the name of Syros' most famous pastry shop.

"What's it look like?" Tassos, dressed in his customary dark suit, white shirt, and bland tie, dropped into the leather chair in front of Andreas' desk.

"Hey, easy on my furniture, I'm not sure that chair's rated to handle the extra weight you're carrying."

Tassos waved his hand in front of his face. "It's an old suit. It makes me look heavier than I am."

"Yeah, sure. I'll have to remember to try that line on Lila. At least unbutton the jacket. It looks like it's going to explode wide open any second."

Tassos waved him off. "I'm fine, it fits perfectly."

Kouros, sitting next to Petro on the couch beneath the windows, pointed at the box. "Speaking of Lila, you're going to be in a hell of a lot of trouble with her when she finds out what you brought the chief."

"He's right. She'll kill you." Andreas lifted the lid and peeked inside the box. He looked up at Tassos and laughed. "Bastard," and turned the box upside down, spilling the contents on his desk.

"Carrots?" said a disappointed looking Kouros.

"Syros' best. I may have been willing to risk Lila's ire, but not that of my beloved Maggie."

Andreas picked up a carrot and pointed it at Tassos. "They're in cahoots?"

"Of course."

"How come they haven't teamed up on you yet?" asked Andreas.

"Because they undoubtedly recognize that with age comes plumpness. It is nature's way of compensating the body for the thinning of other parts." He patted the top of his head with one hand.

"Can't wait to see what you pat with the other hand," smiled Kouros.

"Yianni, stop encouraging him." Andreas bit into the carrot. "Hey, this is good." He looked at Kouros and Petro. "Have one."

"I prefer mine in cake form," said Kouros, gesturing no.

Andreas picked up a carrot and tossed it at Petro. "Don't listen to him, eat your vitamins."

Petro caught it and dropped it onto his lap.

"Great, now I've got all my wacky wabbits together in one place—"

"I just bet you're dying for me to say, 'What's up, Doc?'" said Tassos.

Andreas aimed his carrot at Tassos. "That's a good one. Now can we get to work?"

Andreas described his conversation and a brief follow-up call that morning with the winemaker, and Kouros brought Tassos up to date on the details of his and Petro's investigation.

"Anything to add?" said Andreas to Petro.

"Just that tomorrow's Thursday, so we're hoping to start moving up the supply chain once we get a bead on the new guy supplying *bomba* to Aleko's club in Vouliagmeni."

Tassos nodded. "My guess is you'll dead end at the same place the winemaker did, with an Eastern European name heading up a foreign crime family, but this time in Greece."

"Why do you say that?" said Andreas.

"Because the three names the winemaker got for you through his lawyers are all Eastern European mobsters. Not a single one native to the country they're working in. That sounds like a pattern."

Andreas nodded. "Could be."

"What do you mean 'could be'? It's a sure thing. I'll bet you your carrots."

"No deal." Andreas bit off another chunk. "If you're right, what's the common connection back to whoever's behind it all?"

"Could be the packaging," said Kouros.

"Maybe," said Tassos, "but if the brains behind all this is taking such care to avoid any direct link to the people running all those separate EU country operations, I doubt you'll find a visible hand in the packaging side of the business."

"But it is a place to look," said Andreas.

"I agree," said Tassos,. "And we shouldn't assume perfection on the part of the bad guys. I'll see if I have any friends in the paperhanging business who might be able to give us a lead."

"Paperhanging business?" said Petro.

"Counterfeiters. It all involves putting ink on paper to make the phony look real. It's a small community, so maybe I'll get lucky and come up with something."

Andreas smiled. "I knew you wouldn't disappoint us. No one knows the sordid underbelly of our country better than you."

Tassos shifted in his chair and his jacket rose higher up on his belly, threatening to launch a button across the room. "I think you're trying to compliment me, though it's not quite coming across that way." Tassos undid the button. "I've spent a career showing respect to people on all sides of the law and I'm very proud of that accomplishment."

"For which I'm eternally grateful. Almost as much as I am that…" Andreas pointed at Tassos with the carrot stub, "you unbuttoned your jacket."

Tassos threw Andreas a lazy, open palm equivalent of the middle finger.

"What do you want us to do?" said Kouros.

"For now, precisely as you've planned." said Andreas. "That Thursday *bomba* guy is our only potential link back to whoever's running things in Greece. If we find out who that is, we might be able to sweat him into giving us the big boss."

"Once we find him, I think putting his balls in a wine press will likely get us faster results," said Tassos.

"Or," said Petro, picking the carrot up from his lap, lifting it above his head, and snapping it loudly in half.

Tassos shifted his eyes from Petro's broken carrot to Andreas. "I really like the new kid."

◇◇◇

Two o'clock on a sunny summer day in Athens drew only the hardiest or most foolish to trek from Dionysiou Areopagitou pedestrian promenade at the base of the Acropolis up to the Parthenon at the top. A half-dozen or so young men straddled bicycles as they talked among themselves in the shade of a large plane tree, by the entrance to the path to the Parthenon.

The bicyclists wore the bright yellow tee-shirts of a messenger company, matching racing caps, and all black Ray-Ban Wayfarer sunglasses. All but one carried messenger bags slung across their backs. The lone holdout wore his bag resting on his right hip. Kharon could reach his weapons quicker that way.

He'd paid the others double their normal hourly earnings and given them the sunglasses in exchange for their hanging out with him for a couple of hours, saying he needed them as cover to catch his cheating wife and her boyfriend strolling the promenade at lunchtime. They'd leisurely pedaled back and forth along the promenade for nearly an hour when Kharon told them to stop under the plane tree and take a break. That had been at five minutes before two.

When they'd last passed that same spot, Kharon noticed that a black Mercedes G-class SUV with heavily tinted windows had driven onto the pedestrian way and parked directly across from the entrance to the path up to the Acropolis. The SUV hadn't moved.

Kharon sat on his bike, sipping from a water bottle, scanning every face he could see. None seemed the sort interested in conducting an interview. At precisely two o'clock a bearded derelict dozing under folded cardboard by the path entrance jumped to his feet, startling three tourists into abandoning a nearby bench. He waved his hands and began a dance of what looked to be his own improvised creation. But Kharon did not see it, for he was searching for anyone not distracted by the performance. He found no one.

As abruptly as he'd started, the derelict ended his dance, went back to the bench, and picked up his cardboard. He shuffled to the edge of the path, carefully unfolded the cardboard, held it up above his head, and slowly turned so that everyone in the area could read, KHARON IS HERE, WHERE ARE YOU?

A few tourists laughed. One yelled out, "Do you take silver coins?"

Someone knows his Greek mythology, thought Kharon. *Be sure to have coins for the ferryman.* But the tourist walked away. That was not his contact. No one approached the derelict. After five minutes he carried his cardboard sign to the bench and sat down. It was now two-fifteen. Still no interviewer.

"Hey, are we done yet?" asked one of the bicyclists.

"Almost," said Kharon. "Just one more thing. Follow me."

He put the water bottle back on the bike, pushed off, and pedaled thirty yards past the rear of the black SUV before turning and coming back at it from behind. He skirted in between the passenger side and the edge of the road, burst out in front of the SUV, and pointed at a sign marked NO MOTORIZED VEHICLES.

He pedaled ahead toward the elegant pre-war homes that distinguished Dionysiou Areopagitou from virtually everywhere else in Athens, but turned and circled back before reaching Herodes Atticus theater, pointing again at the sign as he passed close alongside the driver's door. His identically dressed companions followed him, making identical gestures toward the sign. The bicyclists looped slowly around the SUV, like Indians from an American Western film surrounding a wagon train wrongly cutting through their territory.

A few minutes into this routine, as Kharon's bike came head-on past the SUV's front bumper on the driver's side, the driver's door flew open—wedged in place by the driver's left foot—smashed into the bike's front wheel and catapulted Kharon over the handlebars. But, as if he were a gymnast going from one uneven bar to the next, Kharon grabbed ahold of the outside edge of the open door, swung his body around it, and drove his feet squarely into the face of a surprised and instantly unconscious driver.

The big man next to the driver struggled to pull a gun from his right hip, but before he could free it Kharon had pushed the driver across the seat into him, drawn a switchblade from his bag with his right hand, and driven the tip hard up against the big man's throat.

"Uh, uh, Panos," said Kharon as he edged across the seat closer to the ex-soldier. "Play nice, now."

Panos slowly raised his hands. "No problem. Didn't know it was you."

"Then please tell your friend in the backseat to put down the Uzi." Kharon kept the blade pressed against Panos' throat.

"That was a very bold move, young man," said a voice from the backseat. "But foolish, because you would be dead if I wanted you that way."

"Wrong on the last point. You'd be dead by now, and still may be if you don't put that thing down."

"Foolish *and* brazen," said the person in the backseat. "Some might say arrogant."

"Panos, take a look at my left hand and tell your friend what you see."

Panos slowly lowered his head to where he could see Kharon's left hand. "He's got a pistol grip sawed-off shotgun sticking out of a messenger bag pointed at you through the seat."

"You forgot to mention it's a twelve gauge."

"Well done," said the one in the backseat. "My compliments."

"Spare me and drop the Uzi, butt-first, onto the front seat where I can see it."

The gun dropped on the seat between Kharon and Panos.

"Thank you."

"Young man, I think it might be a good idea if we got out of here. Your cycling colleagues have fled, perhaps to get the police. Why don't you come back here with me? Bring your toys with you, and Panos, switch with your unconscious friend and get us out of here before Athens' finest shows up."

Kharon took the gun from Panos' hip, another from the driver, and put them, the knife, and the Uzi in the messenger bag. He slid over the front seat into the backseat on the driver's side, still holding the shotgun. "So, is our interview finished, madame?"

The trim woman adjusted the jacket of her black pantsuit and brushed a stray strand of dark hair away from her sunglasses back toward the tight bun that held the rest of her hair in place. "How did you ever get the derelict to perform precisely at two?"

"I gave him fifty euros and an alarm clock set to go off at two to remind him that if he danced and held up the sign when the alarm went off, he'd get another hundred."

The woman nodded. "You're very good."

Kharon showed no expression. "You knew all you wanted to know about me before you set this up. Why am I here?"

"Not 'all.'"

The SUV pulled away and turned right at the first street off the promenade.

The woman leaned toward the front seat. "Take us back to the plane."

"Whoa, I'm not going anywhere on a plane."

She sat back and turned her head to face Kharon. "I understand, but I must leave, and by the time we reach the airport you and I will have concluded our business, one way or the other."

He met her look, though he couldn't see her eyes through her sunglasses. "And what's that supposed to mean?"

She shrugged. "Nothing more than what it seems. Either we shall reach a deal or decide to go our separate ways. A talent such as yours is too precious to waste, and I assume I'll have your word as a gentleman that if we cannot reach an agreement you will not divulge what we've talked about."

"Why do I think that won't be enough of a guarantee for you?"

"Because you're cautious. But once you know who I am and what I have in mind you'll realize that if you talk about what I am about to tell you, it won't hurt me. It will just show me that I cannot trust your discretion, and that would be a dangerous mistake for you to make."

"You've not yet made me a believer."

"But you have all the guns." She pointed at his shotgun and messenger bag. "What do I have to match them?"

"How about what Helen used to launch a thousand ships?"

She smiled. "Why, Kharon, you're a charmer, too."

"But is it enough to keep the cobra from striking the charmer? That's all I want to know."

She leaned forward, pressed a button, and a dark plexiglass screen rose up out of the back of the front seat to the ceiling. "There. That gives us both privacy to talk and a sign to you of my good faith."

"What sign?" said Kharon.

She smiled again. "That divider screen is made of bulletproof plexiglass. Had you blasted away with your shotgun when it was down, the shot wouldn't have penetrated beyond the back of the front seats. If I'd wanted, I could have killed you anytime I wished."

Kharon pursed his lips and raised an eyebrow. "Make that two thousand ships."

Chapter Seven

"Maggie, come in please," Andreas yelled from his office.

Maggie poked her head in the doorway. "Do you mean all the way in, or is the head enough?"

"Nope, this will require the full-body experience."

"Are you lonely for your playmates?" She walked over to his desk.

Andreas smiled. "Funny you should say that. Yianni and Petro are preparing to chase down our sole lead on Greece's *bomba* kingpin, and your boyfriend is off doing only the devil knows what trying to generate another lead. So, I figured it's time we pitch in too."

"What's with the 'we'? Apparently, unlike some people, I've got a lot of work to do."

"*We* are going to do some Internet research on the counterfeit wine business."

Maggie smiled. "Have you punched 'counterfeit wine' into your browser yet?"

Andreas gestured no.

"Then do so, please."

Andreas inhaled, typed in the words, and exhaled.

"Stop with the passive-aggressive breathing. There's a point to this."

A rush of headline world media coverage—ninety-nine percent of it in English—popped onto Andreas' screen.

"As you can see, Boss, there's more than enough material there to keep you busy all afternoon practicing your English language skills. You've got back issues of the world's leading financial newspapers, a mass of wine industry publications, and recorded British and U.S. television news reports to listen to."

She smiled. "Sadly, my English isn't good enough to be of much help."

Andreas quickly scrolled through the list of articles. "How did you know about all this?"

"I went online after Tassos asked me what I knew about counterfeit wine. I'd told him not much, because it hadn't been a big problem in Greece and I didn't collect expensive French wines, a pursuit fraught with counterfeit-related risks."

"'Fraught?'"

"Yes. I came across 'fraught' in the first sentence of the first English language article I found on the subject. That's about when I decided to give up on my Internet research project. All I can tell you is the amount of money at play boggled my mind. Worldwide annual wine sales approach thirty-four billion bottles, distilled spirit sales run at about the same rate, and demand for both continues to grow."

"That explains the big push into counterfeit."

Maggie nodded. "And I couldn't find anything about counterfeit in the Greek press that we didn't already know."

"Meaning?"

"That it took *bomba*-induced sex in public, crowds on drunken rampages, and a flood of counterfeit euros into one of the country's most notorious, busy tourist locations to get that community united enough to demand police action. The bottom line reality is, only when a *bomba* death of a foreign visitor threatens Greece's tourism image will authorities drop a highly publicized, but selectively administered, hammer on *bomba* sales."

"For a while."

Maggie pointed at the screen. "There's a lot there that might interest you. Let me know when you find something exciting." She smiled as she turned and headed back to her desk.

Andreas thought to ask her just who did she think was the boss, but he already knew the answer.

He began to read, hoping that somewhere in all that information he'd find what drove the counterfeit alcohol market, and from that perhaps deduce a clue to the sort who might be involved in Greece. But what he learned was there were different markets, driven by different motives.

What drove counterfeiting in places like China had nothing to do with lower prices, but with a lack of access to the product. Chateau Lafite Rothschild ranked as the hottest expensive wine in China, yet estimates put only one of every ten bottles sold there as genuine. Counterfeiters rebottled good, fifty-euro bottles of Bordeaux and sold them as fifteen-hundred-euro bottles of Lafitte to palates not used to the difference.

The two identical bottles Theo had shown him in their Skype call—one real, one phony—were an example of how modern technology, designed to aid an industry, had actually made it easier for counterfeiters. Widely available better printing, bottling, and packaging techniques made it so almost anyone could create first-rate copies virtually identical to the originals, and the Coravin syringe system allowed wine to be removed from a bottle without destroying what remained, making it possible to extract from a single bottle of a great vintage just enough to mask any number of bottles of counterfeit with a touch of the real.

Maybe somewhere in all this I'll find the name of someone to talk to, Andreas hoped—a cop or prosecutor who'd successfully brought down a major counterfeiter.

But there wasn't much reported on that score, and nothing helpful. Most of the mainstream media attention focused on the independent efforts of an American billionaire wine collector, fed up at being defrauded by counterfeiters, who decided to take matters into his own hands.

The collector estimated he'd spent four and a half million dollars on four hundred twenty-one bottles of counterfeit wine—out of his total collection of over forty thousand bottles—and another twenty-five million dollars on lawsuits going after his swindlers. One defrauder, called the "Bernie Madoff of the wine world," received a ten-year sentence for fraud tied to his selling thirty-five million dollars' worth of bogus wine at auction. Another of the industrialist's targets, described as a "super counterfeiter," allegedly sold him four bottles of a bogus Chateau Lafite 1787 purportedly purchased by U.S. president Thomas Jefferson in 1790 for four hundred thousand dollars. The American continued to pursue that seller, but he'd given up on collecting wines, saying he'd tired of being swindled by con artists and crooks.

Andreas did find some news stories about various governments' efforts at controlling the counterfeit wines and spirits markets, but in many places—notably China, Turkey, Russia, Eastern Europe, and Southeast Asia—enforcement seemed driven more by deaths brought on by consuming alcohol adulterated with poisons than any serious desire on the part of authorities to go after the counterfeit alcohol industry.

Andreas shook his head and mumbled aloud. "It's the same everywhere. Unless you're stupid enough to piss off the super-rich or powerful, or do something that gets someone killed, this sort of thing simply isn't a police priority."

Andreas pushed back from the screen and swung his chair around to stare out the window. Counterfeit booze offered extraordinary profits with low risk of prosecution. The perfect business for attracting organized crime. No surprise there. But once his unit got an angle on who's behind it all, there would be surprises. Of that he was certain. With something this big he had no doubt there'd be big-time political protectors involved.

Andreas bit at his lower lip. *This is going to get interesting.*

◇◇◇

"If I might offer a suggestion, it would set a far more civilized tone for our conversation if you pointed your shotgun away from my chest. Besides, I can assure you I'd find it most unpleasant if our brief time together were cut even shorter by reason of one of your country's notorious roadway potholes."

Kharon didn't move. He studied the woman's face. As far as he could tell she wore no makeup and he guessed her to be around twice his age. "I have every confidence in your car's suspension system."

"Very well." She brushed another strand of hair away from her sunglasses. "I've heard very impressive things about you. From the performance I witnessed back there, and continue witnessing here, I must agree."

"I don't advertise."

She smiled. "There is no way someone in your line of work can operate in Europe and not come to my attention. Assassins attract interest among those most likely to be their targets. It's rather important we keep informed of who's out there."

"Must be pricey information."

"Yes, but in the long run not as costly as ignorance."

"Should I know you?"

"I'd hope not. I take even greater care than you not to 'advertise.' Notoriety is bad business for both of us."

"I'm getting the impression our conversation has more to do with your business than mine."

She turned her head away from Kharon and faced the side window. Traffic was relatively light along Vassilias Sofias Avenue as they drove toward the Hilton Hotel and the back streets that would connect to the highway taking them to the airport.

"I'm an international businesswoman involved in diversified industries. Recently I expanded into another world."

"I assume you're not talking about time travel or ghosts."

Kharon caught a smile in her reflection in the window. "No. The world of alcoholic beverages."

"What kind?"

"Wine, whiskey, vodka, tequila, rum, whatever sells."

"What brands?"

"All of them."

"You're a distributor?"

"Yes, and a producer of top quality reproductions of the world's leading brands."

"You're a *bomba* bootlegger? That must set you against all kinds of nasty competition."

He saw another slight smile in her reflection. "I'm quite pleased with our progress at increasing market share, though I prefer you not categorize my products as *bomba*."

"Call it what you want, it's still counterfeit."

She nodded. "That I'll accept. Imitated, adulterated, manipulated alcohol has been around since an anonymous lucky soul back in ancient times discovered a wonderful surprise in a batch of moldy grapes unwittingly left to ferment. You may not know, but many of today's accepted practices for creating some of the world's finest wines and spirits were once treated as criminal acts, punishable by death in certain societies."

"*Bomba* kills."

"So can the real thing if you drink enough of it."

"I'm talking about adding turpentine and antifreeze. Stuff that can blind you, if not kill you."

"Yes, yes. I know." Her voice had taken on an edge. "But I'm not talking about that sort of garbage." All at once she swung her head around, pulled off her glasses, and fixed her eyes on his. "No, as a matter of fact *I am*."

He blinked but his eyes stayed drawn to a lustrous amber fire burning deep within dark, almond shaped eyes.

"I am surrounded by shortsighted, grab-the-money-and-run hoodlums who cannot give up their old *bomba*-making ways. They see poisons of the sort you named as a cheaper way of making their products, and never think of the market they're destroying."

She pointed her glasses at Kharon. "The annual worldwide market for alcohol is a trillion US dollars. That means every year there is another trillion dollars to be made, and virtually none of it comes with any of the serious risks or complications of trading in illegal drugs. Virtually all the affluent world finds drug traffickers morally reprehensible, yet they glorify bootleggers as romantics. Drugs draw special prosecutorial attention, but alcohol in one form or another is accepted as a staple in many of those same societies.

"Counterfeit alcohol presents a wide-open growth market at every level. From supplying cheap booze to bars and liquor stores under high-end labels, to offering big-time hustlers the sort of two-hundred-dollar product they can pass off at five or even fifty times more than what they paid for it. Plus every sort of product you can imagine in-between."

She shook her sunglasses at Kharon's chest. "I'm not about to let a bunch of ignorant, macho assholes destroy my potential piece of that pie. One tenth of one percent of that annual market is one billion dollars."

"I get your point, but what do I have to do with any of that? Booze isn't my business."

She smiled and put her glasses back on. "I'm quite familiar with what your business entails. That is why I wish to employ you. To protect my golden goose from those who do not appreciate its value."

"I'm not following you."

"For a modest return above my costs and expenses, I provide my collaborators with identical labels, bottles, packaging, and instructions on how to make my products in their countries. All I ask in return is that they adhere to my specifications. In some instances I've supplemented their marketing methods with my own, successfully eliminating much of their competition. All of them are now far richer than they'd ever imagined."

She shook her head. "But sadly it is the nature of such men to steal. I think it is the risk that excites them, for their rewards cannot possibly match the consequences of failure. And so they manufacture my products using cheaper ingredients than specified, stealing from me in the process, and then from their customers by selling their garbage as mine, hoping the customer won't notice. But they do notice, they complain, and they buy elsewhere. It is not the customer I blame, it's my people."

"Why don't you just switch representatives?"

"It's not easy setting up such an operation, especially in an EU country. All of them have contacts in place, each unique and necessary to their businesses. It's an elaborate network of customers, producers, distributors, police, tax, customs, and other cooperative government officials. Besides, as I said, it's the nature of such men to steal. They're all alike." She shook her head. "No, new collaborators are not the answer. I need another approach."

"And you think I'm that approach?"

"I need a quality-control person, one who can enforce my production specifications."

"And how do you suggest I do that?"

"I'm sure you can come up with appropriate methods."

"You want me to kill someone."

She nodded. "If necessary. Which I think is quite likely. But if done once…or twice…in an appropriate manner, I'm fairly confident that no further significant violence will be required."

"Sounds like you're asking me to kill one of your collaborators as an example to the others?"

She shook her head no. "I don't want any of them killed. As I said, they're too valuable to me. But I want them to think that I will and to know that I could do so at anytime, anywhere I wished. They've grown complacent, think they don't need me anymore, and that their hordes of bodyguards can protect them from me."

"You make it sound as if they should be afraid of you."

She shrugged, modestly. "One can only hope. And that's where you come in."

Kharon moved the shotgun to where it no longer pointed at the woman. "That's quite a story you tell, complete with very impressive numbers, so I assume you're about to offer me a substantial sum to be your 'quality control person.'"

"Enough to set you for life."

"That sort of arrangement always worries me, as it motivates one side of the deal to find a way to reduce the payout period."

She smiled. "Then let's say, tell me what you want and I'll let you know if I agree."

"Please excuse me for saying this, but you're offering me a lot to get a simple 'you better behave' message across to some mobster. That's not a complicated problem. You must know any number of people out there willing to do what you want for a lot less than you're offering me. Many of them already in your employ." Kharon shook his head. "I don't get it. And that concerns me."

"I'm afraid you underestimate yourself, young man. Unlike with alcohol, I'm a firm believer in one getting what one pays for. And in this instance I need someone with a subtle touch, not a machete, to bring my network in line. I'm not looking to start wars with my collaborators. I want them to realize they're better off following my methods."

"Or else the machete will come?"

"Does that bother you?"

"Me?" Kharon gestured no. "What bothers me is that I have absolutely no idea who you are, and I don't like working for people I know nothing about."

"You mean money alone isn't enough?"

"It's never been just about the money."

She nodded. "I see."

"So, who are you?"

"I don't think it's necessary for me to tell you."

"It is if you want me to work for you."

"What I meant was, ask around. I'm sure some of your colleagues have heard of me, and I'm certain my introduction will be far more effective coming from them than me." She smiled. "I wouldn't want you to think I'm a braggart."

"All this mystery….Is it really necessary? Here? Now?"

She coughed. "It's kept me alive."

"So, what is your name?"

The car stopped.

She turned and looked out the window. "We're already here. I'll have my driver take you wherever you wish to go." She reached into her jacket pocket, pulled out a card, and handed it to him.

Kharon looked at the woman's card as the door on her side swung open.

"There's no name on this, just a phone number."

"I no longer have a name. Just call the number and you'll reach me."

Kharon stared into the dark lenses of the woman's glasses.

She patted his hand that still held the shotgun. "They call me Teacher."

Chapter Eight

"Tassos is here," came crisply through the speaker on Andreas' phone.

"Send him in."

"When I'm done with him. He never came home last night and is trying to convince me he was on official business. You're his alibi."

"I'll let you know whether to believe him after I hear his story."

The door to Andreas' office swung open. Tassos stood in the doorway. "Thanks for standing up for me."

"Any time." Andreas gestured to the chair in front of his desk. Tassos dropped onto the couch.

"I'm exhausted. I can't take these all night partying types anymore."

"Where the hell were you?"

"That sums up the difference between a man and a woman. 'Where were you?' is what a man asks, '*What* were you doing?' is all the woman wants to know."

Andreas shook his head. "Just let me know when you get to the part I know you're dying to tell me?"

"In my mind I'm debating that precise point at this very moment. Since I didn't get back to my beloved's place until after she'd left for work, there's a significant chance I may have to stay on this couch indefinitely."

Andreas nodded. "So it's protective custody you're looking for."

"Glad you appreciate my predicament. Last night I went looking for those paperhangers I mentioned. One of the best places to get a line on them is in busy late-night clubs. Those spots are great for distributing counterfeit. The wilder and busier the club, the easier to pass the stuff. Customers rarely count their change, much less study the notes…even if they know what to look for."

"How did you expect to catch a counterfeiter passing paper in those crowds?"

Tassos smiled. "By watching for customers who tip big for their drinks."

Andreas jerked his head quizzically to the side. "I don't understand."

"Busy bars are pretty savvy about counterfeit, so for a counterfeiter to pass large quantities of his paper requires cooperation on the inside. The best connection is an owner, but you can pass a lot working with a hustling bartender. They take in the good bills and give out the bad as change."

Andreas reached for a bottle of water sitting on his desk. "But what's the incentive to the bartender for passing counterfeit?"

"The principle's the same as it is for a bar owner who buys counterfeit at a steep discount. Say the bar bill is fifty euros; the counterfeiter gives the bartender a hundred in bad notes and the bartender gives back a legitimate fifty in change. The counterfeiter tips him with a bogus fifty and the bartender passes all the bogus dough out in change to other customers. By the end of the night all the money in the bartender's pocket and in the register is real."

Andreas nodded as he finished drinking from the bottle. "And the owner never finds counterfeit in his register to charge back against the bartender."

Tassos smiled. "Exactly. Never underestimate the entrepreneurial skills of a bartender."

"I assume you caught a live one."

"It was so simple I'm almost embarrassed. He was in this hot club off Pireos Avenue, playing the big shot, buying drinks for half the women around the bar, and carrying on as if he were a bastard son of Aristotle Onassis. But the bartender made him pay for each round, and he never complained. That tipped me off. True high rollers insist on running a tab; it's part of their routine. But this bartender couldn't let his guy run one because if the guy stayed all night and paid him at the end, the bartender wouldn't have time to pass the counterfeit back out as change.

"The guy must have spent a couple thousand euros while I was sitting there, and every time he paid for a round he'd tip the bartender the cost of that round. He'd do it by putting *twice* the amount for the round on the bar. The bartender would pick up the euros, take them back to the register, and come back with change. That's when the big spender insisted he take the big tip. But the tip *never* came out of the real notes he received in change from the bartender. He'd hand him different euro notes."

"Let me guess, you became high roller's new best friend."

Tassos yawned. "I slid next to him at the bar as he was paying for a round and it went sort of like this. 'Hey, guy, it's an honor to be in your presence. There aren't many generous guys like you around these difficult times.'

"'I believe in spreading the wealth while you have it. No telling what can happen in life.'

"'Amen, brother.' At about that point the bartender gave him his change and the guy put the tip down on the bar. I clamped my right hand on top of the change and the tip, and held my badge out in my left. The bartender looked at the badge and walked away. Big Spender just stared at me. I thought he was going to cry.

"I explained that passing counterfeit euro notes brought big-time EU sentencing attention and perhaps we should adjourn to a quieter place to discuss a resolution of the problem."

Andreas smiled. "He must have thought you were shaking him down."

"Considering the ways of so many of our brethren, how could he not? And I did not discourage him. He offered me a few thousand real euros but I said I was looking for a bigger score. I needed an angle on someone who could counterfeit booze labels. He said he had no idea but knew some guys who might. Turns out he wasn't a paperhanger, but passed the stuff for a few who were."

"And so you spent the rest of the night looking for 'some guys'?"

"Yep. That's my story and I'm sticking to it."

Andreas shook his head. "You better get used to the couch."

"The guy talked to me like I was his father confessor or something. We must have hit a dozen bars, and in every one I got another chapter of his sad, miserable life story. And the guy's not even thirty."

"How much of it was true?"

Tassos shrugged. "Who knows? But I finally told him if he didn't stop with the bullshit and deliver, the next bars he'd see would be those of a cell in Kordydallos. So around sunup we hit this tiny bar in Monasteraki, hardly a soul in it, but my guy said the fellow sitting at the bar was the da Vinci of Athenian engravers."

"Yet, da Vinci was Italian."

Tassos waved his hand in the air. "The guy wasn't an art historian. Anyway he introduced me as a friend looking for someone to do labels. And da Vinci asked 'What kind?' I said, 'booze and wine.'

"That's when he said, 'Seems to be a big market for that sort of talent these days. Hard to imagine why what with all the digital shit taking over the business.'

"Next thing I know, he's telling me his story. Maybe Maggie's right and I should lose some weight. I'm starting to think I look like a priest. Anyway, so now I'm hearing this guy's story, and since he's close to sixty, I figure it will be noon before I hear the end of it."

Andreas picked up the water bottle again. "Sort of how I feel right now."

"Screw you. Anyway, about two hours into it, he says how he'd just finished a really neat job for some 'big-time' Greek hood doing labels of all the big French and American wines."

Andreas paused in taking a sip of water. "Not Greek wines?"

Tassos nodded. "I asked the same question. He said the guy who hired him told him French and American are where the big money is in wines these days, so that's what he wants to get into."

"Did he name the hood?"

Tassos gestured no. "He was bragging about his work while trying to sell me on how discreet he could be. But I have a pretty good idea who the guy is. Da Vinci was pretty blasted by the time he got around to telling me that part of his story, and I kept pressing him for a name. Finally he told me, 'Fuck off, I'd never give your name to Tank, so I'm not going to give you his.'"

"Tank?" Andreas put down the bottle.

Tassos spread his arms wide. "As in built like one. It's his nickname and he operates out of Thessaloniki. Not a big-time mobster, but connected. Sort of the black sheep of a politically very powerful, deep and dirty, battleship gray flock."

Andreas nodded. "I know who you're talking about, but I never knew him to be into *bomba*. I thought drugs and the sex trade were his thing."

"His front operation has always been a small-time legitimate alcohol and cigarette distribution business. He runs it out of a *cafenion* up in Thessaloniki. He got the licenses through his father's connections and they're his cover for his real nightlife-scene operations."

"I guess he's expanding," said Andreas.

"The only thing is, he doesn't fit the pattern. He's Greek, not a Balkan mobster operating in a foreign country like the others."

"Anything else?"

"No. Da Vinci's story is that he's just 'an artist' and takes no part in the business of his clients. If he's as good as he and his buddy said, I'm sure he's also into counterfeiting euros, but I couldn't raise that without sounding like a cop and burning the guy who introduced me. Besides, he'd never answer me, anyway, and I figured I knew where to find him if I ever needed to talk to the great artist again."

"How'd you leave it?"

"I told da Vinci I'd check with my boss and get back to him. I told the thirty-year-old that if he wanted to make thirty-five rather than serve thirty-five, he'd better land a different line of work."

Andreas smiled. "What did he say?"

"If I could find him a job he'd take it. I said that's a great one-liner, but I doubted the judge will be moved by it."

Andreas laughed. "Indeed."

Tassos looked down at his tie and brushed away a bit of lint. "I guess I should go out and make up with my beloved."

"I'm sure she believes you about last night."

Tassos cocked his head. "How can you be sure?"

"Because if she didn't she'd have taken her ear away from the door, stormed in here, and killed us both." Andreas raised his voice. "Isn't that right, Maggie?"

A few seconds passed and the speaker crackled. "Damn straight."

◇◇◇

"Well, if it isn't my hotshot, in-demand buddy," called out Jacobi from a table in the rear of his taverna. "How'd the job interview go? I thought I'd hear from you yesterday."

Kharon sat down at Jacobi's table and slid a backpack across toward his friend. "I had some thinking to do. Thanks for the use of your shotgun."

"I assume you didn't fire it." Jacobi pulled the bag off the table and onto his lap.

Kharon nodded. "What do you know about a woman named Teacher?"

"Teacher? What kind of teacher? There are a lot of them around here, what with the university practically next door."

"No, not a real teacher. I'm talking about a serious mobster type, but a woman who looks around fifty, who calls herself Teacher."

Jacobi stared at Kharon but said nothing.

"What's wrong with you? Didn't you hear me?"

"Yeah, I heard you. I just wish I hadn't."

"Stop messing with me. Tell me what you know."

"That kind of telling can get someone hurt real bad, even killed."

"So can silence. But she told me to ask my 'colleagues' so I assume by that she meant you."

"Fuck." Jacobi looked down at his hands. "Promise me you'll keep this to yourself."

"Done."

Jacobi kept looking at his hands. "Everything I know is second-, maybe thirdhand. But I've heard the rumors enough times to stay as far away from anything having to do with Teacher as possible. She's said to bankroll quite a few of the biggest criminal enterprises in Eastern Europe. Ones that didn't have the good fortune of ex-KGB connections."

Jacobi looked up at Kharon. "I'm sure the pay's great, but there's a story about her that should make you think long and hard before going to work for her. Doing business with Teacher is a lifetime commitment. There's no way out unless she ends it."

"I get your point. Now tell me the story."

Jacobi cleared his throat. "An Albanian mob boss built a hugely successful digital pirating network using Teacher's money and contacts. But he decided he'd shared enough of his profits, hired on a small army of muscle to protect him, and told Teacher to go fuck herself.

"Less than a month later he watched as his wife and three children were doused with gasoline and burned to death. One by one. But he wasn't killed. Instead, his every other toe and finger were snipped off with pruning shears and his penis and tongue burned with a blowtorch. The man now pays on time.

"End of story."

Kharon stared across the table at his friend. "Do you believe it?"

Jacobi shrugged. "Even legends have a basis in fact. I'd prefer not to learn firsthand how much of this one is true."

Kharon kept staring. "Aren't you curious to find out what she's heard about me?"

Jacobi leaned forward. "No need to, my farmer friend. I can guess. 'You're a brilliant, ruthless, nutjob.'"

Kharon smiled.

◇◇◇

"Come in."

Kouros opened the door to Andreas' office.

"I'm surprised. You actually knocked," said Andreas.

"Maggie wasn't around and I didn't want to barge in on something."

"She must have gone out to buy me a present," said Tassos.

"Probably a GPS to keep track of your late-night wanderings." Kouros dropped into one of the chairs in front of Andreas' desk.

"You heard about it too?" said Andreas.

"Only the part about our friend here staying out all night. Nothing about what happened."

"Enough about me," said Tassos. "Did you come up with anything?"

"Not much. Petro and I followed the guy to what seemed every hot bar and club in town. He knew his way around but never carried more than a bottle or two of booze into any place."

"Sounds like he was dropping off samples and picking up orders," said Tassos.

Kouros nodded. "That's what we figured. About three hours ago he headed north out of Athens toward Rafina, got off the highway, and made his way to an old warehouse not far from the port."

"What sort of warehouse?" said Andreas.

"A busy one surrounded by razor wire, with trucks going in and out, and forklifts loading and unloading pallets. It had the sort of high security you'd expect for a place holding valuable goods. Or illegal ones. The gate had a guard, so we couldn't get close enough to verify what was inside, but our guy went through a door marked OFFICE and stayed there for about a half-hour. A half-dozen other salesman-looking types went in and out the same door while we waited for our guy to come out.

"When he did, we followed him to Kifisia. He parked next to an apartment building listed as the address for the car. He went upstairs to an apartment, and from the street we could see him with what appeared to be his wife and two young children."

"Just your typical, hardworking, Greek family man," smirked Tassos.

"Trying to make ends meet selling bootleg," said Kouros.

"From the neighborhood you tailed him to, I'd say he's making a hell of a lot more than any liquor salesman I ever knew," said Andreas.

"I checked him out. He's connected through his wife to a political clan up north."

"Let me guess." Tassos gave him Tank's family name.

"How the hell did you know that?" said Kouros.

"Lucky guess."

Andreas answered for him. "An informant told him that a member of that family had gone into the bootleg business. It all fits. His nickname is Tank and he keeps his organization tight by using family members wherever he can."

"The warehouse looks like it could be a major distribution point for his booze. We could hurt him real bad with a raid," said Kouros.

"He'd probably claim he uses it for his legitimate booze business and didn't know anything about the counterfeit," said Tassos. "But even if you nailed some of his relatives in the warehouse in the act of putting phony tax stamps on *bomba*, I doubt you'd catch more than small fry."

Andreas made a fist. "We have to yank this network out by its roots. That means shutting down his producers and distributors, not just taking him out. Otherwise, all we're doing is making it easier for another bootlegger to step into his shoes."

"Not sure we can ever avoid that from happening," said Tassos.

"We can try," said Andreas.

"Sounds like you don't want him to know we're onto him," said Kouros.

Andreas nodded. "Not until we see if we can get a shot at bringing down the whole operation."

"Works for me," said Kouros. "Just tell me where to go from here."

"Have Petro stay on the Kifisia relative. I want a list of everyone he contacts. And once Petro has those names, tell him to do the same for the other salesman-looking types you saw at that warehouse. That should give us a handle on the distribution side of his business."

Kouros made a note in a pocket-size notebook. "Got it."

"I want you to head up north and see what you can find out about the production end. But be careful who you talk to, because with all the money involved, anybody could be in Tank's pocket."

Tassos nodded. "And he won't take kindly to someone he thinks might be trying to shut him down, even a cop."

"Especially a cop," added Andreas.

"When do I leave?"

"As soon as you can."

"Guess that means I'm out of here. Got to get home and pack. It's been a pleasure, gentlemen." Kouros stood and smiled at Tassos. "Amazing how a man of your age can still manage to stay up all night."

Tassos shrugged. "It's simple. Don't take care of your prostate."

Chapter Nine

Teacher sat in her study surrounded by things. All very expensive, immaculately maintained, and scrupulously accurate in presentation. Not one offered her a memory of her past. Any that did, even fleetingly, were banished to an auction house. Even the lone photograph in a silver frame on her desk pictured a young girl, someone she never knew, symbolizing a life she'd never lived.

She would have preferred never returning to Greece. Certainly not in search of another headstrong man to work for her, given the bitter disappointment of her last experience on that score. But this new one came highly recommended, too much so to ignore. More than she needed his help, she knew that it would be bad business for him to end up working for one of her competitors.

Too many mad religious zealots, preaching terrorism as the primary reason for existence in this life, wanted her dead. She and they appealed to the same recruits, for she also saw terrorism as a tool; but as one to better the lives of her followers in this life rather than simply as a means for transporting believers to the next.

She drew in and let out a deep breath. The young man had demonstrated the necessary physical skills and courage, and was clever too. He could be a sociopath, a trait common to his line of work. The question was, would he follow orders or look to run his own game? Children forced to raise themselves could go either way.

She knew that all too well. She'd had parents. Just never knew them. At the thought, memories came at her in rapid, flip-book fashion. Instinctively, she focused on the anonymous girl's photograph to fend them off, but some other instinct made her pause, and she let them come:

An Eastern European child, stolen away so young that her first memory was of her hands making knots for carpets and her body serving the much larger hands of faceless men. She'd survived as a trafficked slave by learning to obey orders in whatever language they were given, and emerging as the unquestioned ruler of her fellow captives' tiny universe by adopting the cardinal principle of her enslavers: *Do as I say or die.*

When her enslavers found more profit to be made from her as a full-time whore, she'd used her beauty to escape the life of those forced to take on all comers on a shantytown cot, and ultimately her wits to escape slavery by marrying the police protector of her captors.

She shook her head as if to stop her thoughts, but they rolled on. Now came the memories of her two fine sons, a kind husband who encouraged her education, and the day she found all three slaughtered in their home by a still unknown enemy.

On that day she became a nameless refugee fleeing to a foreign land, abandoning all connections to her past. In time she no longer feared death, and with that newly discovered liberty, took absolute control over her life for the very first time.

She made friends among the many like her that she met in shelters and on the streets. She'd lived their lives; she spoke their languages, and they had bonded. She taught them how to overcome and unite, weaned their fears into strength and their innocence into power. She used the skills she'd developed as a trafficked child to harness their rage at society's empty promises and focused them in violent attacks on those she presented as symbols of their oppression. She offered them a simple satisfaction for otherwise belittled lives: revenge. And in return they called her Teacher.

It did not take long before prospective targets saw the wisdom in paying Teacher for protection from her followers' ire. That's when money started rolling in and Teacher's life became infinitely more complicated. It led to bankers, lawyers, and investment advisers. Teacher had become part of the very system her followers despised.

But they saw her as different, for she brought them a better life, something no government had ever done. In exchange, they ruthlessly spread her methods of doing business across Eastern Europe, taking advantage of power vacuums that accompanied distracted, corrupt governments. And those who went to prison found new followers for her inside. No opportunity was missed. Teacher had become the quintessential, multi-national corporate leader.

She'd achieved far more than she'd ever dreamed. And none of it had been about the money. For her it was all about protecting the marginalized and oppressed; a mission that today made it *all* about the money. Today she faced off against fanatics possessing seemingly unlimited resources, recruiting the gullible from around the world with grand promises of a glorious afterlife for all who followed them in their violent path against the non-believers.

Her competition financed their proselytizing with oil and drug money. Teacher relied on counterfeit booze—and a global network of loyalists channeling its profits into bettering the day-to-day street-level lives of the exploited. All she asked of those benefitting from her largesse was the simple commitment of absolute fealty to furthering her vision. If that meant some had to die in the process, so be it. Her goal was just.

Teacher shifted in her chair and thought about what Kharon had said to her in the car. "It's never been just about the money." She smiled. *Perhaps he is the right choice.*

◇◇◇

At a casual pace, the drive from the hotel near Athens' Omonia Square to Kharon's home in the modern village of Delphi just beyond ancient Delphi took approximately two hours. For most travelers, entering modern Delphi meant a two-lane highway splitting into twin one-way streets, each a third of a mile long, one taking you away from the ancient site toward the towns below and one bringing you back. The streets stood lined with hotels, restaurants, snack bars, tourist shops, an occasional market or bakery, the random private home, and on one road, a post office. Much like most tourist areas, the locals lived away from the main streets, in this case up the mountain. There they'd find the goods and services necessary for sustaining a normal existence amid a tourism-driven economy.

But, for Kharon, entering Delphi today meant that he'd made the trip from Athens in one and a half hours, a near record, in large measure due to the BMW motorcycle he'd borrowed from Jacobi.

"Why not, you paid for it?" was all Jacobi said when Kharon asked to borrow it.

The rush of the high-speed ride cleared Kharon's helmetless head and got him thinking about Teacher's offer. No question if he accepted it he could say good-bye to being his own boss. She'd own his soul. And if she somehow thought him disloyal or inept, that would be the end of him. Or maybe there wouldn't even have to be a reason; simply an instinct on her part to get rid of him would do the trick.

But—and it was a big but—if he refused her offer, she'd likely kill him now. Her story about them parting ways amicably if he declined her offer was pure bullshit. Someone as powerful as Teacher, and used to dominating the lives of all about her, did not take rejection well. Rejection made her type worry about the motive and, rather than worry, elect to remove the source of concern. She'd probably already lined up his killer, just in case she had to pull the trigger. He thought about that last point. He thought about it a lot.

Know thyself, he thought, *and thy enemy better.*

By the time Kharon reached home he'd made up his mind. If he had no choice but to work for the devil, he'd damn well better have the devil's respect from the start. That meant pressing the devil hard. Extremely hard. Kharon now knew his price, and how far he might have to go to get it.

◇◇◇

Sunset colors in the Athens sky depended upon a lot of things. Some of which the city tried to control by limiting vehicular traffic in the city center according to the last number on a license plate. Those with even numbered plates could enter on even days, odd ones on odd days. But no matter what colors happened to be performing on a particular night—orange, magenta, crimson, rose—staring out his apartment windows at the Acropolis, backlit against a sunset sky, never failed to remind Andreas of how very blessed he was.

He sat in his living room holding his son on his lap, pointing at the Parthenon and telling of the glory that once was Greece.

"Daddy...do gods live on the Acropolis?"

Andreas kissed Tassaki on the top of his head. "We Greeks certainly hope so."

"My teacher said all gods are myths."

"Do you know what a myth is?"

"A story. Like fairy tales."

"You're very smart for four."

"Do you think my teacher is right?"

"I think your teacher believes they are myths. Other people do not. That's something for you to decide for yourself when you're older and can read about them." He kissed him again.

"I know how to read."

Andreas smiled. "I know you do, but some books may be a little too difficult for you to understand right now. I'll see if I can find one for you about the gods. Okay?"

"Okay."

Lila poked her head through the doorway from the dining room. "Marietta said dinner is ready."

Andreas put Tassaki on the floor, and the boy ran to his mother. "Daddy is going to buy me a book all about Greek gods, so I'll be able to find them when they come to the Acropolis."

Andreas caught a wondering look on Lila's face. He shrugged. "It beats raising an Xbox junkie."

Lila took Tassaki's hand, led him to the table, and helped him into his booster seat. "Tomorrow, right after preschool, we'll go to the bookstore and find you a good one."

Andreas gave Lila a kiss on the cheek. "Thanks for saving me the trip."

"Thank you, too, Mommy."

"You're welcome." Lila gave her son a kiss on the cheek and sat down between him and Andreas.

Marietta came into the room, carrying a bottle of white wine and a juice box. She put the juice box down in front of Tassaki. "Now you be careful not to squeeze the box or else you'll spill the juice and your mother will not be happy with either of us."

Lila smiled as Marietta poured some wine into her glass. "I'll be careful too." She turned toward Andreas. "Theo sent us a case of his best wine as a thank you for your helping him."

Andreas stared at his glass as Marietta served him the wine. "I haven't helped him yet, and I'd have preferred he'd not have done that."

"Why, do you think someone might think he's trying to bribe you?"

Andreas shot Lila a quick glance, moving his eyes to Tassaki and back to her.

Lila silently mouthed, "Whoops," followed by saying, "I meant, do you think someone might think he's trying to ride you into taking action?"

Andreas smiled. "Nice recovery, but yes to both formulations."

"Should I send it back?"

Andreas gestured no. "Let's just thank him and ask for the name of his favorite charity so that we can send a check in his name in appreciation of his gesture."

"Isn't that a bit of an overreaction for a case of wine?"

"Far less has brought down honest cops." *Like my father.* "No point in giving folks angles on me. Right?"

Lila nodded. "Absolutely. No problem, I should have realized that in the first place."

"What's a bribe?" said Tassaki.

Lila bit at her lower lip and looked at Andreas.

Marietta picked up a small plate filled with salad from the sideboard and placed it in front of Tassaki. "Eat all of your greens and I'll give you rice pudding for dessert."

Tassaki's face lit up in a smile, "Rice pudding's my favorite."

"Yes," said Marietta, "and giving it to you for eating your greens is what's called a bribe."

Andreas leaned over to Lila and said in a stage whisper, "She gets a raise first thing tomorrow."

Marietta smiled, did a brisk curtsy, and continued serving.

Lila tasted the wine. "Very good."

Andreas took a sip and nodded. "I sure hope I can do something for Theo. This is shaping up to be something a lot bigger than just Greek bootleggers. We're going to need quite a bit of cross-border cooperation."

"Doesn't seem to be much of that happening these days from what I see in the news."

"Europol is still pretty helpful. It's local authorities that make things tough in these situations. There's so much money available for bad guys to spread around that it seems practically impossible to root out the protected ones."

"I take it you're saying this isn't some Greek version of a cartoon showing an American hillbilly moonshiner trying to outwit the revenuers?"

"Definitely not."

"So I guess that means I root for the revenuers."

Andreas grinned. "That would be nice."

"I want to help, too, Daddy."

Andreas smiled. "Thanks, son."

"I'm going to ask the gods to help you."

Lila looked at Andreas but spoke to Tassaki. "How are you going to do that?"

"In my prayers."

Lila turned and faced Tassaki. "We only pray to one god."

"Mommy, I know that. That's why I'm going to ask our God

to speak to his friends who live in Greece to help Daddy. After all, isn't that what Greek gods are supposed to do, help Greece?"

Lila tousled Tassaki's hair. "Out of the mouths of babes."

Andreas lifted his wineglass. "From your lips to God's ears, my son."

Tassaki lifted his juice box. "*Yia mas.*"

Lila stared at Andreas as she lifted her glass. "And he's only four!"

◇◇◇

Teacher picked up the phone on the third ring. She could have on the first, but delay suggested nonchalance on her part and many times triggered unconscious anxieties in the caller. Both good things in negotiations. And she knew that's what this would be, for it was Kharon calling. Only he had the number for this line, scrambled and untraceable to her.

"Hello."

"Teacher?"

"Yes."

"It's Kharon."

"How nice to hear from you. I had expected a call from you sooner. You have patience."

"I have a price, too."

"I like someone who gets right to the point."

"As do I."

"So, what is it?"

"It's complicated."

Teacher cleared her throat. "Complicated?"

"There are olive trees and an olive oil production facility near where I live for sale. I want you to buy them for me."

"Why don't I just give you the money so you can buy them yourself?"

"No way I could explain how I had the money to do that."

"It's that expensive?"

"Of course."

Teacher smiled. "And you have to live there. I understand your concern."

"What I want you to do, is buy them in the name of a company ultimately owned by me but not traceable to me."

"That's a more sophisticated request than I imagined coming from you."

"I watch a lot of television."

She laughed despite herself.

"Anyway," Kharon went on, "the company will hire me to look after the operation for its supposed absentee owners."

"Very clever. Just how much will this little subterfuge cost me?"

"They're asking sixty euros per tree."

"Per tree?"

"That's how olives are sold here."

"How many trees are you looking to buy?"

"Ten thousand."

Teacher paused. "That's six hundred thousand euros. I understand the reason for your concern. I also think you place a rather unrealistic value on your services, young man."

"Plus, another four hundred thousand euros to acquire and modernize the olive-pressing facilities."

She let her tone turn cold. "There are many who do what you do."

"Then hire them."

Teacher bristled. "Perhaps I have."

"Undoubtedly. But before we cross that bridge, understand the full context of my offer."

"Please, proceed."

"Unless I misunderstood your offer of employment, you're asking that I work for you exclusively until death do us part."

"Interesting way to put it."

"But accurate?"

"Go on," she said.

"The second part of our arrangement is that you never have to pay me anything more than what's necessary to meet yearly property taxes on the olive trees and production facility. No matter what you ask me to do, you'll never have to pay me another euro."

"Your arrogance is not becoming."

"You're confusing arrogance with confidence."

Teacher drew in and let out a breath. "You talk a good game and have a distinguished reputation among those who know you. But frankly, you've only performed before local yokels on a very small stage. You've done nothing to show me why I should consider such an elaborate request, one I would have a hard time entertaining even if put to me by the very best in your business."

"Perhaps I should pass along an example of just what you'll be buying."

"Meaning?"

"Why don't you tell the two men in the beat-up black Fiat parked up the road from my place to stop by and say hello."

"Spotting those two is hardly worth the price you're asking."

"For sure. But that's not the example I'm offering. I have something I want to show them."

"Why don't you just tell me?"

"I don't think that will be quite as effective in moving our negotiations along."

"I think we've just about reached the end of any negotiations."

"Sorry to hear that."

Anger rose in her voice. "But I shall be sending someone around to see you."

"I'm sure you believe that."

The anger remained in her voice. "You'll find he is very good at what he does. Some say he's the best."

"Too bad, I wish I'd known that."

Teacher's anger faded into a tight smile. "Would that have made you ask for less?"

Kharon sighed. "No, but out of professional courtesy I'd have put a marker on his grave, 'Here lies the best, Michael C. Dillman.'"

◇◇◇

Teacher put down the phone and looked at the photograph of the young girl on her desk. She shook her head, laughed, and rubbed at her eyes. She kept laughing as she drew her hands away from her face and scraped her fingers back through her hair to the tight bun holding it in place. She undid the bun. Still laughing, she ran her fingers through her free-falling hair until abruptly clenching fistfuls of it in her hands and pulling wildly.

As quickly as her laughing had begun it stopped, and she dropped her hands onto her lap. She stared at the photo, drew in and let out a deep breath, then spoke aloud. "I can't believe he spotted Dillman. He's been with me since the second Bush's Iraq War. My deadly American chameleon. Just like that. Gone."

She shook her head again, but this time without laughter. She'd survived and prospered by following her instincts to whatever ruthless extremes they'd led her. Kharon's demand was preposterous even though the amount he'd asked for was meaningless to her. But, if her instincts were correct, and he was as he appeared, his value to her would be priceless.

She bit at her lower lip. For one who'd once said it was not about the money, he'd set quite a high price. She saw that as a good sign, that he'd recognized the value of aligning his principles with hers.

She looked at her phone. Greeks were notorious for picking asking prices out of thin air. With the right local lawyer and connections, she should be able to get the trees and business Kharon wanted at a much better price.

She smiled as she reached out and touched the photo. "I think we have found us a bargain in this man from Delphi."

◇◇◇

Kharon had taken a gamble, but he'd seen no other play. Teacher either would own him outright or see him dead. His only leverage was if she needed him badly enough to give him what he wanted in exchange. So, he told her about Dillman, betting that her urge for revenge couldn't compete with her thirst for someone with the skills he'd demonstrated in dealing with Dillman. Kharon had detected and anonymously eliminated a professional killer sent to target him by a person he neither knew nor had any reason to know might want him dead.

Twice he'd seen Dillman's car in the vicinity of his home before Dillman offered him a ride. And when the ride came it was in a very out-of-the-way place, almost as if Dillman had been following him. The coincidence struck him as too great. But he wasn't about to kill a man based on that alone. He'd need a sign; something to show him that Dillman was a professional setting him up for an unexpected hit at another time.

That sign had come in the form of Dillman's hand on Kharon's thigh. Sexual intimacy would be Dillman's pretext for their next and final assignation. Kharon knew that ploy. He'd used it himself. Most pros had. Which meant someone like Dillman would be suspicious of another pro succumbing so quickly to the bait. That left Kharon with no choice but to do all that he did on that plot of grass out beyond the cypress trees to get Dillman to drop his guard.

It wasn't until his bracing motorcycle ride back from Athens that Kharon had realized Teacher had sent Dillman. She'd arranged to have someone killed she'd not yet met, on the chance he might turn down an offer she'd not yet made. He admired her style, and hoped she'd admire his too.

His mind played through the final moments of their negotiations.

There'd been a decided pause on Teacher's end of the phone following Kharon's mention of Dillman's death, and he'd held his breath until she said, "Complete your first assignment, young man, and the property is yours."

"Terrific," he'd shot back, "but I'll need to own everything free and clear. I want you to have an investment in me, one that makes my living more important to you than my dying."

"That's acceptable, provided everything reverts to me should you die."

"Yeah, right, that would make me feel real comfortable," led to laughter on her part and an agreement: In exchange for no strings attached to his property, his life now stood as hers to control.

Kharon shut his eyes. He'd struck his deal with the devil.

Now to live with it.

Chapter Ten

Thessaloniki came to be 2,400 years ago, named for a half-sister of Alexander the Great. From the first years of the Byzantine Eastern Roman Empire until the early fifteenth century, Salonika, as it's also called, ranked next to Constantinople as the Empire's second city in terms of wealth and population. A leading trading, manufacturing, and shipping center in the days of the Empire, today Thessaloniki served as a major trade and business hub, with the largest number of students in Greece, a municipal population of 320,000, and more than a million in its metropolitan area. Though it was second in size to Athens and two hundred miles north, Thessaloniki residents proudly boasted of their city as Greece's cultural capital.

Kouros wasn't familiar with Thessaloniki and on his morning flight up from Athens toyed with the idea of a quick bit of sightseeing before heading off to find Tank, but settled on "maybe later." He'd ignored customary procedures calling for visiting cops on official business to inform local police of their presence, thinking if he had, for sure someone would have spread the word about a Special Crimes Division cop snooping around Thessaloniki.

He rented a car from an agency that emblazoned its name across its cars, making his tiny white hatchback as nondescript as the tens of thousands of other identical-looking Hyundais, Fiats, Peugeots, Nissans, Volkswagens, and Chevys driven around Greece by wandering tourists.

GPS got him to the address Maggie had found for Tank's *cafenion*. It was a nondescript coffee shop in what looked to be the sort of area every city allowed to exist in order for really bad guys to have a place to play, away from the nice folks. Omonia Square served that purpose in Athens. In Thessaloniki you went to Vardaris Square on the northwest edge of the city limits.

He parked, went inside, found a scruffy wooden table along the faded, pale green rear wall that abutted an open kitchen area, and sat facing into the room. He nodded at a man sitting at a similar square table next to him on his left. The man nodded back and continued reading his paper, taking his time eating his breakfast.

Kouros looked around the room. Eleven in the morning and still half the eight small tables crammed together closest to the front door sat packed with what looked to be locals, all of them men. In Athens, locals with jobs would be at work by now. Some of the men made no attempt to hide their curiosity about him, a proverbial Greek trait toward strangers.

"What would you like?" said a perky, very red-haired, thirty-ish woman bounding toward him with a pad in her hand.

Kouros smiled, "Just coffee, *metrio*."

She ticked her stylus along a small, touch-screen pad. "One Greek coffee, medium sweet. Got it." She put away the stylus.

Kouros nodded. "Thank you."

As she scurried off the men looked away, their curiosity apparently satisfied. He took out a map and studied it as if he were a tourist. The waitress returned with a glass of water, as always accompanies Greek coffee.

"Can I help you find something?"

"Thank you. I have no idea where I am. I'm trying to get here." He pointed at the map.

"Man, you should invest in a GPS. That's almost twenty miles from here." She looked at him. "You're way lost. That's down by the jail."

Kouros smiled. "I have to visit my mother."

"Your mother's in jail?"

Kouros reached out and patted her arm. "Shhh, someone might overhear you. It's embarrassing."

"Come on, you're putting me on. Besides, most of these guys call that place home." She jerked her head back toward the tables by the front door.

He smiled. "Yeah, I'm kidding about the part about my mother. But if the crowd's so bad, why are you working here?"

"You're really not from around here, are you?" She didn't wait for an answer. "Otherwise you'd know jobs are scarce, and you take whatever you can find."

A bell rang in the kitchen.

"I'll be right back with your coffee."

This time when she left, some of the men who'd looked away now stared at him. Kouros ignored them and looked at his map.

She returned and slipped the coffee onto the table between the map and his chest. "Sure you don't want something else?"

"How about a toast?"

"With ham and cheese?"

He nodded and she left. Now most of the men in the room stared at him openly. Kouros felt like the proverbial pair of brown shoes at a black-tie affair: he was in a place he didn't belong.

Which made it the right place. He just hoped he wasn't making an indelible impression on guys he might soon be following. That would really piss off the chief.

The waitress strolled over, pulled out a chair, and sat down. "Do you mind if I tell the assholes in here that you're my cousin?"

"Why would you want to do that?"

"Because they're just what I said. They don't like strangers here. This is their place of business."

"What kind of business?"

"Nothing you want to know about. Trust me. It's all bad. Do yourself a favor and leave now to visit your mother or let me tell them you're my cousin, because I can tell they're about to bust your head."

Kouros smiled. "But they won't believe you. You didn't kiss me hello."

She jumped out of her chair ran around and began kissing and hugging him. He started to laugh and she smacked the back of his head. Then she kissed him some more.

With her arms around Kouros' neck she turned to the room and yelled, "This *malaka* is my long lost cousin I haven't seen in twenty years! He came all the way up to Salonika, just to surprise me." She kissed him again.

Kouros offered a sheepish smile and wave to the room. The men nodded and went back to ignoring him.

"Thanks," said Kouros. "But why'd you do that for me?"

"Because you're cute and I'm horny."

Kouros blinked and she laughed. "Only kidding. But around guys like this you have to be willing to give as good as you get." She smacked him on the arm. "You stumbled in here and gave them no reason to give you trouble. They're just bored. All they do these days is sit around and wait for their boss to give them something to do."

Kouros nodded, trying not to look at the men." I guess you're not the only one having trouble finding work."

"Yeah, their boss hasn't given his men much to do. Everything's been calm and peaceful."

Twice she'd mentioned a "boss." As if pressing Kouros to ask about him.

"That sounds like a good thing."

"Why are you really here?"

"To meet you, cuz." Kouros smiled.

"We both know that's not true."

"Would coffee and toast be an acceptable answer?"

"No, but that reminds me," she hurried off to the kitchen and returned with the toasted ham and cheese sandwich.

She sat at the table and slid the plate across the table. "Now, tell me, why are you here?"

A motorcycle screamed to a stop by the front door and a barrel chested, clean-shaven, dark-haired man in his late thirties stepped off the bike and walked through the door. He wore blue-mirror aviator sunglasses, a blue oxford cloth dress shirt, and khakis.

"A bit preppy for this neighborhood," said Kouros.

"Be careful what you say," she whispered.

She didn't say why to be careful but Kouros already knew. He'd recognized Tank from his photo.

Tank looked at Kouros and gestured with his head to the waitress. She leaped out of the chair and over to his side.

So much for being inconspicuous. Andreas would be pissed.

Tank spoke to the waitress and walked over to Kouros. "So, you came to visit your cousin."

"Is that what she told you?"

"In this place I ask the questions."

Kouros smiled. "Any particular answers you'd like?"

Tank sat down. "You're a wiseass, huh?" The men behind him stood up.

"No, just a customer who foolishly thought the sign outside reading CAFENION meant a place to get a coffee."

"I don't believe you."

Kouros shrugged, picked up his toast and took a bite. "Food's not bad."

"My sister doesn't trust you."

"You mean the waitress? She has a lot of relatives, that one." He took another bite of toast, followed by a sip of water.

"She said you're looking for the jail."

"I never said that, she did."

"Are you calling my sister a liar?"

Kouros smiled and put his hands in his lap. "Oh, so that's where this is headed?"

"I wouldn't be smiling if I were you." He took off his sunglasses, showing tiny, mouselike eyes, and motioned for the men at the tables to step forward. Eight did.

"Impressive. One problem."

"What's that?"

Kouros smiled again. "They take one more step forward and you're dead."

"Tough talk, asshole." He waved for the men to step forward.

Kouros lifted his right hand from his lap and pointed a nine-millimeter semi-automatic at the middle of Tank's chest.

"*Stop,*" shouted Tank.

The men stopped.

"And back up, please," said Kouros.

They moved without waiting for Tank to tell them.

"As I was saying, sir," keeping the gun firmly pointed at Tank's heart, "I have no idea what the problem is with your sister, but I just came in here for a coffee and directions. So why don't you leave me in peace?"

The man at the next table cleared his throat. "I don't mean to pry, sir," he said looking at Tank, "but I've been here the whole time and this gentlemen is telling the truth."

"Who the fuck are you?" said Tank, aiming his bravado at the man without the gun.

"Just another customer who happened to be the primary subject of curiosity on the part of your friends before this gentleman with his gun pointed at your chest entered your establishment."

"Are you guys together?"

The man said, "Never saw him before in my life. But he does present a small problem for me, one that I hope we can resolve."

Kouros glanced at the man's hands, not moving the aim of his gun.

"You see, I was sent here to deliver a message to you." His eyes remained fixed on Tank as he folded his newspaper and put it down on the table. "It's a very personal message. One from someone who feels you betrayed trust. And trust is a very important thing to maintain. It is a very firm message, but one not intended to bring physical harm to you."

The man turned to face Kouros. "I hope, sir, that you appreciate the meaning I'm trying to get across."

"You don't want me to kill him."

The man nodded. "Yes."

"Fine with me. My only reason for pulling the gun was to stop him from having his friends rearrange my dental work."

"A wise decision that I fully understand. But perhaps now you'd be best leaving."

"Good idea," said Kouros.

"Don't worry, I'll pay your bill." The man nodded toward the waitress. "And I'll tip her appropriately."

Kouros had no idea what was going down, but things looked guaranteed to end badly if he stayed around. Besides, this was a room filled with bad guys pissed off at each other, not some place where he had to jump into a fight to save a law-abiding citizen.

Deciding discretion would be the better part of valor, Kouros stood. He kept his gun focused on Tank and gestured for everyone else in the room to move to his left, toward the stranger's table. Kouros kept his eyes on the crowd and gun on Tank as he backed toward the door opening onto the street.

"Close the door, please," said the stranger.

Once outside, Kouros closed the door as the stranger had asked, crossed the street to his car, slid his gun back into the holster hidden in the front of his pants, and drove away. Whatever happened next wasn't his problem. At least not yet.

◇◇◇

The moment Kouros left the *cafenion,* Tank lunged at the stranger, but pulled up abruptly when the stranger sprang up from his chair and brought the point of a stiletto snug against Tank's throat with his left hand.

"You seem to continually underestimate people," said the stranger. "First that cop and now me."

"What cop?"

The stranger shook his head. "You're supposed to be a bigtime mobster and yet you can't spot a cop? Who but a cop would come in here, in a shit hole neighborhood like this, on the lame excuse of looking for directions and sit around having coffee, chatting up your waitress for information?"

"You're here. Does that mean you're a cop too? Or just an asshole."

The stranger pressed the knifepoint hard enough against Tank's throat to draw blood. "I'm not supposed to kill you, but if you continue to press me, I just may have to make you look as ugly as your manners."

Tank tried leaning away from the tip of the blade, but the stranger pressed harder and Tank stopped. "What do you want?"

The man shook his head again. "Do you ever listen to what you're told? I don't want anything. I'm here to deliver a message, that's all."

"What message?"

"One to get your attention, so that you realize it's not a good idea to betray your teacher."

"My tea—" Tank froze in mid word. "Teacher sent you?"

"Did you think she'd forgotten about you? Or your promise to cherish, honor, obey, *and pay* until death do you part?"

Tank's eyes remained wide. "Okay, I got it. We can work this out, right?"

"Of course we can. Just do as you've agreed and all will be forgiven."

Tank smiled. "Great, terrific."

"But first I must give you the message." Without moving the knife point, he drew a .380 semi-automatic out of his pants pocket with his right hand, pointed the gun at Tank's head, and in the instant before firing shifted his aim to Tank's sister.

She dropped to the floor, a bullet hole centered in her forehead.

No one moved to stop the stranger as he strolled out of the *cafenion* to a motorcycle parked in front and drove away.

Message delivered, thought Kharon.

Chapter Eleven

Kouros drove around for about an hour before parking down by the harbor, close by the city's most famous landmark, a white tower literally called that in Greek, *Levkos Pirgos*. Thoroughly renovated on the inside, broad steps wound from one level up to the next, offering a mesmerizing exhibition of the history of Thessalonki to the climber. But Kouros never left the car. His thoughts weren't on touring.

He'd left multiple messages with Andreas and Maggie for Andreas to call him ASAP. Kouros tried making sense out of what he'd just witnessed. Whoever the stranger, the guy had balls. Huge ones. Which likely meant he worked for someone Tank feared. You just don't walk into a mob place like that and act as if you owned it.

Right. I should listen to my own advice.

Kouros' mobile rang and he picked up on the first ring. "Hi, Chief."

"Don't tell me you were in the middle of that *cafenion* mess?"

Kouros stared at the phone. "How the hell did you know about that?"

"From Maggie."

"How did she know?"

"Our beloved boss, the Minister of Public Order, had her pull me out of a department heads meeting to tell me how all hell had broken loose in a *cafenion* in Thessaloniki. I had her stay on the line to take notes and after Spiros hung up she told me that the address of the place he'd gone on about was the same as she'd given you for Tank."

"But what was there for him to go on about? Nothing happened."

"I'll take that to mean you're the stranger who left just before another stranger put a bullet hole into the forehead of a beloved female member of one of Greece's most prominent political families."

"Tank's sister?"

"You got it."

"Holy Mother. I wouldn't have left if I thought he'd kill her." Kouros told Andreas all that had happened.

"Sounds to me if you hadn't left there'd have been two bodies sporting bullet holes in their foreheads. The shooter was a definite pro."

"He said he had a message to deliver to Tank."

"As in a bullet to his sister's head?"

"I'm not sure how he came up with that, but he definitely said he was sent there to deliver a message to Tank."

"'Sent?' By whom?"

"Didn't say, except it was from someone who felt Tank had 'betrayed trust.'"

"Well, if that was the goal, it worked," said Andreas. "According to our minister, who obviously didn't know the facts you just told me, it got the attention of Tank's entire family and media all across Greece."

"I shouldn't have left." Kouros' throat tightened as he paused to compose himself.

Andreas spoke. "The shooter killed her right in front of her brother and a shitload of bad guys with guns, but got away without anyone laying a hand on him. How in the hell could that happen unless the brother knew whoever sent the shooter, and what sort of hell would follow if he went after him?"

"I can't believe he killed the girl."

"What's the matter? Because the victim was a she instead of a he, you think an innocent died? Okay, she flirted with you, but that only meant she was charming. There are a lot of real charmers out there who are deadly characters, both male and female. You know that. And I'll lay you hundred-to-one odds that Miss Congeniality was the one who told her brother to come by after acting like your snuggle buddy."

"Yeah, but...."

"Think about it. The sister had options. Thanks to her family's money and influence she could have made any kind of life for herself that she wanted. But she chose to get her kicks out of being part of her brother's mobster lifestyle. Those sorts of decisions come at a price, and she paid the ultimate one."

"That's still not a reason to kill her. I should have stayed. At least identified myself as a cop."

"Of course it's not a reason to kill her. But stop beating yourself up over this. The shooter was a pro. He never said or did anything to indicate he was going to harm anyone. In fact, he stepped in to stop you from harming Tank. At best you'd have delayed him from killing her until after you'd left. At worst he'd have killed you on the spot for being a cop who could identify him. You went with your instincts and they saved your life. The only coincidences I believe in are the nasty ones that get cops killed. You were in the wrong place at the wrong time, and only by the grace of God didn't end up with a bullet in your brain. Be thankful and move on. Period."

"End of story?"

"No, not quite. The minister wants us to get to the bottom of this, yesterday. 'We can't tolerate foreign mobsters intimidating legitimate Greek business owners,' were his precise words."

"Where did the minister get the idea foreigners were involved? The shooter was Greek."

"From Tank I assume. Tank described the killer, and get this. According to him, you have a twin brother out there somewhere. But Balkan."

"The killer looks nothing like me. He's tall and wiry and one hundred percent Greek."

"Well, Tank obviously needed a description to run with his story, but didn't dare point at the guy who actually did it."

"Not so sure that's a bingo card I'm happy to win once the local cops pull my prints off the crime scene."

"I doubt that will happen. You're Tank's mystery man cover story for a big mess. Not just to the press, but his family. I doubt he'll want you appearing as a witness to tell what really happened, and if he finds out you're a cop in Special Crimes, for sure he won't want to draw you in and ruin his little fantasy explanation for his family. My guess is he'll bury any connections to you."

"As long as he doesn't decide to bury me along with them."

"Don't see any reason for him doing that. But if he does, I can assure you I'll find some pretext for arresting him."

"That makes me feel all better."

"Since you raised the point, though, just to be on the safe side, I want you back in Athens ASAP."

"What about my tailing the guys connected to Tank's counterfeit booze operation?"

"After this episode, I think you best forget about tailing anyone tied to Tank around Thessaloniki. I'll get Petro to pick up on that. You have to focus on identifying the shooter. If you do, it might give us an idea of who sent him. Maybe even a link to whoever's behind this multinational counterfeit booze empire."

"You really think so?"

"One can hope. But just identifying the shooter will give us a real angle on Tank. We already know he's afraid enough of our shooter's connections to let him walk away from murdering his sister. A police ID of the killer should scare him shitless. Maybe get him to do something stupid."

"I can't imagine Tank and his people backing me up, even if I identified the killer."

"But think of the glorious possibilities. I, being duty bound, will of course pass your match along to our minister who, being the ass-kissing, favor cultivator he is, will undoubtedly race to the dead girl's family with his record time, Sherlock Holmes-like solution of the mystery. Tank will then have to decide between denying or agreeing with what he'll know we know is the correct identification of his sister's killer. If he denies your pick and it comes out that he's lying, he risks ostracism from his family's power and fortune. And if he agrees with you, he knows he's face-to-face with whatever nightmare is lurking out there behind the killer."

"Both wonderful choices," said Kouros. "The kind that might drive a fellow like Tank into striking a deal with us that doesn't require him to choose."

"Precisely. And it all begins with little old you coming back here to go through mug shots until you find our guy."

"Funny, you say that. Now that I think about it, something about that guy's face struck me as familiar. I didn't have much of a chance to study him in the *cafenion*, but definitely something about him made me think I'd seen him before."

"That's why the good Lord invented mug shots. They give you the chance to reconnect with old friends."

"Sort of like Facebook for felons," said Kouros. "All right, I'd better run. Got a plane to catch."

"Later."

◇◇◇

Teacher sat smiling at the photo on her desk. "We chose wisely."

She'd not wanted Tank as her collaborator in Greece. She preferred a Balkan foreigner, same as in her other Western European operations. Balkan mobsters were far easier to control than those native to their countries. Not because they were less dangerous. To the contrary, Balkan mobsters were among the most ruthless on earth. No, the key difference was the manner in which they operated and stayed in power. As foreigners, they maintained their influence with bribes to corrupt local police and government officials. If a lesson needed to be taught to one of her Balkan collaborators, Teacher could out-bribe them with the authorities, destroying their operations if necessary.

Local mobsters, however, had family and friends to protect them, presenting far more complicated ties to overcome than those based on corruption. As Teacher saw it, working with local mobsters put her at a distinct disadvantage should they misbehave, especially in a country like Greece with its historically entrenched, narrow-minded attitudes toward foreigners doing business on Greek soil.

But that wasn't Teacher's only concern with Tank. She saw him as a self-absorbed egotist, the worst example of a spoiled child of a connected family. He thought he could do anything, and no matter how many times he failed, his family would be there to bail him out.

When Tank had learned of Teacher's interest in entering the counterfeit booze business in Greece, he'd claimed his involvement in the legitimate side of the business made him perfect for her and pressed hard to work with her there. So hard that potential non-Greek competitors for the position who didn't withdraw found their residency permits unexpectedly revoked and their families deported.

Reluctantly, Teacher took the risk of going with Tank. It was a mistake she would not have made back when she relied upon her instincts in building her empire, instead of presuming that all who now chose to work with her knew to fear her iron fist. At first, it all worked smoothly, but having been insulated by his family all his life from any fear of consequences, within six months Tank was cheapening the formulas and skimming money.

I must send Tank a thank you note, she thought. *After all, it was his misbehavior that prompted my finding Kharon.*

Her instructions to Kharon had been simple: "Don't kill him. All I want is for my other collaborators to get the message that if I am willing to do this in Greece to a member of a powerful Greek family who defies me, imagine what I'm prepared to do to those of you who are strangers in foreign lands."

She'd left it to Kharon to decide how best to get that message across.

Teacher sat in front of her computer, waiting for the first international news report on what Kharon had called to tell her he'd achieved. As if summoned by her will, a headline popped onto her screen: ASSASSIN MURDERS DAUGHTER OF GREEK POLITICAL GIANT IN FRONT OF BROTHER.

Well done, young man, well done.

◇◇◇

Five minutes after leaving the *cafenion*, Kharon abandoned the stolen motorcycle he'd used to get there, stole another to take him to where he'd parked the one he'd borrowed from Jacobi, and called Teacher with a brief, cryptic description of what had happened. He kept below the speed limit all the way back to Delphi and wore a helmet, though he doubted any cop would stop him if he hadn't. Still, he saw no reason to take chances. One coincidental meeting with a cop today was enough.

From what he'd overheard of the cop's conversation with the sister, he hadn't been able to make out what was on the cop's mind, but he guessed the man's purpose for being there had something to do with her brother.

Kharon couldn't believe his good luck when Tank walked into the place and decided to play Rambo with a cop cool enough to handle him. That gave Kharon the dramatic opportunity he'd needed to focus everyone in the room on his purpose for being there, and inspiration for a new ending to the scene. Let the cop walk, and drop the sister.

Not many who knew of Tank's sister's role in his operations would mourn her. According to Kharon's connections in Thessaloniki, she was Tank's "black widow," using her sweetness-and-light act as an innocent waitress act to set up many a man for the wrath of her brother's macho temper. Watching her perform her routine with the cop was what had inspired Kharon to rethink his big finish.

One must always be open to improvisation.

Chapter Twelve

"It's your favorite minister, Chief," came through the speaker-phone on Andreas' desk.

"Thanks, Maggie." Andreas picked up the phone. "Kaldis here."

"One moment please for Minister Renatis."

Andreas looked at his watch. How long it took for his boss to pick up generally proved a reliable inverse indicator of his agitation level. The shorter the wait, the greater the likely explosion.

Spiros jumped on in less than five seconds. "We've got a catastrophe on our hands. We've got the prime minister, and every media outlet in Greece breathing down our necks to capture the killer of that poor woman in Thessaloniki."

"You mean that hardworking Pakistani mother of three dragged off the street on her way home from work, sexually abused, beaten to death, and carved up with swastikas by home-grown Nazi skinheads?"

Andreas listened to his boss draw in and release a deep breath.

"You know that's not what I'm talking about."

"I guessed as much, but it does make me curious."

"Curious?"

"That Pakistani mother died less than a month ago, and when I suggested *we* look into it you said, '*We* have more important things to do' and that 'local cops handle those sorts of cases far better than *we* do.' I'm just curious about what's changed your mind."

"Stop busting my balls, Andreas. You know as well as I do they're two very different situations."

"Yeah, one involves a member of a poor immigrant family of color offering little of continuing interest to the press, while the other has rich, connected Greek parents and hordes of reporters falling all over themselves in a twenty-four/seven media feeding frenzy."

"It's the world we live in, Andreas. You might think you can change it, but I have no such delusions I can. One thing I do know, though, is that if *we* don't pull out all stops at solving this, what will change is our employment status."

Andreas smiled. "I can't believe you're actually trying logic to convince me that your thinking is right, and not just screaming into the phone when I disagree."

"I've decided reason may be a better way to deal with you. But don't get too carried away, the bottom line's the same. We have to find the foreign bastard who killed her in front of her brother."

"Why do you say he's 'foreign?'"

"That's what the brother told the local police. He said he saw the whole thing from beginning to end. A brutal, horrific experience."

"Are those his words or yours?"

"His, according to the police. He said he was sitting at a table at the far end of the room facing the door and having coffee with customers. His sister, who liked helping out as a waitress, was taking an order from a table next to the front door when the killer opened the door, took two steps inside to where she stood, shot her in the forehead, and left."

"Sounds like a professional."

"Precisely my thinking. The brother said it was like watching a movie, and in the few stunned seconds it took for him to comprehend he'd just seen his sister murdered, the killer had escaped on a motorbike parked with its motor running just outside the *cafenion's* front door."

"That's definitely a story I'd call 'horrific,'" said Andreas. *And phony too*, he wanted to add, but decided it best not to let Spiros know just yet what had actually happened. Spiros might be trying to change his ways, but Andreas doubted whether he'd quite reached the point of overcoming his sycophantic dependency on the press. His boss had mastered the art of justifying to himself how passing along juicy bits of inside information endearing him to the media actually benefited rather than impeded a pending investigation.

For the time being Andreas wanted Tank thinking the police had no reason to disbelieve his story, giving him all the rope he needed to hang himself and snare those behind his sister's murder in the process. With that in mind, Andreas decided to keep his questions for Spiros to the expected routine.

"How did the brother know the killer was foreign?"

"What do you mean?"

"From the story you told me no one ever heard the killer speak."

"Good point. Maybe there was a verbal exchange. That's why I need you. To catch things everyone else misses."

"Nice try, but flattery's not going to work."

"I don't think you understand, Andreas. I need you on this case *now*."

"Your voice is rising, Spiros. Do something before you lose your zen state."

Andreas heard forced breathing on the other end of the phone.

"This isn't funny. I'm trying. It's difficult." More pronounced breathing. "But if you can't get up to Thessaloniki today, send Kouros. I need your best man on this one right away."

Now Andreas paused to draw a breath. "Yianni is in the midst of a delicate, long-term investigation that requires his presence in Athens at the moment, but don't worry, I've the perfect guy for this."

"Are you sure?"

"Spiros…"

"Fine. Do what you think is best, but do it *now*. I really, really, really need your help on this one. And quick results. Thank you. Bye."

Spiros hung up before Andreas could say good-bye. Still holding the phone he yelled, "Maggie, come in, please."

She opened the door as Andreas hung up the phone.

"From the look on your face it must have been a pretty shocking call."

"I think *amazed* better describes my state of mind at the moment." Andreas shook his head. "Spiros actually kept his cool and behaved like a sane human being under pressures that usually send him bouncing off the walls."

"Maybe he's on medication?"

"God bless the pharmaceutical gods if he is. All I can say is that he literally did not seem himself."

"Hmm. That is strange. Want me to see what I can find out?"

"In your, quiet, old girl network way, please."

"I'll have lunch with his secretary today and let you know what she tells me."

Andreas cocked his head and looked at her. "Dare I ask what you'll be telling her in return?"

"Oh, nothing really important. Just about how your office is filled with booze and men wanting to sleep on your couch."

"That's nice."

"Don't worry about it, she won't be surprised."

"How come?"

Maggie turned and walked toward the door. "You were once police chief on Mykonos. Need I say more?"

◇◇◇

"It's late, Yianni," said Andreas peeking his head into Kouros' office. "How's it going?"

Kouros sat behind his desk, staring at a computer screen. "If you ever forget how many bad guys are out there, I have something to remind you." He pointed at the screen. "I've spent two hours looking at faces without so much as an inkling of recognition. I know I've seen the shooter before, but I just can't get a fix on him."

"Maybe you should try working with a police artist?"

Kouros reached for an envelope on his desk and handed it to Andreas. "Already did, first thing after I got back. I figured it might help me set my mind on what I'm looking for."

Andreas pulled out a digitally rendered composite of a man in his mid-twenties with jet black short hair, a close-trimmed beard, and dark eyes. Andreas stared at the face. "I see what you mean. I think I've seen him too."

"Maybe we think we know him because he looks like some celebrity, a soccer player or television actor?"

"Could be," said Andreas. "And practically every Greek boy who can grow a beard these days has one. Makes them all look alike."

He put the composite back on Kouros' desk. "Pass this around and see if anyone can come up with a possible name to go with the face. But only show it to cops you trust not to talk about it. If this guy's off the radar and as deadly as he seems, we don't want to show it to snitches yet. Too risky. All we need is for one of them to decide it's safer to warn our killer we're on to him than to cooperate with us, and he'll vanish."

Kouros nodded. "I'll start on that after I finish this. I should be done in a couple more hours."

"You sound like you don't think you'll make a match."

Kouros shook his head, eyes already fixed back on the screen. "I doubt it. I've gone through the photos of everyone vaguely resembling his description up to age thirty-five, and back to the youngest on record at thirteen. No luck."

"Maybe you're right, and he just looks like someone we know from the media." Andreas bit at his lip. "But hard to imagine a killer as cool as this one with no arrest record."

"He spoke Greek like a native Athenian, but perhaps he never got arrested here?"

Andreas shrugged. "Could be. Though most guys aren't *that* good. Let's send the picture on to Europol and see what they come up with."

"With luck, something before his beard turns white."

"That's it. I recognize him."

Kouros jerked his head around to look at Andreas. "You do?"

"Yes," said Andreas. "Santa Claus."

Kouros refocused his eyes on the screen. "I bet in your diet-induced state of diminished capacity you actually thought that was funny. I have a suggestion. When you get home, hug your four-year-old, get down on your knees before him, and beg him to write you better punch lines."

◇◇◇

When Andreas got home he found Lila sitting on a couch in the living room reading.

"You're home early," she said.

"I missed you."

"Nice try. What's up?"

"Where's Tassaki?"

"My father and mother took him to dinner."

"To plot against their common enemy, no doubt."

"If you haven't noticed, our son needs no assistance from my parents on ways to combat us."

He dropped onto the couch beside her. "I wasn't suggesting he was the one who needed the help." He kissed her on the cheek and looked out the window at the Acropolis.

Lila closed her book and stared at his face as he bit at his lower lip.

"What's wrong, Andreas?"

He spoke without looking at her. "Maggie had lunch today with Spiros' secretary. He'd acted strangely when we spoke this morning and so I asked Maggie to find out if something's wrong."

"I assume there is." She reached for his hand.

He took it. "Yes." He paused. "He's ill."

"Oh God, I pray it's not serious."

"I'm afraid it is. The bastard's made my life miserable in virtually every imaginable way, and yet I can't help but feel sorry for him."

"I should hope that's how you'd feel. Otherwise you wouldn't be the man I married. Besides, as you've often said, he's not a bad or corrupt person, just weak."

"Uh, let's not get carried away here. He has a lot of other traits I'm not too fond of, but I agree this is horrible."

"I must call his wife."

Andreas turned his head toward her. "No, don't do that."

"Why not? She needs support as much as he does at a time like this."

"But she doesn't know."

"*Doesn't know?*"

Andreas nodded. "As hard as it is to believe, he hasn't told her. His secretary only knows about it because he needed her to cover for him when he went for treatments."

"This is all too bizarre."

"What can I say? Apparently he's afraid his wife will leave him if she knows he's sick."

"How could he possibly think that? He must be deranged."

"A man unexpectedly confronting his mortality can turn paranoid. His wife is the one with the family money that got him his position in the first place. He probably sees his whole world falling apart, and imagines things only getting worse in every possible way."

"But how could he think his wife wouldn't notice he's ill?"

Andreas shrugged. "I wondered the same thing. But who knows what sort of relationship they have?"

"For him to even *think* she wouldn't notice says it all about that relationship. Can you even imagine how he must feel going through what he is alone, fearing all the while what else might happen should his wife find out?"

Andreas squeezed Lila's hand. "I'm one lucky guy."

"Damn straight. And don't you forget it." Lila leaned over and kissed him on the lips. "What is the illness?"

"His secretary said she didn't know."

"He didn't tell even her?"

"Maggie sensed she didn't want to say any more about it, even if she knew."

"Understandable. She probably felt bad enough for betraying her boss' confidence."

Andreas smiled. "You're pretty smart. That's precisely what she told Maggie. She also said the only reason she was telling Maggie was so that Maggie would tell me."

"Tell *you?*"

"Yes. And get this. Because 'Andreas is the only friend Spiros has.' The son of a bitch actually thinks of me as his friend."

"To his way of thinking, you probably are. My guess is you're the only one he can trust to tell him the truth. Everyone else around him likely has his own agenda."

"Considering what I'm keeping from him at the moment, that just goes to show you how poor a judge of character he is."

Lila shook her head. "You're not convincing me, Kaldis. I know you better than that. You'll be the one guy in his corner through whatever he's going through."

"But I still won't trust him."

"I doubt he'd expect you to. What he needs is to be able to trust you."

"Okay, I get it."

"Fine. And by the way...."

"Yes?"

"Just so I'm certain you're not hiding anything from me—"

"What sorts of things?"

Lila stood up and pointed toward their bedroom. "Get in there and strip. I want to make an up close and personal inspection of my biggest investment."

"Ah, now I know what you're looking for." He stood, taking her hand as he did.

"And what, pray tell is that?"

Gently pulling her in the direction of the bedroom, he whispered. "Hard assets."

She patted his butt. "Welcome to my portfolio."

◇◇◇

Spiros sat in the dark on the edge of his bed staring out the window toward the heart of the city. Athens was lovely now. He wished he had more time to enjoy it. His wife certainly knew how to do that.

No reason to plow those thoughts again.

They'd each made their own beds and now they were lying in them. Alone. At least not with each other. She had her parties and he had his career. When they'd met in university, she was searching for a husband who'd advance her pretensions to social prominence and he for someone to buy him a career. They settled on each other, and used her family's money to achieve both. Now, it was all about maintaining appearances.

He reached over to open the bottom drawer of the nightstand and pulled out the bottles of pills. He shook one from each into the palm of his left hand and stared at them.

"Whatever dreams I have left for my life depend on you."

There were no children to hug, no family left to talk to, just the pills. He put them in his mouth and swallowed. Gagging, he reached for a bottle of water on the nightstand and drank until the gagging passed.

He put the bottles back and sat staring at them sitting in the open drawer.

Why am I so afraid to talk to her? He already knew the answer. His wife's life followed an immutable plan, known only to her, with no allowances for the slightest sidetrack or delay. He wondered if she'd had an unscripted moment their entire life together.

He sighed, stood, and walked to the window. He studied his hands in the moonlight passing through the curtains. No one else was in the house, just him and his thoughts. He felt very much alone, that he'd gotten old, and more foolish. He worried about his image, how he'd be remembered. But by whom? He could not think of one soul out there who cared a damn about whether he lived or died.

Spiros shook his head. There must be more to life than this. "*There has to be!*" He shouted the last few words so loudly they'd echoed back at him.

"Ah, a voice I can understand. Perhaps I should listen to you more often." He rubbed his forehead with his right hand, reached out with that same hand, and pulled back the curtain.

The other voice he heard in this house only spoke the truth to distract or assuage him, and never without motive. He wondered whether his wife's depressions were a distraction too? Or were they real? She seemed so lost, so unfocused at those times. And he would concede whatever issue troubled her so, no matter how trivial to her but meaningful to him. What choice did he have? After all, life was all about her and no one else.

He let the curtain drop back into place. "I want to share my problem with you. I *must* share my problem with you. *You are my wife.*"

There was the sound of a door opening somewhere in the house. Spiros hurried back to bed. He did not want to talk anymore.

Chapter Thirteen

Andreas looked at the calendar on his desk. Kouros had finished going through mug shots and came up empty. He'd had no better luck spending another two days showing the artist's sketch of the killer to every cop he'd thought might recognize him.

On top of that, even magical Maggie couldn't manage to hook Andreas up with his old friend who'd once headed the ministry's organized crime division.

As Andreas saw it, nothing was going right, but Maggie kept telling him to trust in the stars.

"Everything will improve as soon as Mercury comes out of retrograde."

Andreas was considering the implications of astrology as an aid to police work when his mobile rang.

"Hi, Chief, it's Petro."

"Still in Thessaloniki?"

"Yep, into my third day watching the carryings-on of Tank and his merry men."

"Any better luck than with the first two?"

"Wish I could say yes, but Tank's spending all his time playing grieving brother. He's working every opportunity to put the image of his *slaughtered* sister in front of the media and demand that the government clamp down on what he calls a *foreign terrorist element* trying to muscle in on legitimate Greek businessmen."

"I know. I'm getting calls from virtually every member of the three-hundred."

"The what? I assume you're not talking about the Spartans of Thermopylae."

"No, those three hundred we could use. I'm talking about the three hundred members of our illustrious Parliament."

"We could use less of those."

"A lot less. Can't you at least come up with something exciting to tell me to justify your three days on the road at taxpayer expense?"

"I've trailed Tank's crew to a long list of places buying bootleg. Amazing how many bars, clubs, liquor stores, restaurants, and hotels are into counterfeit."

"That's the best you can do? They'll all swear they didn't know it was counterfeit."

"Chief, you asked me to come up with something exciting. Whether or not it'll get someone put away is a different story. Besides, that's just the intro to my report. I spotted some trucks unloading what looked to be booze at the same warehouse Tank's crew uses for making deliveries. I traced one load back to a ship out of Northern Cyprus, another took me up to the border with Bulgaria. He kept going, I didn't."

"A wise decision."

"A third truck took me straight to a place making the stuff. It's in the boondocks of Salonika and looks like a small-time operation."

"With our legitimate economy cratered everywhere but in tourism, I'm surprised more Greeks aren't into manufacturing *bomba*," said Andreas. "I'm also willing to bet, if we don't put a stop to whatever Tank's got working, that operation and a lot of others won't be small-time for long."

"Wish I could say I'm any closer to getting a line on whoever's behind Tank, but I'm not."

"Join the club." Andreas fluttered his lips. "I'm open for suggestions on how we can get Tank to arrange a face-to-face meeting with the big boss."

"I don't have any ideas off the top of my head, but how about a tap on his phones? We might catch them talking."

"Ah, yes, a phone tap. And let's not forget to add to our little wish list of judicial and ministerial cooperation, permission to access Tank's bank transactions and financial history. Trouble is, between his family connections and all the publicity over his sister's death, I can't conceive of us getting that sort of authorization."

"Maybe we'll get lucky and catch Tank making payments to his boss in a suitcase filled with cash?"

"I'll add that one to my prayers, but I doubt they're doing transfers that way. Without Tank's cooperation, tracking down who's getting the money will require us to wade through a mess of offshore corporations and cooperative bankers that these types of international bad guys use to launder money upstream. Our getting permission to conduct that sort of full-scale forensic investigation would be seen as setting a precedent for looking into the financial shenanigans of a lot of other people. Something I don't see our distinguished politicians letting fly."

"Sounds like you think we've hit a dead end."

"Not quite dead, but comatose. Yianni's come up dry on identifying the killer. We need a break. I don't care if we dig one up or stumble upon it in the dark. But we need one that doesn't require the cooperation of our government to nail the bastards."

"Should I take this conversation as a sign for me to return to Athens?"

"You might as well." Andreas looked at his watch. "If you hustle to the airport, you could be back here by lunchtime."

"Okay. Will do, Chief. Bye."

"Bye."

Andreas put down the phone and stared out his office window. *I sure wish I had better news to pass along to Spiros.* He shook his head and said aloud. "Damn, I wish I had better news to keep for myself."

◇◇◇

Kharon knew it would take weeks, perhaps months, before all the property would be his. It could be done more quickly if one paid the right people, but that would be unwise. Aggressive buying interest would raise the price, but of more concern to Kharon, attract attention and trigger gossip. Two things he definitely did not want. No matter, he knew the property would be his and so he wandered the groves as if they already were. No one cared or took notice, for he'd long been a familiar figure among the trees.

He walked along a patchy mat of green grass and brown dirt amid rows of hundred-year-old olive trees planted in parallel to tens of thousands of others. The trees spread north for miles from the Gulf of Corinth's harbor town of Itea, filling the broad flat valley with endless green. They stretched northwest to the town of Amfissa, and northeast to below Delphi at the picture perfect village of Chrisso—all surrounded by mountainsides of brown and gray, flecked in green, rising up from the sea and rolling back toward limestone Mount Parnassos.

In this Amfissa-Chrisso-Itea triangle grew the finest olives in the region, each tree yielding over five liters of oil in a good year. Ten thousand trees meant a potential annual production of nearly fifty thousand liters of prime grade olive oil. On top of that, once Kharon owned the olive press, the standard price in the community for any grower using his facilities would be fifteen percent of the grower's crop, plus ten euros per hundred liters.

Kharon had never even dreamed of such a life, one of profit and at peace with the land. Now all he had to do to make it real was stay alive.

Kharon turned north between the rows of olives and aimed slightly west of Chrisso toward its looming mountain backdrop. He moved quickly across the valley floor. The hills close on his right appeared greener to him than those in the distance to his left, but all shared the same hazy beige and chocolate markings reminiscent of shadows that did not exist at this time of day.

Could there be a more beautiful place on earth? He quickened his pace.

Just beyond the northern edge of Chrisso, Kharon turned east and climbed a steep hillside toward a group of boulders perched high above an aqueduct carrying water down from the mountains to the valley. He sat among the boulders and looked south across the valley toward the Gulf of Corinth. From this height, none of the trees he'd just walked among stood out from any other, except for random cypresses spiking the sky. He saw only a broad canvas of olive green, framed on three sides in beige and brown with touches of ochre and terra cotta, its far side bordered by sapphire blue sea and bright blue sky.

He leaned back against a boulder and watched doves soar up to where gulls drifted lazily overhead, only to scatter at the sight of a hawk rising in the sky. He inhaled deeply and caught a distant scent of the sea blending into aromas of wild herbs and lavender. The only sounds a chirp, a caw, or a rare distant bark. He closed his eyes, lifted his head and faced straight into the sun.

She was the first woman he'd ever killed. Strange, it didn't bother him at all. Why should it? Why should a woman's life be more precious or meaningful than a man's? If one could be said to *deserve* to die, why could it not be said of the other? Are there not good and bad amongst both genders? Yes, a man was more likely to harm with brute force, but a woman had her subtleties, and if both shared the same deadly intention, where was the distinction justifying mercy for one and not the other?

All this he had learned through one who claimed to have pledged herself to saving lives.

He opened his eyes.

He must thank Teacher for the lesson.

Chapter Fourteen

"Chief, It's Ted Rousounelous on the line."

"Who?"

"He said you knew him."

"Never heard of him."

"Gimme a minute," said Maggie.

Andreas picked up a pencil and began drumming the eraser end on his desktop. He'd barely slept last night, and not for a good reason. No leads meant no sleep. And no sleep meant a likely cranky morning.

"Chief?"

"What you got, Maggie?"

"He said, 'Tell him it's 'Rolex.'"

A smile burst across Andreas' face. "Why didn't he say so in the first place? Put him through."

"Hello?" The voice sounded tentative.

"Rolex, you old son of a bitch. How are you?"

"I'd thought you'd forgotten all about me."

"I can't remember the last time I heard you called by your real name."

"Yeah, nicknames stick like you-know-what to a shoe. I lost it at my new job. No one here knew me from our school days."

"You have to admit, a seven-year-old wearing a solid gold wristwatch to class had to attract attention."

"Tell me about it. My mother thought it looked cute. And since it was a fake, she thought what harm could it do."

"How is your mother?"

"She passed away a couple of years back."

"Sorry to hear that." Pause. "I gotta ask. Did she know?"

"Know what?"

"About the nickname."

"How could she not? She heard all my friends calling me 'Rolex,' so she asked them why they called me by the name of a watch, and they told her."

"Did she mind?"

"No, she laughed and said it could have been a lot worse. Imagine what I'd be called if she'd made me eat raw garlic everyday before school to ward off illness."

"God bless her soul."

"And the strange thing about it is, I threw away that damn watch on the way home from school that very first day and never wore one again."

"Funny, how, when we're kids we don't realize how a seemingly little thing on a single day can brand you with a nickname for life."

"Too bad we never came up with one for you."

"Yep, that's me, just plain old Andreas."

"We ought to call you Lucky, with that wonderful bride of yours."

"That's right, I haven't seen you since our wedding."

"How's that working out?"

"Terrific."

"Damn well better, she's the best thing that ever happened to you."

"Why does everyone always tell me that?"

"I think that's something you can figure out for yourself, Chief Inspector."

Andreas laughed. "My secretary told me she'd finally tracked you down and that you're doing something hush-hush with the Defense Ministry."

"It's so secret I can't tell you that it has to do with keeping track of potential terrorists."

Andreas laughed. "Thanks for not telling me."

"Your secretary left a message that you wanted to speak with me about something important."

"Yes, I wondered if you've heard anything about a big move by international organized crime into the European counterfeit alcohol market?"

"Sure wish I could help you, but I've been out of the loop on that sort of thing since they replaced me as head of organized crime at GADA. I don't have to guess why you're not running this past the guy who took over for me."

Andreas snickered. "I'd only talk to him if I wanted to make sure the bad guys knew I'm interested in them."

"Yeah, he's not exactly known for discretion."

"A nice way to put it." Andreas let out a deep breath. "Oh well, it was worth a try. Thanks for calling back."

"No problem, and just so your effort's not a total loss, I may have something for you on a different matter."

"What sort of thing?" asked Andreas.

"We've been watching a taverna in Exarchia for about a year. It's a gathering place for the sort of home-grown terrorist characters we're interested in."

"Like November 17 and Conspiracy of the Cells of Fire?"

"Yeah, but mostly wannabes. A week ago we picked up a telephone conversation between the owner named Jacobi and a male called Kharon. It sounded interesting."

"What did they talk about?"

"Here, I'll play the tape for you. Jacobi is the first voice you'll hear."

Andreas heard Rolex fiddling with some buttons.

"Kharon?"

"Did he show?"

"Yes, and with all the money."

Silence.

"Kharon, did you hear me? He showed with a hundred thousand euros!"

"Yes, I heard. So did all the world by now."

"*Come on, this isn't the United States, no one's listening in on calls from my shitty little taverna in Athens.*"

"*Where is the meeting?*"

"*You're to be at the foot of the Acropolis at two. At the start of the path up to the top.*"

"*Who am I looking for?*"

"*He said they'll initiate contact.*"

"*Bye.*"

"*Wait a minute. What about all this money?*"

"*Hang onto it for me.*"

"*Until when?*"

"*Until I ask for it.*"

"*You definitely are nuts.*"

"That's all of it," said Rolex.

"Sure sounds suspicious to me," said Andreas.

"That's what we thought, so we had people stake out their meeting."

"Did he show?"

"I'll say. With bells and whistles. It was as if James Bond had come to town and put on a show." Rolex described how an acrobatic Kharon went from incognito bicycle messenger to uninvited passenger in an ominous SUV.

"He sounds like a real pro," said Andreas.

"For sure. We followed the SUV out to the private air terminal at Venizelos."

"Where'd he fly?"

"He didn't. He stayed in the SUV. A woman got out."

"Any ID on her?"

"No, and we couldn't get a photo of her."

"Tough break."

"But we did manage to identify the plane off its tail number. Not much help though, it's owned by some offshore, likely shell, corporation."

"What about the James Bond character?"

"We followed him to a hotel by Omonia, and the next morning to Jacobi's place in Exarchia."

"Any idea what they talked about?" said Andreas.

"Nope. We don't have the necessary equipment."

"Let me guess. Crisis cuts."

"Too bad the bad guys aren't feeling the pinch too," said Rolex.

"What about the others in the SUV?"

"Two men returned it to a place that rents out high-security vehicles, caught a taxi to Venizelos, and took a commercial flight to Sofia."

"Bulgaria?"

"Yes. No idea where they ended up. We had no authority to follow them out of Greece."

"Out of sight, out of mind. A wonderful philosophy on fighting terrorism."

"Tell me about it," said Rolex.

"Which brings me around to asking what this mysterious stranger Kharon has to do with me?"

"Patience, dear boy, I was just getting to that. We followed him to a place up by Delphi. Apparently he lives in the area. Thank God we had a tracking device on his bike. The guy rides like a bat out of hell. Three days ago we followed him from there to Thessaloniki. But we lost him when he switched bikes on us."

Andreas felt the hair on the back of his neck start to rise.

"How'd you get the tracking device on his bike?"

"He picked up a BMW at Jacobi's taverna and rode it back to his hotel in Omonia. In the time it took him to get his things out of his room, we stuck it on the bike."

"Too bad you lost him in Thessaloniki."

"It wasn't a total loss. We stayed with the bike and he came back for it. We'd lost him for three hours, and then followed him back to Delphi. On the way back he kept to the speed limit. Even wore a helmet. Like he didn't want to be noticed."

"And would those three hours have been after breakfast, say between ten and one?"

"I see you're getting the picture."

"Speaking of pictures, do you happen to have any of this Kharon guy?"

"I'm emailing them to you as we speak."

"I guess I don't have to ask why you thought I might be interested in him."

"I do read the papers and watch the news. Not sure if he has anything to do with the mess you have on your hands, but when I saw the call from your secretary I wondered why you were calling. That's when it hit me that I should have called you about this sooner. I guess it was one of those out of sight, out of mind things."

"I'll take that as your gentle way of saying let's stay in touch. Duly noted, Rolex."

"Uh, there's just one favor I'd like."

"Sure, name it."

"It's not a big one, and you know that I'm not the sensitive sort, but for someone in my position to be called 'Rolex' suggests I might be on the take. If you need a nickname for me, can't you come up with something less flashy?"

"You mean like Patek?"

"I see that marrying Lila has elevated your sense of humor."

A new email popped onto Andreas' screen. Attached to it were a half-dozen photos of a dark-haired, clean shaven man in his mid-twenties. It was a face Andreas had definitely seen before.

"I have the photos, my friend. Thanks. I owe you big-time," Andreas paused, "Ted."

◇◇◇

"Is he in yet?"

"Chief, as I told you five minutes ago when you hung up with your watch friend, I'll tell Yianni to go straight to your office the moment he gets in. Just because you decided to come into work an hour early doesn't mean the rest of the world does too."

"But, you were here."

"In case you haven't noticed, I'm always here early. It's the only time I can get any work done in this place."

Andreas listened to Maggie hang up. He looked at his watch. Almost nine in the morning. Still a lot of time left in the day to be cranky. He looked at the photos on his computer screen. This had to be the guy who did Tank's sister. No beard on this one, but definitely the eyes and facial structure of Kouros' composite. Andreas kept staring at the face. *I know I've seen you somewhere before.* That thought had helped keep him awake last night.

"Damn," he said aloud staring at the screen. "Who are you?"

"The one you wanted to see," said Kouros peeking in the slightly open door.

"Get over here and take a look at this."

"And a good morning to you, too, Chief," said Kouros walking over to Andreas' desk.

"Okay, so I'm not in a good mood." Andreas pointed at the screen.

"Hard to tell," said Kouros as he turned to look at the screen. "You're always so full of happiness and—Holy Mother, it's the guy from the *cafenion*."

"I was hoping you'd say that."

"Where'd you get the photos?"

Andreas told him of his conversation with Rolex.

"It sounds as if this Kharon character was hired to do the hit on Tank's sister," said Yianni.

"Too bad we can't prove it."

"What do you mean can't prove it? We've got the tape of his conversation with the taverna owner, the meeting by the Acropolis, Kharon followed to Thessaloniki, my identification of him in the *cafenion*—"

"Your leaving the scene of the murder before it happened, and not a soul in there when it did go down willing to point a finger at Kharon, including the deceased's brother."

Kouros walked over to the couch and dropped onto it. "I guess it's wishful thinking to hope we can somehow put enough heat on Tank and his crew to get any of them to turn against Kharon."

"Especially since it's not Kharon they fear."

"Then who do they fear? The mysterious woman in the SUV?"

Andreas shrugged. "Could be, or she could be representing whoever wanted the message delivered to Tank. But no matter who sent Kharon, I'm betting this is no coincidence, and that it all somehow ties into Tank's counterfeit booze business."

"What makes you think that?"

"From the way Tank is screaming about foreign terrorists muscling in on his legitimate business."

"But he's asking for all of Greece to go after Kharon's boss. That doesn't sound like he got the message."

Andreas gestured no. "He got it loud and clear, but he needs political cover to explain why a mobster-style execution of his sister right in front of him doesn't paint him as tied into something dirty. It's a typical political misdirection ploy intended to cover the first thing that ordinarily comes to the Greek public's mind: a conspiracy. To counter that, you tell enough of the truth for your version to be believed without implicating any of your real bad guy buddies. As long as Tank doesn't identify the real killer, there's no way to trace anything back to who ordered the hit. And if Tank does as he's told and pays on time, the big boss in charge couldn't care less what he says to cover his ass."

"This is all way too crazy."

"Come on, Yianni, it's not all that different from the sort of intrigues we see Greeks and our government involved in every day."

"This still seems wilder to me."

"Really? Remember when our government in its wisdom imposed that special real estate tax you had to pay with your electric bill?"

"Of course. The government knew if it just sent a tax bill no one would pay it, but this way if you didn't pay, your electricity got shut off."

"Precisely. And if you happened to be a property owner who received electricity from a private company, that provider was required to collect your tax payments and turn them over to the government. Back in the early days of our financial crisis, one of those private electric companies collected over three hundred million euros in taxes and solemnly announced one day that it was transferring all of those funds to Cyprus for 'safekeeping.'

And guess what happened? *Poof.* The entire three hundred million vanished without a trace."

"Four guys went to jail, didn't they?" said Kouros.

"They were arrested, sat in jail for eighteen months, but never came to trial."

"Son of a bitch. So the court had to let them out. Just like those terrorists who walked out of jail for the same reason."

"And in a midnight session of Parliament the four of them received amnesty." Andreas bit at his lower lip. "Don't get me started on my rant about the Greek justice system. I just arrest them."

"Don't worry, I'll bitch for you. But I never saw anything in the media about the three-hundred-million-euro men walking away."

"Nor will you likely ever. Three hundred million euros buys a lot of cooperation. From everyone. Including the press. And with no 'clawback' law in Greece, I wouldn't bet on the country ever seeing a cent of the missing money."

"Maybe the tax boys will decide to go after the original taxpayers. I can hear them now: 'Hey, you still owe us, we never got your money.'"

"That would lead to one thing for sure. A rise in Molotov cocktail sales."

Kouros shook his head. "I can't believe all that could happen right under the eyes of Greece's European and IMF Troika watchdogs."

"Yeah," said Andreas. "Sort of makes you wonder, doesn't it?"

Kouros shook his head. "But what's all this have to do with our problem with Tank?"

"It's meant as a lesson in the rigors of combating political power."

"Meaning?"

"Care to guess the family behind the company responsible for the missing three hundred million? Here's a hint, they never received a line of blame in the press."

"Tank's?"

"Bingo, you win. Tank's family is all about maintaining appearances as it pillages and plunders."

"And how do you expect us to bring them down?"

Andreas shrugged. "Not sure yet, but let's start small and see what happens. Petro is supposed to be back around lunchtime. As soon as he's in, grab him. I want us to take a little ride together."

"Why do I sense trouble?"

"Because you're a good detective."

Chapter Fifteen

"Why are you driving?" asked Kouros. "You never like to drive."

Andreas smiled, "Because you and Petro would refuse to go to where I'm taking us." He made a right turn out of GADA and drove west along Alexandras Avenue.

Kouros turned and looked at Petro in the backseat. "The son of a bitch is taking us to watch his soccer team play."

Petro gestured no. "Too early. Besides, they're still in mourning over last night's loss."

"Laugh while you still can, guys, because you won't be laughing long." He turned left off onto Trikouri Street.

Kouros stared at the side of Andreas' face. "If you're headed to where I think you are, what suicide wish possessed you to drive a marked blue and white screaming Athens police?"

"I want everyone to know who we are. It'll surprise them. They aren't expecting us to be so bold."

"I think you mean crazy. May I remind you that cops haven't been welcome in Exarchia since 2008 when two of our less than gifted brethren shot and killed an unarmed, sixteen-year-old demonstrator."

"Frankly, Yianni, cops haven't been welcome in this neighborhood for a lot longer than that."

"Then what makes you think things have changed?" said Kouros.

"I guess we'll find out soon enough," said Andreas. He drove past the southwest corner of Exarchia Square, made a left at Benaki and another left at Arachovis.

"So, now we're making a loop around the neighborhood, just to make sure no one misses us?" said Kouros.

"Of course, I want everyone to know we're headed to Jacobi's."

"Are you out of your mind? You mean we're actually going to stop?" said Kouros. "In case you haven't noticed, every pair of eyes in the neighborhood is fixed on us."

"Yeah, I know. They can't believe we're here in a blue and white." Andreas stopped by the eastern edge of the square and parked on the sidewalk right in front of Jacobi's front door.

"You really do want to be obvious," said Kouros.

"Okay, guys, it's show time. We're all going to act as if we're old-time buddies of Jacobi's just stopping in to have a coffee and say hello."

Kouros looked at Petro, held up his hand, and pinched his thumb and forefinger nearly together. "I came this close to getting my ass blown away in a *cafenion* up in Thessaloniki, and now I get to relive the experience at some shithole taverna in Exarchia. Where did I go wrong?"

"Don't worry," said Petro. "I know how to get us to the nearest hospital."

"Comforting." Kouros opened his door and got out.

Petro did the same and they followed Andreas toward the taverna, each man scanning the area as he did. So far no one had picked up a rock to throw at them. Or a Molotov cocktail. But for late night revolutionaries it was early yet, and they needed their beauty sleep.

As soon as Andreas entered the taverna a swarthy, bearded, bowling ball of a fellow waddled up to him. "What the fuck are you assholes doing in my place?"

Andreas opened his arms, embraced the man, and kissed him on both cheeks. "Jacobi, *mou*. How we've missed you. It's been way too long. I promised you we'd stop by and thank you personally for all you've done to help us."

Jacobi's eyed jumped frantically among the faces of his customers, then fixed a glare on Andreas. "What the fuck are you talking about? I never saw you before in my life."

"Oh, *to pedi mou*, how can you be so ashamed of your old friends?"

"I'm not your child, asshole."

Andreas leaned down and whispered, "If you want me to say a lot more in front of your customers, things that will probably have you burned out by sundown, just keep pushing me. Now hug me and let's sit where we can talk."

Jacobi paused for a moment and grunted them with a nod toward a table as far from the door and the other tables as possible.

"Okay, I'll pass on the hug." Andreas nodded Petro toward the door. "Keep an eye on things."

Andreas and Kouros sat with their backs to the wall, facing into the room. Jacobi stood facing them.

"Sit down," said Andreas.

"I don't sit with cops."

"Your choice, but I think you'll want to hear what I have to say sitting down."

"Fuck you."

Andreas shook his head from side to side and smiled. "Jacobi *mou*—"

"Don't call me that."

"Okay, we'll call you shithead," said a smiling Kouros. "Fits you better anyway."

Jacobi clenched his fist.

"A very unwise decision," said Kouros.

"Especially for a man who is about to lose a hundred thousand euros given to him for safekeeping," said Andreas.

Jacobi blinked.

"Yeah, I'd love to hear how you're going to explain losing it to the guy who left it with you," said Kouros.

"I don't know what you're talking about."

Andreas patted the chair across from him. "Sure you do, and if you don't start cooperating we're going to tear this place apart until we find the money and what I expect will be a lot of other interesting things."

Jacobi sat.

"Good," said Andreas. "We're really not interested in you."

"That's what cops always say."

"And we really don't want your money."

Jacobi raised an eyebrow. "That's what cops never say."

Andreas nodded. "That should let you know we're here for a very serious reason."

"What do you want?"

"A simple name."

"There is no such thing as a 'simple name.'"

"Well, let me make it simple for you. Due to your most kind cooperation, we know who killed the pride and joy young woman of one of Greece's most prominent political families."

Jacobi shifted in his chair. "I don't know what you're talking about. I haven't told you a thing."

"Of course you have. How else could we possibly know the shooter's name?"

"Beats me," shrugged Jacobi.

"No, no, I think what you mean is that when he finds out what you told us *he* beats you," said Kouros.

Jacobi shrugged again.

"I'm sure you and he go way back together," said Andreas. "Otherwise why else would he trust you to hold all the money he got just to show up at the Acropolis?"

Jacobi tugged at his beard. "I don't know what you're taking about."

"You've already said that twice," said Andreas. "But actually you do. And you also know that your buddy's going to figure out that you're the only one who could have fingered him."

"You don't know shit. You're fishing."

It was Andreas' turn to shrug. "I know enough to get you killed."

"Fuck you do."

"When I leave here I'll be smiling and happy and blowing you kisses. But the moment I get in the police car I'm on the radio putting a call out across Greece for the immediate arrest of the person identified as the Thessaloniki woman's killer. And I'll make sure that word leaks out through unofficial channels that, in exchange for the information, the informant got to keep the hundred thousand euros paid for the hit."

Jacobi jerked forward in his chair. "He'll never believe it."

"Of course he will. Maybe not completely, but at least enough to think *maybe* you turned him in. And *maybe* to a guy like him can be deadly for a guy like you."

"I'll never tell you his name."

"His name? I don't want his name. I don't even want to arrest him."

"Then what do you want?"

"I want the name of the person who hired him to kill her."

Jacobi leaned back in his chair and laughed. "Oh, I see you want me to commit suicide."

"No, I want to spare you from certain death. The other is just a distinct possibility."

"You're crazy."

"Of course I am. Just enough to pin a bullseye on your forehead that your buddy couldn't miss. I want a name."

"No way."

"Then I'll give you one. And after I say it I'm walking out of here, making my radio call, and spreading that name and yours all across Greece."

Jacobi swallowed. "You're bluffing."

Andreas nodded to Kouros and the two cops got up and headed to the front door. Petro stood waiting for them. A couple of sixties-throwback student types stood near the police car, staring into the taverna as if waiting for reinforcements.

Andreas turned and watched Jacobi rise from his chair.

"Jacobi *mou*, next time we'll actually let you buy us that coffee you promised."

"Fuck off."

"And don't forget to say hello to our buddy," Andreas threw him a kiss, cupped his hands around his lips and shouted, "*KHARON*."

The three cops strolled out of the taverna and into the police car. Andreas turned on the ignition, put the microphone to his lips and said, "One, two, three, four, five, six—"

A pounding on the front passenger's side window startled Kouros before Andreas had reached seven.

"Just as I thought. I never got to ten. Open the window, Yianni."

As soon as Kouros did, Jacobi leaned in. "Have you called yet?"

Andreas held up the microphone, "Just about to."

Jacobi bit at his lip. "You promise not to say it was me."

"Promise."

Jacobi lowered his eyes and leaned further into the car. "Teacher," he whispered.

"I didn't hear you," said Andreas.

Kouros looked at Andreas. "He said, 'Teacher.'"

Andreas now swallowed. "Do you mean Teacher as in *Teacher?*"

"Yes, that one. She's who hired him." Jacobi pulled back from the window and waddled back inside.

"Uh, Chief," said Petro.

"Yes."

"Now there's a half-dozen of those whack jobs behind the car with more coming. We ought to get out of here before all hell breaks loose."

Andreas put the car in gear and pulled away. "Too late, it already has."

◇◇◇

Andreas spoke with Maggie on his mobile as he drove back to GADA while Kouros brought Petro up to speed on what he'd missed of Andreas' conversation with Jacobi.

After Andreas hung up, Petro said, "Sounds like your plan worked, Chief. He gave you the name you wanted."

"No, he definitely gave me a name I did *not* want. I can assure you I'd have preferred just about any other name on earth but that one."

"Why? Who's Teacher?"

Kouros answered. "A couple years back, before you were in the unit, we had a run-in with her on Mykonos."

"I wouldn't exactly call it a 'run-in,' Yianni. More like, let's hope she doesn't notice we exist while we try to manipulate her."

"But it worked," said Kouros.

"Or so we thought."

"The problem went away."

"But now she's back with all new players, as far as we can tell. And if this counterfeit booze business is as big as it seems, it's a natural fit for what she does, which is providing financing for much of Europe's big-time criminal activity."

"So, who is she?" said Petro.

"Maggie's pulling a file containing the little we know about her. But, the truth is, I've never met her, spoken with her, or even seen a photograph of her."

"Then how do you know she's as bad news as you say?"

"Sometimes it's prudent to believe what you hear. Like don't jump into a swimming pool filled with angry, hungry crocodiles."

"Or get between an Athenian housewife and a pair of crocodile shoes on sale," said Yianni.

Andreas slowed to turn into GADA's parking area. "As you can tell, just the mention of her name is enough to cost Yianni his sense of humor." He parked, and the three cops went inside the building and up to Andreas' office.

As Andreas passed Maggie's desk she held out an envelope for him.

"Thanks."

"You're welcome. Sorry you had to ask for that one," she said.

"Me too."

Andreas went inside his office and sat behind his desk, Kouros and Petro sat on the couch.

"I see Maggie's down on Teacher, too," said Petro.

"Hard to imagine anyone who knows anything about her who'd feel otherwise." Andreas opened the envelope and took out a thin document. "And now you, too, are about to know why we all feel as we do. This is a transcript of an anonymous telephone call that came to us courtesy of Europol. The question put to the informant was, 'Who is Teacher?' This is his answer."

Andreas cleared his throat. "'My answer requires somewhat more of an introduction than you might think warranted, but it is necessary if you wish to understand the phenomenon that is Teacher. And I say phenomenon because she is far more than just a mortal being. At least in the world to which she belongs. And rules.

"'The world is no longer linear. There are no straight-line rules to follow, or confining borders to observe. Not in communication, not in business, not in political loyalties, and certainly not in crime. Those who seek to retain parochial influence within strictly drawn political borders fail to appreciate the implications of this new order. Today vast numbers live within various countries' legal borders but owe their allegiances elsewhere, to leaders outside borders and beyond a government's reach. Their loyalty is to a thought, an idea, one not offered in any embraceable form by the land in which they now live.

"'It is the West's greatest nightmare. An insoluble situation many say. And one Teacher has exploited as ruthlessly as anyone on earth. She has convinced an army of the exploited that they have the power to change their lives. That any who desire simple protection from those who would do them physical harm should join her on the path to a better life.

"'She preaches that words alone are not enough for those in mortal fear, and that praying for a better life is not the way. She proves her point by telling them what they already know: that the criminal beast can never be killed off in this world. Far too many want the sex and slaves and drugs that it offers. What *she* offers, on the other hand, is to tame the beast a bit. To teach those who traffic in evil that it is far wiser to pay the small share she asks for on behalf of her flock than face the assassination and torture she would bring upon them and their families.

"'She lives in no one place. She has no family. She lives a private life away from prying eyes. It is said she has no vices because she's done them all and has attained a state far above what they promise.'"

Andreas stopped. No one spoke for a moment.

"That's all the information we have except for one bit of gossip. And I quote,

"'Virtually all in Eastern Europe who fear her are praying the rumor that she's terminally ill is true. They believe no one who assumes her role could be as ruthless as Teacher.'"

Andreas looked up from the transcript and stared at Petro. "Got the picture?"

Petro nodded. "I'll take the swimming pool with the crocodiles."

Chapter Sixteen

"So, my friend, to what do I owe the honor of this phone call?" said Tassos.

"Sorry to disturb your siesta," said Andreas, "but Maggie said you won't be back in Athens until tomorrow and I wanted to give you a heads-up on a development in that *bomba* business with Tank."

"No problem. At this point in my life all my day is siesta time. I could solve these island homicides in my sleep. Same story line, different players. Follow the passion."

"I thought it was 'follow the money'?"

"That's in big city Athens. Here on the islands we think more with our pricks and pussies."

"You do realize that's not a very politically correct approach to police work."

"I'm open to broadening my thinking. Why just the other day I collared a gay guy who'd planted a hatchet in his boyfriend's... or was it girlfriend's...head."

"Enough. I've got something serious to tell you."

"Okay, what is it?"

"Teacher's back in play."

A few seconds passed before Tassos spoke. "Are you sure?"

"I can't imagine that the guy who gave me her name would have been insane enough to point the finger at Teacher if it weren't true. Sort of like purposely stepping on Superman's toes. As I'm sure I don't have to tell you, her appearance is not a good development."

"For anyone involved. She'd wipe out your life, my life, our families' lives, all without even knowing our names. Or caring to know them."

"That's why I'm calling you. To tell you we have a problem and we need to come up with a strategy."

"I think we should follow the example of the cockroach," said Tassos.

"Which is?"

"They've been around for 280 million years because they know how to hide and adapt."

"Okay, very funny. Now why don't you tell me what's really on your mind."

"Seriously, we can't be caught out in the open in daylight."

"Tassos—"

"Okay, okay. Teacher can never know that we're on to her, so whatever we do we have to make damn sure she thinks Tank is our target and not she. That snitch, the one who named her to you. What's the chance he'll get religion and confess that he told you?"

"If he were Catholic, I'd say he'd only confess if he were looking for his last rites."

"Good," said Tassos.

"But Tank's her guy in Greece, which likely means part of her deal is protecting him from cops like us."

"Remember when we talked about how he didn't fit the profile of her guys in other countries? Tank is local, and I'd bet you anything he sold himself to her, claiming he could protect his own operation and she needn't worry about any of that."

"He's just arrogant enough to think that way," said Andreas.

"The more significant question at the moment is, are we arrogant enough to think we can bring down Teacher?"

"If the opportunity presented itself, I'd love to, though I'm guessing the odds on getting that chance are about the same as on achieving world peace."

"Well, the good news is that whether our goal is to nail Tank, his sister's killer, or Teacher, as I see it, everything starts with the same thing—shutting down Tank's operation. If we're right, and Teacher is behind it all, threatening her investment puts a hell of a lot of pressure on Tank. My bet is that once that happens he's likely to make a mistake we can use to put him away and, possibly, get him to identify his sister's killer. Who knows? We might even get lucky and Teacher will make a mistake, too."

"I put those last two scenarios in the categories of wishful and extraordinarily wishful thinking. The more likely result of shutting Tank down is an immediate spike in the body count among his nearest and dearest. With our esteemed politicians screaming for our heads over the murder of one member of Tank's family, would you care to guess which parts they'll be aiming to slice off once that happens?"

Tassos snickered. "Since when has that ever bothered you?"

"Okay, assuming shutting down Tank's business is the place to start, how do you suggest we go about doing it without getting Teacher pissed off at us, too? After all, as you pointed out, it is ultimately her operation and investment we'd be trashing."

"Hey, why ask me? I'm the siesta-loving cop. You're the Athens hotshot."

"Sometimes you're a real pain in the ass."

"Okay, I get your point. My only suggestion is that you keep giving Tank all the rope he's willing to take. Sooner or later he'll tie himself up in knots, and make what you have to do so obvious and downright simple, that if you didn't do it, Teacher would think you're brain dead."

"In other words, make it so that she blames Tank for the screw-up, not vigorous police work for taking him down."

"Exactly. People like Teacher don't get angry with dumb cops who bring them down because of someone else's stupid mistakes. It's the smart ones they resent, because those who outthink them make them look bad to themselves. Professor Moriarty would never have given a second thought to doing battle with Watson. It was Sherlock Holmes who drew his ire."

"Thank you, Watson, for telling me in such an eloquent way to do absolutely nothing."

"Essentially, yes. But that will not be easy. There will be great trials along the way, challenges to your resilience and character. But in the end you will prevail and cut off Tank's fucking balls."

"I'm glad you finally dropped the Yoda impression. It was getting me a bit worried."

"Good-bye, Andreas. And may the force be with you."

"I knew you'd say that."

"Of course you did." Click.

Andreas smiled. It was a good idea calling Tassos. The world seemed better now. *Do nothing and things will work out on their own.* It was Greece's national motto. Perhaps this time it would actually work.

◇◇◇

Andreas heard the secretary say, "Minister, it's Chief Kaldis on the line."

Spiros picked up the phone immediately. "Any news?"

"Excuse me while I take a moment to say hello."

"And hello to you, too."

Andreas had expected a bit of a bite back, not a cheery reply. It wasn't like Spiros to give Andreas a pass on sarcasm.

"I have some news, Minister. But it's...how shall I say... complicated."

"What do you mean *complicated*?"

"We know who killed her—"

"Terrific. Have you arrested him yet?"

"No, that's the easy part."

"Then why haven't you?"

"Because of the complicated part." Andreas paused, not sure how much he should tell him. "Minister, I don't know if I should tell you this, but—"

"Are you crazy? I'm your boss." The words were as he'd expected from Spiros, but the tone lacked its customary outrage.

"If I tell you what I know and word gets out—because you may feel obligated to tell the prime minister, who'll then undoubtedly tell others—your life, my life, and a lot of other lives will be in danger." Andreas saw no reason to say that the prime minister would tell Tank's family, as that seemed obvious.

"Are you suggesting I can't be trusted?"

"No, not you."

"Then who? The prime minister?"

"Let's put it this way. He's a politician, and politicians far too often make decisions based on the expediency of the moment. Especially now, with an election looming that polls have him likely to lose, and a hungry press out there screaming for a name to blame for the murder, I'm not betting on him or any politician seeing a bigger picture than his own reelection."

Andreas braced for an explosion.

"I understand." Spiros' voice was flat. "So what can you tell me?"

If Andreas hadn't personally dialed the minister's number he'd have sworn he'd called the wrong man. "We don't want anyone knowing we've solved the crime. We also don't want to do anything that might discourage Tank and his family from screaming at us for not catching his sister's killer or protecting Greek businessmen from 'criminal elements.'"

"That's quite a bit to ask, Andreas. If you think the press is attacking us now, they'll go nuclear if we can't show them any progress."

"I know, but at the end of the day, you'll look like a hero."

"That assumes the prime minister doesn't replace me by the end of *this* day."

"Is it that bad?"

"Yes."

"Well, then tell him I'm trying to come up with answers that won't destroy the credibility of his party."

"What does that mean?"

"No idea, but being the politician he is, his mind will run to all the possibilities and he'll come up with something to justify your strategy."

"But even assuming he doesn't want me to press you for details, he's going to want a timetable for when he'll have his answers."

"Tell him, we expect it all to break for us within a matter of days."

"Is that true?"

Andreas looked at his free hand, remembered an American gesture, and crossed his fingers. "Absolutely."

◇◇◇

Spiros hung up on his call with Andreas and stared at a deep brown Chesterfield armchair in the far corner. He stood up, walked across his office, and dropped down into the chair. His wife hated the big, cushiony leather thing, which was why he insisted on keeping it—though in his office, not at home.

He sighed. He'd restrained his curiosity over wanting to know all that Andreas knew, and wasn't sure Andreas was correct in his strategy, but he'd let it all pass. Despite all the bad blood between them over the years, he knew he could trust Andreas not to set him up. *It's a shame*, he thought, *that he couldn't say the same thing about me.*

Spiros leaned his head back against the chair, shut his eyes, and whispered, "That's why I owe him this."

Chapter Seventeen

Four days after his sister's death, Tank and his family held a memorial service practically canonizing her. Every politician, cleric, and business leader who mattered in Greece seemed to have made the pilgrimage to Thessaloniki for the service. And every journalist—mattering or not—attended with camera and pen in hand feasting on the spectacle. Two TV channels carried the service live.

Tank did not miss the opportunity to make his point. He delivered an eloquent eulogy, ending with a message that would be repeated endlessly in sound bites across Greek television.

"My fellow Greeks, as hard as it is to accept, I must accept that my sister is gone and that I shall never see her again in this life. But what I cannot accept and will not accept is that any of you must needlessly suffer as my family and I have suffered.

"I want none of you *ever* to witness one of your own loved ones slaughtered before your eyes. I want none of you *ever* to find your property, your business, your very way of life targeted by those who'll tell you, 'Give us what we want or watch your family die.' That is the message my sister's murderer meant to send to all of Greece.

"But how can we, a simple people unschooled in violent ways, resist such men? We cannot. For that protection we must rely upon our government and our police. I call upon you, Mr. Prime Minister, Mr. Mayor, and Mr. Public Order Minister, to tell me and my family why in the time since my sister's death you have accomplished absolutely nothing toward bringing her slayer to justice? The murderer is not a phantom. I have personally described him in detail. *Shame on all of you.*

"But my fellow Greeks, when I speak of shame, I speak of national shame, for if we allow our government to continue doing nothing, if we allow this violent criminal element to fester and grow, if we allow this scourge to further undermine the basic values of our beloved Greece, then I say to you, my countrymen, *SHAME ON US ALL.*"

The applause that followed was spontaneous and deafening, joined in even by the politicians singled out in Tank's excoriation of their ways.

"Sounds like he's running for office," said Andreas nodding toward the television in his office.

"And if we're wrong in our strategy, there will be a hell of lot of them to fill," said Tassos.

"Plus a few chief and detective slots I can think of," said Kouros.

"Aw, don't worry," said Andreas. "He's percolating along just fine. Pretty soon he'll be ready."

"To devour or explode?" said Tassos.

"Ah, yes, it's those small details that make life challenging," said Andreas.

Tassos nodded. "Yep, 'the devil is in the details.'"

Kouros pointed at the television showing Tank standing by the podium basking in a standing ovation. "Nope, today I'd say he's right up there in Thessaloniki."

◇◇◇

"Hello, Teacher, it's Tank."

She checked to make sure the scrambler was operating before answering. "What can I do for you?"

"I know you don't like to chit-chat so I'll get right to the point."

He paused as if waiting for a response, but Teacher said nothing.

"We've had a bit of a disagreement recently, but I want to assure you I received your message loud and clear and all that media talk you've heard from me since then is only meant to benefit our mutual interests."

She checked the scrambler again. "From what I hear, you're demanding that Greek authorities bring your sister's killer to justice and protect you and your countrymen from foreign criminal extortionists. How could I possibly see any of that as intended other than 'to benefit our mutual interests'?"

Tank gave a nervous laugh. "You have no reason to worry about the police finding your man. I gave them a completely wrong description." He swallowed. "Honestly, it's been a great opportunity for gaining political cover for our business. No one will touch us with all the sympathetic press we're getting. And if anyone does, I'll scream that I've been set up by the very criminal element I'm pushing our politicians to attack."

Teacher paused. "I have only one question for you. Why do you always find it necessary to seek your own path on every journey, even when there is a direct, reliable road taking you straight to all you could ever possibly hope to gain from whatever you're pursuing?"

"I don't understand."

"I was afraid you'd say that. Let me give you one example. I have given you the means for duplicating the best Greek wines, yet you have this infatuation with copying the highest level French and American wines, something far beyond your abilities."

"I don't know how you knew about those plans, but I intended to surprise you."

"I'm sure. But haven't you learned by now that you're wasting your time trying to keep secrets from me that concern my business?"

Tank swallowed again. "The way I've handled the media has made me so popular that people are saying I should run for public office. I'm thinking of running for mayor. After all, our current one comes out of the wine business, so why couldn't I be next?"

"He's honest."

"So what? People get tired of honest politicians. They want mayors they can work with."

"Didn't the mayor before this one get a life sentence for that sort of thinking?"

"He was sloppy and arrogant."

Teacher paused and cleared her throat. "I think you should consider getting a realistic grip on your ambitions. All this press coverage I'm sure is exciting for you, but the press has a way of eating its favorites."

"I can handle them."

"Fine, so let me put this differently. I have given you a program to follow that yields great profits everywhere it's employed. I expect you to adhere to the product formulas, but if you wish to pursue your love affair with the media as a means for enhancing our business I shall not oppose you."

"Thank you."

"But if one day you should *again* conclude there is a way to cheat me, or your actions deny me the full measure of all you've agreed to pay me, I can assure you that the press you see venerating you today will be reporting on speeches demanding justice for your assassination."

"That's a wholly unnecessary approach for you to take with me."

"I think not. You just called the murder of your sister a 'bit of a disagreement' and raved on about how you've turned it into a 'great opportunity' for 'our business.' You should be cursing me, hating me, fearing me. Instead you're trying to hustle me with your bullshit delusions of grandeur. I've seen it all, I've done it all, I've been it all. My bottom line is simple: I don't care what sort of little masturbation games you want to play with yourself, but if you ever even *think* of screwing with me or our arrangement again, I promise to cut your balls off. Literally. Slowly. Painfully."

Silence.

"Understand?"

"Yes."

"I didn't hear you."

"*Yes!*"

"Good. Your next wire transfer is due tomorrow." Teacher hung up without saying another word and slammed her hand on the desktop.

She drew in and let out a deep breath. She hated when she lost her temper. She swallowed and looked at the photo on her desk. "This one just doesn't get it. He's a narcissistic sociopath, coddled and protected by his parents for so long he thinks he can get away with anything."

She rubbed her forehead with the hand she'd slammed onto the desk. "I hope he's right, or if he's wrong that his parents remain prepared to be there for him. Losing one child is more than any parent should ever have to bear."

◇◇◇

"My, aren't we home early," said Lila looking up from the computer screen on her desk. She sat in her study, framed from behind by a lightly draped floor-to-ceiling window view of Athens' majestic Likavitos, sister hill to the Acropolis. She glanced at her watch. "It's still midafternoon."

Andreas leaned across the desk and kissed her on the forehead. He stepped back and dropped onto a beige and crème damask Queen Anne sofa set back against five wall-spanning rows of lacquered bookshelves.

"That's all I get, a forehead kiss?"

"I'm practicing restraint in all aspects of my life."

"Come again?"

"It's that mess up in Thessaloniki. We're letting that asshole Tank wail away at us and not hit back. It's emotionally exhausting. We can't even swear at him."

"That doesn't sound like you."

"It isn't me, but the strategy is to let him punch away at us as often and hard as he likes until he makes a mistake that we can use to bring him down."

"I get it. A variation on 'rope-a-dope.'"

Andreas blinked. "You never fail to amaze me. I didn't know you were a fan of American boxing."

"'Thrilla in Manila.'"

Andreas smiled. "You should have stopped while you were ahead. 'Thrilla' was Muhammad Ali and Joe Frazier. 'Rope-a-dope' came out of Ali's fight before that one, when he beat

George Foreman to regain his heavyweight championship in 'The Rumble in the Jungle.'"

Lila shrugged. "Okay, so you caught me. Besides, those two phrases exhaust my knowledge of American boxing."

"But you're right about us and rope-a-dope. Ali let Foreman bang the hell out of him while he curled up against the ropes, letting the ropes absorb most of the shock from Foreman's punches. That's sort of our plan with Tank. Let him pound away at us until he knocks himself out."

"Sounds like a painful strategy."

"You've no idea."

"How's Spiros holding up?"

"Considering he's taking most of the punches on his chin, amazing."

"He must be on drugs," said Lila. "Or else he's found a guru the entire world should be following."

"Or it could just be that his health problems have put everything else in perspective. Whatever the reason, so far he hasn't cracked."

"How much longer do you think he can take the pressure?"

"No telling. But if he caves in now, after Tank's televised eulogy today, the whole country will think Tank was right about him. Make that right about *us*. We'll all be out of work. Let's just hope he hangs tough for at least a bit longer."

"How long is a 'bit longer'?"

"Until Tank makes a mistake that gives us an opening to hit him as hard as we can with the best we have."

"How long did it take Ali to find his opening?"

"He knocked Foreman out in the eighth round."

"Ouch, that's a lot of pounding to take to get there."

"And we've no way of telling which round we're in with Tank."

"Only one more boxing question. If Spiros is playing Ali, who are you?"

"Today, I'd say I'm the ropes."

Lila stood up from her desk, walked over to the sofa, and sat down beside him. She put one hand around Andreas' neck, the other on his upper thigh, and kissed him on the cheek. "Are you sure you want to practice 'restraint' in *all* aspects of your life?" She squeezed his thigh.

He smiled, still staring off in the general direction of the window. "At the moment, sadly, yes."

She kissed him again on the cheek. "Too bad you didn't decide on doing that sooner."

He turned his head to face her. "What's that supposed to mean?"

She nodded toward the desk. "I was just checking my emails. One is from my doctor."

"What's—"

Lila stopped him with a finger to his lips. "Shhh, I'll tell you." She sat back and took his hands in hers. "I'm pregnant.

Andreas' face lit into a smile. "I can't believe it. That's terrific!" He squeezed her hands, dropping them only to hug and kiss her. "Tassaki's going to have a baby…baby what?"

"Too soon to tell."

"I'm so excited." Andreas hugged her again.

Lila took his hands in hers. "Me, too. And I think there's a sign to be drawn from this."

"What sort of sign?"

"That your rope-a-dope strategy is working."

Andreas gave her a 'what are you talking about?' look. "How could such wonderful news about your being pregnant possibly be a sign of anything having to do with that piece of garbage Tank?"

"I see it as a sign of the power of your knock up punch."

Andreas burst out laughing. "It's '*knockout*' punch."

Lila smiled. "Oh, well. That too."

Chapter Eighteen

So far Teacher had kept her word. Kharon had his offshore company, and with it contracts to buy most of the olive groves he wanted. The olive oil production facility's owners were playing cute over price, but Teacher told him not to worry. "They'll come around."

Her reassurance came in the course of a telephone conversation about another "simple message" she had for him to deliver. She said the details would be in a package in the helicopter she'd arranged to pick him up at a place of his choosing. "I assume you don't want to be seen by your neighbors flying about on a helicopter like a shipowner bouncing between girlfriends and family on summer holiday."

He met the helicopter in a deserted, burned-out olive grove between Delphi and Amfissa, and it brought him to a private airport near Greece's northern border with Bulgaria. From there, a private plane flew him to Kiev, and armored transport courtesy of the Ukrainian military brought him as close to its eastern border conflict with Russia as the soldiers would dare go. Kharon's instructions described his target, its anticipated location, and a suggested method of transmitting her message. He was free, though, to vary the delivery means should he so choose. His army escort would wait for his return. At least that was the promise.

Arms smuggling stood as big business in the Ukraine. Players from around the world used it as a staging area for supplying many Middle Eastern and North African hotspots. The armed conflict between Russia and Ukraine brought unintended, unappreciated consequences to the region's arms dealers. Russia was back in the game. Not directly, but with its war machine gearing up, black market, sophisticated product now found its way into the flow of commerce. The Bear's illicit profiteers were cutting in heavily on Teacher's share of arms-dealing profits.

Teacher's efforts at reaching a deal with those in the Russian military now profiting off trade in their army's weaponry were flatly rejected. "Tell the bitch to fuck off," was the actual message conveyed to her emissary by the Russian General in charge of Russia's unofficial military operations in the Ukraine. He saw no reason to share the benefits of his position with those he regarded as beneath him.

The General's visit to the Ukraine that day had been a last-minute affair arranged to satisfy a buyer from the Middle East intent on purchasing a missile system capable of bringing down high-flying aircraft. The buyer had balked at paying until he received personal reassurances that the product was "truly Russian." He would settle for nothing less than a face-to-face meeting with the General.

No matter, it would be a brief late afternoon excursion, one affording the General an opportunity to reacquaint himself with the young Ukrainian girls he'd put in charge of keeping his buyers happy. Middle East men loved his blond, busty, blue-eyed entertainers.

The General's helicopter landed next to a warehouse about ten miles inside the Ukraine. A phalanx of armed men surrounded him at the helicopter pad and stayed with him to the warehouse door, then remained posted outside.

Fifteen minutes later, the door opened, and the General, accompanied by a man dressed in traditional Arab garb, stepped outside. The armed men immediately formed around the two and accompanied them to the helicopter. At the helicopter the Arab bowed and shook the General's hand. The General smiled, patted him on the arm and got inside the helicopter. The men moved back and all but the Arab stopped to watch it take off. The Arab walked quickly toward the warehouse waving at the rising chopper as he did.

He reached the warehouse door just as a contrail seared across the sky from a hillside one mile from the warehouse. The explosion showered what remained of the helicopter down on the armed men scattering for cover.

The troops who reached the hillside minutes later found evidence of the sort of handheld surface-to-air missile used by the Ukrainian army. The Russian spokesman announcing the General's death made no mention of the missile or the Ukraine, only that the General had died in a tragic helicopter accident "far from any conflict zone."

As far as the world would know, it was an accident. But for those in the Russian military prepared to step into the General's black marketeer shoes, there was a lesson to be heeded. A lesson that Teacher would reaffirm in red letters emblazoned upon a gold ribbon stretched across a massive wreath of flowers delivered to the General's funeral: "Sharing is good."

◇◇◇

Kharon sat staring out the window of the private jet carrying him back to Greece. He still preferred the up close, personal approach to ending a life, one that allowed him the opportunity of affording a potential victim a reasoned means for survival. But with his assignments from Teacher, any opportunity for the target's survival had long since past. For her, Kharon's role was simply to function as executioner. He wondered at what point she'd lost her moral center. She must have had one. Did she lose it quickly, or did it degrade over time? *And when will mine disappear?*

He'd toyed with the idea of killing the General while he enjoyed the women, but that would have been needlessly risky. Besides, Kharon lacked the time, local contacts, and language skills necessary for carrying out such a sophisticated assassination.

So he did it Teacher's way. Just as her instructions promised, the missile had been waiting for him on the hillside, programmed to take down the General's helicopter. All he had to do was watch through binoculars for the signal wave from her Arab colleague, count to five, and fire. It was all too simple. Anyone could have done it. There was no reason to bring Kharon all the way from Greece simply to pull a trigger.

Which meant Teacher had a very important reason for bringing him.

She wanted the Ukrainians to see an actual foreign assassin, one the Russians would later hear described in detail by their spies in the Ukrainian military.

He shook his head, admiring her technique. Teacher had used him as cover for Russians she'd involved in arranging the assassination. Most likely some of the General's underlings, anxious to get in on the profits he'd kept only for himself and his bosses.

Yes, sharing is good.

◇◇◇

"Have you told anyone else?" said Maggie.

"Only my mother and sister."

"Don't worry, I'll get the word out around here."

"I bet," mumbled Andreas from behind his desk.

"What was that?"

"I said, 'go ahead.'"

"I bet."

Andreas smiled. "It's exciting. A new baby on the way."

"I wish I'd had the experience," said Maggie, uncharacteristically wistful.

"You're always welcome to change diapers."

She nodded. "Which reminds me, Tassos told me to ask you how things were going with Tank."

"I won't bother to ask how one thought reminded you of the other."

She chuckled. "The mind works in mysterious ways."

"Like I said, I won't ask. Just tell him Tank's set up a press conference for this afternoon."

"About what?"

Andreas shrugged. "No idea."

"Maybe to announce his candidacy for Parliament?"

"That would go a long way toward making the rest of Parliament look good by comparison."

"Son of a bitch gets his sister murdered because of what he did, lets her killer walk away free, and makes himself into a martyr as her perpetual mourner."

"Modern family values at work," said Andreas.

Maggie waved her hand in the air as she walked out of his office.

Andreas stared at the photo of Lila and Tassaki on his desk. *I'll need a new photo. Will our baby be a girl or a boy?* he wondered. *As long as it's healthy.* He glanced at the door Maggie had just passed through. He'd realized why his little joke made Maggie think of Tassos: Tassos' only child had died in childbirth along with his wife. Tassos, like Maggie, had never had the opportunity of changing diapers.

Life wasn't fair. That wasn't news. Every cop knew that.

Andreas looked at the document on his computer screen, a press release announcing a "major announcement" by Tank later that afternoon.

What is it that makes some children good and some children bad? For sure the parents must play a part. But it's hard to imagine even the worst of parents as solely responsible for an asshole like Tank. Or the best of parents as wholly blameless.

◇◇◇

For as long as Spiros could remember, Sunday mornings meant church, first alongside his parents, later beside his wife. Like clockwork, they would find a place close to the front where Spiros would listen for the word of God. His loss of faith came gradually, much as a beach yielded ground to the sea. Ultimately, church meant nothing more to Spiros than the last remaining public pretext for his marriage.

Although his mind was on prayer, today wasn't Sunday, and in five minutes Tank's press conference would begin. Spiros walked from behind his desk to the leather armchair across from a big-screen television.

The days when he'd believed faith and prayer important seemed so very long ago, as if they'd simply vanished from his memory. He longed for the comfort of those times.

Spiros looked at his watch as he sat down. No time for such thoughts now. He'd lost all room to maneuver. The prime minister had given him forty-eight hours to "break the case wide-open." That was thirty hours ago. There was no "or else" at the end of the prime minister's curt call. It was understood without being said.

Spiros leaned his head back against the chair. He dreaded what was about to come. He shut his eyes and pressed the remote.

Then he prayed.

◇◇◇

A shimmering blue and green sea touching up against a robin's egg blue sky and a lightly fluttering Greek flag filled the TV screen. The final notes of the Greek National Anthem played in the background as a stern-faced Tank stepped into the frame, blue shirt, blue blazer, no tie.

"My fellow Greeks, good afternoon. It is a truly beautiful day. One befitting our glorious Greece. We have much to be thankful for, much to be proud of, and much to defend.

"I do not have to tell you that we are a country in crisis, put upon by nations who call us friend while they drain us dry. I do not have to tell you we struggle to find work, while illegal immigrants take our jobs for slave wages. I do not have to tell you our children see no future, while foreign investors buy our precious resources for their own children.

"Today, our politicians serve foreign masters. They do not share the concerns of our people. They are only interested in emptying our pockets to fill their own. Foreign bank accounts, expensive cars, lavish boats, and mansions on Mykonos—not keeping Greece alive and strong for Greeks—are the goals of Greece's political leadership.

"We are nothing to them but sheep forced to fend for ourselves. To be bought. To be sold. To be slaughtered."

Tank touched his eyes with the thumb and forefinger of his right hand, as if holding back tears.

"Almost a week has passed since I lost my sister." He swallowed. "We shall never spend another day together in our beloved Greece."

He pressed at his eyes again. "She died because the police did not care. She died because the minister of public order did not care. She died because the prime minister did not care.

"When big foreign money is in play, our government is indifferent over who gets hurt, as long as those that matter get their share. My sister stood up to all of that, and now she's dead. A bullet through her forehead from a foreign assassin. But it was our government that held the gun.

"Why is it the police have done nothing to catch her killer? They must know who is behind it? I do. It is no secret.

"Our country has no place for mafia types. That is neither our culture nor our history. We need a fair playing field for our honest businessmen and it is up to our government to provide one.

"I am calling on the prime minister in the name of my sister to destroy the vicious foreign criminal element behind her murder."

He reached inside his jacket pocket, pulled out several sheets of paper, and held them up to the camera. "Here are the names and addresses of those who terrorize us, some of whom, I'm sorry to say, are working in complicity with our countrymen."

He waved the list. "These are the ruthless gangsters responsible for the murder of my sister. Mr. Prime Minister, if you really care about making Greece a better place for the honest to do business, now is your chance to prove it. I'm giving you these names, unafraid of what retribution those named might seek against me for pulling them out from beneath their rocks."

He dropped his hand and stared straight into the camera. "And if you ignore this list, I promise you that every day I shall publicly ask you, 'Why?' And pray for the people of Greece to join me in holding you accountable."

Fade to black.

◇◇◇

"That was a nice crisp three minutes of television," said Kouros from the couch in Andreas' office.

"He looked quite sincere," said Maggie.

"Just goes to show you how gullible humans can be." Andreas looked at his watch. "Any bets?"

"Within five seconds," said Maggie.

Kouros said, "Fifteen—"

Andreas' desk phone rang. Andreas looked at the number. "Maggie wins." He hit the speakerphone button. "Hello, Spiros."

"I'm dead. The prime minister will kill me. I'm dead."

"Relax, you're not dead yet." Andreas grimaced at their unintended references to Spiros' mortality.

"I'm not sure he'll even give me the remaining eighteen hours on my deadline to solve the case."

"He said to 'break it wide open.' Not solve it," said Andreas.

"What's the difference?"

"Solving means nailing the killer. No one on that list will get us to the killer. I'd bet my pension on it."

"Why don't you bet something that's worthwhile, so that we know you're convinced?"

"Who said that?" asked Spiros.

"Detective Kouros."

"Oh."

Andreas and Kouros braced for a harangue about taking the situation seriously. None came.

"Then who's on the list?" said Spiros.

"I don't know. Not the real killer or anything likely to lead us to him, that's for sure. That would be suicide for Tank." Andreas paused for a moment, wondering if he should say more. He decided not to. "How long until you can get us the list?"

"I assume I'll get it the moment the prime minister does and you'll get it a minute later."

"Great. Tell him it's the break we've been waiting for."

"You just said it won't likely help."

"Not to solve the case, but as I said, it might be what we need to break things wide open."

"How's that?" asked Spiros.

"No need to get everyone's hopes up until I've seen the list."

"No one's hopes but the prime minister's?" said Spiros.

"Right," said Andreas. "I'm just trying to buy you some breathing room," said Andreas.

"I won't need much in a casket."

Andreas cringed. "Let's just pray we get lucky."

"I'm already doing that," said Spiros.

"Good. Let me go, I want to get things organized just in case the list is the break we're looking for."

"Enough with the drama already. Just save my ass."

Andreas hit mute on the speakerphone, "That sounds more like him." He hit mute again. "We'll do our best. Bye."

"Bye."

Andreas checked to make sure the phone was off. "I still can't believe it's him."

"A brush with mortality can change a man," said Maggie.

"So can unemployment," said Kouros. "Something we're all likely facing in eighteen hours. How are we going to break this case by tomorrow morning?"

"As I said, it all depends on the list."

"And like the minister said, enough with the drama. Just tell me what the hell you're thinking," said Kouros.

"In a minute. Maggie, get Petro in here right away, and scramble every precinct in Athens and Thessaloniki to have men ready for a major operation beginning in," Andreas looked at his watch, "eight hours. And alert the tax guys too."

"They're not going to listen to us," said Maggie.

"Tell them it's under a direct order from the prime minister."

"How can we say that?"

"Who's going to question you? Besides, the list is coming from the prime minister, so how can we not consider it his direct order that we go after everyone on it?"

Maggie nodded and headed toward the door. "Suicide takes many forms."

"Thanks for the sign of confidence."

"Any time." Maggie opened the door and left.

"But why are we alerting half the police in Greece over what could be a very short list?" asked Kouros.

"If the names on Tank's list are what I think, it's our chance to blow up his entire operation."

"And is there a name for this magic you plan on using to turn Tank's list into his demise?"

Andreas smiled. "Nuts and bolts, my boy. Just good, old, basic, boring, nuts and bolts police work."

Chapter Nineteen

Tank lay in bed switching between television channels covering his press conference. He was the central subject of conversation on all the network news shows; old faces, old ideas, old agendas all screaming at one another trying to make points with a public fed up at hearing them. But in this case the talking heads were all in agreement: Tank had scored a winning goal. He'd punched the sitting government in the eye by playing to the Greeks' natural propensity for seeing a conspiracy in the number of raisins in a cereal box, and for assuming their government was in cahoots with monied bad guys. Best of all, he'd successfully portrayed his own politically powerful and suspect family as part of Greece's victimized suffering masses.

All day he'd been receiving congratulatory calls from politicians of every party. Even members of the prime minister's own party called playing up to him. Hedging their bets, no doubt, with elections on the horizon. This was not a time for party loyalty, but for tending to your own ambitions. Politics stood as practically the only surefire way of making money in Greece these days, even for the honest. It was a matter of self-preservation.

Tank was in heaven. It was the greatest moment of his life. He was no longer his family's black sheep bad boy, but a cunning politician, as good as any of his cousins, or brother. Too bad his sister had to die, but her sacrifice made all this possible. He'd erect a statue to her. Yes, a grand statue.

He smiled as he listened to another commentator rave on about how "Tank's List," as the press had come to call it, would help "rid Greece of a great curse." It certainly would. It would finish off his Athens and Thessaloniki competitors in the counterfeit alcohol business. Every single one of them was on that list. Names and locations.

He laughed out loud at the brilliance of his ploy. At the image of the Greek police wiping out his biggest competition without touching a hair on his head. His demonstration of true Greek ingenuity at work would impress even Teacher. *The arrogant bitch*. Daring to speak to him as if he were a child. He wished he could be there to see her face when she learned of his masterstroke. He wouldn't be surprised if after this she asked him to participate in *all* her European operations. Of course, he'd only agree if she made him an equal partner.

His mobile rang. Probably another congratulatory call. He didn't recognize the number. He looked at the time. It was after two in the morning. He took the call.

"Whoever this is, why are you calling me at this hour?"

"Tank."

"Xenophon? I didn't recognize your number."

"It's not my phone. I left it in the warehouse when I went out the back window."

"What? What are you talking about?"

"The police are raiding everywhere. Not just our competitors, they're hitting *us* too. Knocking out our warehouses, production facilities, distributers, even our customers."

"Did you say '*us*'?"

"Yes, *US*."

"But how could they? I only gave them information on our competitors."

"I have no idea, but they're busting up everything, and by that I mean *our entire illegal operation*. Tax authorities are with them shutting down our retail outlets in Athens and Thessaloniki, padlocking clubs and discos, and putting customers out on the streets."

"That can't be happening." Tank's voice cracked.

"Look, I don't know what the fuck went wrong. But we're out of the counterfeit business and a hell of a lot of people tied into our operation see your little play on TV today as wiping them out. They think you've snapped, decided to become a hero good guy, and they want you dead."

"But I didn't turn them in. You know that."

"Yes, I know, but I'm not about to tell any of them that. At least not now. They're angry enough to kill anybody they think was in on this with you, and I'm not saying anything to anyone that might get them thinking that way about me. I'm calling you just to warn you to hide out until the smoke clears. There's talk among our own people about taking you out tonight, before you can do them any more harm. Whoever did this set you up magnificently. The cops had a list of every place tied into our operation. Someone really wanted to fuck you. Someone really—"

Tank shut off the phone. He didn't want to hear any more. He had to think. He had to think. He had to—

I have to get out of here.

◇◇◇

At precisely ten the next morning, all Greek television networks interrupted their regularly scheduled programing for an announcement from Minster of Public Order Spiros Renatis.

"Ladies and gentlemen, good morning. It is with enormous pride in the Greek people that I speak to you today. Yesterday you heard one of our countrymen speak of the tragic death of his sister, and call upon his government to bring those responsible for her death to justice.

"I am pleased to tell you that last night, in daring raids across much of mainland Greece, your government did just that."

Spiros cleared his throat. "But we could not have done it without her brother's help. The prime minister and all of us in your nation's police force share your desire to make our country a better and safer place, free of the criminal element corrupting our democracy. But as in so many situations, unless members of the community are willing to come forward and identify those who prey on them and their neighbors, we have no way of knowing whom to go after.

"Yes, I know many of you think police are all-knowing, but we are not. We need your cooperation in order to help *you*.

"All of Greece is by now familiar with what is called 'Tank's List.' Thanks to that list, last night we struck a mortal blow to a deadly, nationwide, counterfeit liquor business lying at the very heart of one of Greece's largest, clandestine, criminal enterprises.

"That list has done a great service for Greece, and shines as an example to our countrymen of what a single individual can do to better our country, our neighborhoods, ourselves. Police will do their job if you identify those robbing you, corrupting your politicians, and stealing your tax dollars out of your pocket. And you can do all of this anonymously. Simply send us your own Tank's List of names and addresses, and we'll take it from there.

"Your policemen and women could not have done what we did last night without Tank's List. Having said that, and at the risk of sounding ungrateful, I do have one other slight favor to ask of its author.

"We are amazed at your grasp of those engaged in Greece's illegal alcohol trade. With your help we've closed much of it down in Athens and Thessaloniki. But as I'm certain you know, during tourist season there is significant counterfeit alcohol activity taking place in the islands and elsewhere. Your country would greatly appreciate your providing us with a similar list of persons and places engaged in those criminal acts in those places. I assure you we'll act on that information the moment we receive it.

"We look forward to your helping us again, and once more, thank you—" Spiros coughed as he pronounced Tank's name. He left the podium, taking no questions.

Andreas jumped out of bed fully dressed, and pumped his fist in the air in front of the television. "Fantastic, beautiful, perfect."

"How come you never say those things after we make love?" said Lila from the bed.

"Because you always leave me speechless." He thrust his fist in the air again. "Spiros left Tank drawn and quartered. The bastard has no place to run."

"Except home to daddy."

"Not sure that will help him with all the people pissed at him after this."

"The rich always find a way to take care of themselves."

"But at a price."

"Yes. For sure." Lila patted the bed. "Why don't you come back to bed? You've been out all night."

"It's been a night of sheer joy." He glanced at Lila. "I mean professional joy."

Lila smiled, "I knew what you meant. Were you in the office all night?"

"Yes. Yianni, Petro, and I stayed on the phones making sure the local cops did what we'd told them to do, even if it meant crossing serious bad guys who'd been paying them for protection."

"How'd you manage that?"

"By scaring the shit out of them and their bosses if they didn't do what we said."

"And it worked?"

"A couple wiseass chiefs told us to 'fuck off,' so we had to get Spiros to tell them they'd best not report to work in the morning if they didn't do what they were told that night."

"Spiros was in your office?"

Andreas gestured no. "Up all night at his home. He seemed even more excited than we were. He'd met his forty-eight-hour deadline. We'd saved his ass."

Lila frowned. "But he didn't mention you once in his announcement. I didn't like that."

"He did exactly as I'd asked. I didn't want my name near this story. We had to make it look like it was all Tank's doing in bringing down his competitors and his own operation." He smiled. "No brilliant police work involved this time." There was another reason for keeping his name out of the story, but not

one he wanted to share with his pregnant wife. He didn't want
his name appearing on Teacher's radar screen.

"Still, it was you who guessed Tank would only put his
competitors on his list, and came up with the idea of adding
on Tank's places and people from what Yianni and Petro had
compiled on his operation."

"Yes, but it was the obvious play for someone like Tank to try.
He thinks of himself as smarter than everyone else in the world."

"But not smarter than my husband."

Andreas offered a modest shrug. "It also served as an object
lesson to Yianni and Petro that boring, basic police work sometimes pays off in unexpected ways."

"From the way Spiros choked simply saying Tank's name,
you must have had a hard time convincing him to give Tank so
much credit."

"Not 'so much,' but *all* the credit. Yes, he hated the idea, but
he came around to seeing it as the only way of ruining Tank
with his bad guy business associates. Then Spiros thought up
the idea of turning the whole episode into a how-to commercial
on helping your local police to help you, and he was off and
running on working up his speech."

"Who thought to have Spiros ask Tank to turn over a list of
bad guys operating in other places, like the islands?"

Andreas smiled. "You liked that idea, huh? It was mine. I
figured if you wanted to turn Greeks against Tank, just get them
to thinking he's going to shut down their summertime cheap
booze fun at their favorite vacation spots. Greeks who think their
hangouts might be selling untaxed booze and *bomba* aren't going
to take kindly to anyone trying to close them down."

"Ah, yes, the modern Greek's motto: 'I hate corruption except
when it benefits me.'"

"Cynic." Andreas stood by the edge of the bed.

"What do you think Tank will do now?"

"If he's smart, disappear. This morning, a lot of very dangerous
people are very angry with him, and with Spiros pitching him
for a list of more names and locations, quite a few of them will

do just about anything to make sure he doesn't get the chance to turn in that list."

"You mean like have him killed?"

Andreas nodded.

Lila sighed. She patted the spot next to her. "Come, lie down."

"I have to get back to the office. I just came home to shower and change."

"And of course to say hello to your loyal wife who was up all night worrying about you."

Andreas paused. "Yes, of course."

She patted the bed again. "Then come. Say hello."

Chapter Twenty

"How the hell did I ever end up like this?" Tank mumbled to himself.

"Silence," admonished a wiry, gray-haired monk.

Tank nodded and went back to sitting quietly among the row of chanting monks. His coarse, brown monk's cassock scratched at skin accustomed to Egyptian cotton shirts; the rough leather straps of his sandals irritated feet used to handmade Italian loafers. But what other choice was there? Too many persons outside these walls wanted him dead. This was the safest place for him.

At least that's what his father told him. He was the only one who knew Tank was here and neither man trusted telling anyone else. Tank's first choice was to flee Thessaloniki sixty miles southeast to Mount Athos and find sanctuary among one of that Aegean peninsula's twenty monasteries, but his father said no. Too many others had sought refuge in that place. A sophisticated hunter would think to look for him there, and for a price he might be betrayed. That was not unknown, even among the faithful.

He'd been here for only a couple of days, but it seemed like an eternity. No contact with the outside world except through his father, and he expected none until his father sent word for him to return. Tank's father said he'd work things out with everyone involved in this "business dispute." His father knew how to make big problems disappear for important people, and said Tank's situation would be "child's play" for him, resolved in a matter of months at most.

Months…I might have to sit here for months. His mind wandered back to the political phenomenon he'd become. No one wanted him to succeed. Not even his father. He thought that's why his father had told him to stay in hiding until the matter stood forgotten by the press. He wanted all the attention back on Tank's brother, the heir apparent to his father's influence. *Damn them. I have nothing to fear from anyone. When I leave here I'll crush them all.*

He lowered his head and closed his eyes.

The old monk nodded at what looked to be the newest monk finding solace in prayer.

I should have told my father about Teacher.

◇◇◇

"So what's happening?" said Tassos strolling into Andreas' office without knocking.

"You mean aside from my forgetting to bolt my door shut from the inside?"

Tassos plopped himself down on the couch. "I know you've missed me, admit it."

"You've been away? Oh yes, my secretary's been unusually happy these past few days."

"No, I haven't been at Maggie's, I've been home on Syros."

"That's what I meant. She's been happy." Andreas smiled.

Tassos shot him the open palm.

"So, are you still all at peace with becoming a daddy again?"

"Sure am. Just waiting for the January estimated time of arrival."

Tassos nodded. "Wonderful."

Andreas leaned back in his chair. "Things have been very quiet since the raids. Make that eerily quiet. No sign at all of Tank, Teacher, or the killer. All that serenity has my cop instincts anxiously waiting for something to explode. That wouldn't, by chance, be what brings you here today?"

Tassos looked away as he gestured no. "Just wanted to say hello."

"Yeah, right. Okay, 'Hello.'"

"You could say it with a bit more sincerity."

"Tassos—"

Tassos raised his hands, "Okay, okay." He put his hands down. "It's about Spiros."

"Our boss Spiros?"

Tassos nodded. "Maggie told me you think he's ill."

Andreas nodded.

"Well, I hate to tell you this, but on top of everything else I think he's got some serious people gunning for him."

"You mean of the shooting kind?" said Andreas.

"No, the political asshole kind."

"He's used to that sort."

"But this is different. Someone is trying to spin your raids closing down Tank's business into a calculated plan by Spiros for financing his retirement."

"Huh?"

"Someone somehow knows Spiros is ill and is selling that to the press, along with the implication he's about to retire, as Spiros' motive for taking money from Tank's competitors in exchange for shutting him down."

"That will never fly. We went after his competitors too."

Tassos shook his head from side to side. "Not all of them. You only went after those Tank listed. There are others, like the ones Spiros asked Tank to name in his speech announcing the raids. Setting up a good guy like Spiros to look worse than the bad guys he's chasing is an old tradition here."

"Not just in Greece." Andreas picked up a pencil and began drumming the eraser end on his desk. "What has you thinking Spiros is a target?"

"A newspaper publisher on Syros called me all friendly-like to join him for coffee." Tassos shook his head. "I never trust those guys. They're always in the hunt."

Tassos crossed his legs. "Anyway, one sip into the coffee he started bombarding me with personal questions about Spiros, his wife, his health, their finances. When I said 'Whoa, what's this all about?' he told me it was confidential and he couldn't tell me."

Andreas smiled. "I can imagine how you reacted to that."

"I told him that what he's working on might be 'confidential,' but for damn sure the time I caught him with his pants down and an underage *Roma* behind the town hall wouldn't be for long."

Andreas shook his head. "You always know just the right thing to say."

"It comes with age. Anyway he told me every newspaper in Greece is in the hunt on this story. Someone is working very hard to get the heat off Tank and onto Spiros."

Andreas rolled his eyes. "Wonder who that could be?"

"Yep, Tank's pappy. He's not even trying to hide he's behind it. He knows all the newspapers want to remain on his good side."

"And he pays well," said Andreas.

"That too."

"I guess I better tell Spiros to be prepared."

"That's why I'm telling you. He'll probably panic. Might try to push the blame onto you. Claim that you're the one who came up with the list of Tank's places and the idea of setting him up."

Andreas nodded. "The old Spiros would have in a minute, but the new model I'm not so sure about. Besides, it's all true. We did set up his bastard son. Though not in exchange for a payoff."

"Once the press learns you set him up, they'll jump to whatever conclusion serves their story. They'll substitute 'good old common sense' for facts, saying it's obvious no one can show cash actually changing hands between 'Chief Inspector Kaldis and X, Y, and Z' but—wink-wink—we all know what happened."

Andreas shook his head. "I guess I'm fated to hear that sort of thing for the rest of my career."

Tassos gestured no. "Nah, sooner or later they'll get around to A, B, and C."

"Thanks for the encouragement."

Tassos nodded. "You're welcome. I've put out word that I want to know the moment anyone hears any chatter about somebody trying to set up a big-time government official."

"Good luck on hearing anything back on that."

"What else is there we can do?" said Tassos.

"Not much. As long as Tank's father is pushing, we're going to feel the pressure. And if word ever gets out that we're who added Tank's operations to the list he'd prepared of his competitors…" Andreas waved his right hand in the air. "The fact the places we added were all part of his son's illegal business operations will get lost in the noise of 'police set up' and a mass of lawyers claiming all of Tank's businesses are legitimate and that Tank had no knowledge of any illegal activity involving any of them. That will play especially well since Spiros never mentioned anything about any of that when he practically called Tank a hero in announcing the raids."

"And our suggesting he had a hand in his sister's murder…"

Andreas again waved his hand in the air.

"Yeah, that will just make us look desperate," said Tassos. "It's Tank's and his buddies' word against Yianni, who wasn't even there when it happened."

"It will be a hell of a media shit storm when it hits."

"At least you didn't commit a crime," said Tassos.

"No, but we committed a horrible political mistake likely to embarrass the prime minister. Tank's father now has an angle for claiming that the prime minister's handpicked minister of public order and the police were paid off to add Tank's *legitimate* businesses to the places raided." Andreas put the pencil down on his desktop. "But, we're not there yet. A lot of things can happen between now and Armageddon."

"Like what?"

"I'll tell you as soon as I know." Andreas pressed his intercom button. "Maggie, the delightful gentleman in here has kindly delivered me a terrific headache. Could you please bring me two ibuprofen, wait five minutes, and call Spiros?"

"Do you expect the headache to be gone in five minutes?" said Maggie.

"No, but with any luck its delivery boy will be."

Andreas ducked as one of the couch pillows whizzed past his head.

◇◇◇

Andreas let the phone go into voicemail. "Spiros, call me when you have the chance. Sorry to bother you on your mobile, but I tried you at the office and your secretary said you're not in."

No reason to say any more on a recording. Spiros would know it was important.

Maggie's voice came through Andreas' speakerphone. "Chief."

"Yes?"

"It's Spiros."

"Thanks."

Andreas picked up. "Spiros, I—"

"They're everywhere, like flies. I can't get rid of them. I have to hide. I can't go out, I can't answer the phone, I can't—"

"*Spiros*," Andreas shouted. "Get ahold of yourself. What are you talking about?"

"The press. They're everywhere. They're asking questions like I'm some sort of secret mafia chieftain who robbed the bank of Greece. No respect for me or the office, they just keep goading me with accusations."

Guess it's a bit late for the warning, thought Andreas. "It's Tank's father, he's stoking the press with stories that you were paid off by Tank's competitors to stage the raids. I was calling you to tell you to be ready for it."

"That's preposterous. We went after his competitors. Besides, what motive would I have for becoming corrupt at this point in my career?"

Andreas paused. "They're saying you did it to finance your retirement."

"Retirement? I'm not retiring. Why would I retire?"

Andreas drew in a deep breath and let it out as he said, "Because they know you're ill."

Silence.

"Spiros?"

"They know?"

"Yes."

"You know too?"

"Yes."

"How do these things get out?"

"It's hard to keep that sort of thing secret from people who know you. From people who care about you."

Spiros' voice cracked. "There's just so much pressure a person can take. And now…to have to defend myself from claims that my illness is what made me corrupt as I try to beat it…."

Andreas swallowed hard. "I think you should ignore them. Issue a statement that there will be nothing coming from your office on what is a continuing investigation into an elaborate criminal network threatening Greece, because to do so would compromise the case."

"That won't stop them."

Andreas swallowed hard a second time. "Just keep telling them that the person in charge of the investigation, and the only one authorized to speak on the subject, is me."

"That sounds like I'm trying to pass blame off onto you."

"I know, but don't worry about it. I can handle it."

Andreas heard what sounded like a suppressed sniffle.

"You're being very kind to me. Far more so than I deserve."

"Don't bother going there, Spiros. It's not necessary. Water under the bridge and all that. I have only one question. It's a tough one to ask, a harder one to answer, but I need to know."

"I didn't take any money from anyone. Ever."

"That's not my question." Andreas paused. "How sick are you?"

Spiros cleared his throat. "It's pretty serious. But the doctors caught it early enough to give me a fighting chance."

"Why are you even working?"

"Because I can. I prefer it to staying home. It's best for my wife too."

"I just wanted to know where things stood with your health. And frankly it sounds good. A fighting chance is all you Spartan types need."

"I'm from Tripoli."

"Close enough." Andreas laughed.

Spiros did too. "You do realize you're jumping into the middle of a shit storm without a parachute?"

"So, what else is new? You've kicked me out of that plane many times before. At least this time I get to jump by choice."

Spiros laughed again. "I can't ever repay you for what you're doing."

"No need to. Just get better, that's all the repayment I want. Make that all that Lila and I want."

Another sniffle. "Thanks, Andreas. And please thank Lila, too. Good luck."

"You too, my friend."

"Bye."

Andreas held the phone for a moment before putting it down. He'd voluntarily put his neck into the guillotine in place of another's, and not just anyone's, that of someone who'd betrayed him many times before. He closed his eyes. *How am I ever going to explain to Lila what I've just done?*

His eyes popped open and he smiled. The answer was obvious. He'd quote from the closing lines of her favorite English novel, "It is a far, far better thing that I do, than I have ever done."

The smile began to fade as Andreas realized that the speaker of those words from *A Tale of Two Cities* lost his head in the end.

Chapter Twenty-one

Thirty miles southeast of Thessaloniki the once undiscovered region of Chalkidiki reached out its bony, three-fingered hand into the northern Aegean, each digit separated from the next by a gulf or *kolpos*. The peninsula of Kassandra, at the far west, sat separated from the middle peninsula of Sithonia by the Toroneos Gulf, which in turn looked east across the Singitikos Gulf to the easternmost finger, the independent monastic state of Mount Athos forbidden to all but adult male visitors with permission.

Kassandra and Sithonia peninsulas served as summertime holiday retreats for many. Kassandra was the more developed, in part because it lay closer, by road, to Thessaloniki, but also because it had experienced massive forest fires that had paved the way for once forbidden development. Local populations swelled ten-fold or more during the season, and elaborate resorts, golf courses, a casino, and marinas set amid the island-like feel of Chalkidiki continued to attract monied foreign and domestic investors intent on building vacation homes along its picturesque shoreline.

Many who came were Russians, some claiming to share their leader Vladimir Putin's deep religious commitment to Eastern Orthodoxy's Mount Athos and its Russian Monastery. More and more Russians chose to build here, seemingly oblivious to the irony of erecting hedonistic palatial residences in homage to a Holy Mountain sacred for its fifteen-hundred-year-old customs, vows of poverty, and prayer.

Some of the more expensive homes in northern Greece could be found along Chalkidiki's shores, including the summer residence of Tank's father. He'd built a compound on Sithonia away from its succession of fisherman's hamlets, harbors, and tourist-attracting beaches, on the green northeastern edge of Dragoudeliou-Karra wildlife refuge, a mountainous swath of land cutting though the middle of Sithonia from its north-to-south coastlines. Protected by the European Environment Agency, the refuge comprised more than one quarter of that middle peninsula's two-hundred-square-mile area.

The compound offered him absolute seclusion. Only the invited could enter his property. It suited those times when security mattered. Like now.

The war he'd mounted against the minister of public order to save his son did not concern him. He could handle the politicians, and he saw himself on schedule to destroy that silly minister in a matter of days. Only an idiot would refuse to talk to the press, delegating that duty to an underling.

What worried him was what he *didn't* know. He was not a fool. He knew his son had not told him everything. Tank didn't want him to know he'd expanded his legitimate booze business into the counterfeit trade. He'd have preferred that his son made money in less risky ways, but he'd long ago accepted Tank's lifelong attraction to the criminal side of life. After all, who was the father to judge the son? But for the corrupt, the father would still be a pauper.

No, what troubled him was the possibility that his son had crossed people who did not share the father's belief that any dispute could be resolved through the exchange of money. Those types were dangerous and required special handling. That's why he came here today. To meet with someone who could tell him what unknown dangers his son faced. His ex-KGB neighbor had arranged the meeting. "Ex" to the extent one ever could be from that sort of past.

He looked at his watch. His driver had picked up the man at

Thessaloniki airport an hour and forty-five minutes ago. They should be here any minute, depending on traffic.

He picked up a walkie-talkie from his desk and pressed TALK. "Hello."

"Yes, sir."

"Any word?"

"The driver just called to say they're five minutes away."

"Good. When my guest arrives I want you to treat him with the utmost respect."

"Of course, sir."

"But I also want you to search him thoroughly. Make sure he is not armed."

"Yes, sir."

"And I mean *make sure.*"

"Understood, sir."

"Good. Then show him down to the pool. We'll be meeting there."

He hung up without saying more.

He fidgeted with his tie. *One can't be too careful these days.*

◇◇◇

"Mr. Vladimir, a pleasure to meet you, sir." Tank's father stood to extend his hand across the table. "I understand you speak Greek."

He took the father's hand and shook it. "Yes." He stood about a head taller than the father and looked about a third his age.

"Where did you learn to speak our language?"

"You mean your boys couldn't figure that out from our little pat and probe dance party?"

"Sorry about that, but I'm sure you understood the reason."

He shrugged. "In Greece, to an invited guest? Not really."

The father looked at his three steroid-sculpted bodyguards standing behind his guest. "I told you to treat him with respect."

The guest sat down in the chair across from the father. "They did. One even promised to send me chocolates. But that little scenario revealed a lot more to me about you than it could possibly tell you about me."

"I wouldn't say that. I now know your name and where you live." The father sat down.

"No, you know the name and address of a dead Russian general. But I know you're seriously afraid of something. Scared enough to reach out to strangers for information, and then be frightened of the messenger." He leaned across the table. "Now why don't you tell me why I'm here?"

The father smiled. "For someone who claims to know so much about me, you mean you don't know?"

"Of course I know. I just want to know if you know."

The father's face tightened. "I'm not one to play games with."

"Nor am I." Vladimir gave him a thin smile. "So why don't we skip the part about how your son is a misunderstood little boy who only gets into trouble because he's trying to please daddy, and get to the part you really want to know about?"

"Which is?"

"Who's going to kill your son?"

"You know?"

"Of course I know. Why do you think your friend contacted my boss? My boss knows everything."

The father's lips grew taut. "You're not the boss?"

Vladimir nodded.

"Then I should be dealing with your boss."

"If my boss gets directly involved, I'd say things are close to terminal for you."

"Are you threatening me?" The father glanced at his body-guards.

"Of course not. I was just telling you why you don't want to meet my boss."

"All right, enough of this bullshit. Who wants to kill my son and why?"

"Well, to answer your second question first, your son Tank entered into a business arrangement with my boss—"

"You mean you're with the people after my son?"

"You told your neighbor you wanted to know what's happening, so he went straight to the source. These KGB types are very efficient. But that's beside the point. Anyway, your son didn't listen to my boss when my boss told him how to run their mutual business. Even tried to steal from my boss. My boss gave him a second chance and he blew that one too. Now my boss is out a lot of money and your son has set a very bad example for my boss' other business associates."

"And for that your boss is going to kill my son?"

"No, not my boss."

"Then who?"

"The same person who killed your daughter."

The father leaned forward. "Are you fucking serious? You say that and think you're going to leave here alive?"

His guest shrugged. "Ask one of your boys to take my wallet out of my back pocket. I want to show you some photos."

The snarl stayed on the father's face, but he nodded at one of the men to do as the guest had asked.

The guard took out the wallet.

"Here, give it to me, not him," said the father.

"Good choice."

The father rifled through the wallet until he found the photos. His mouth dropped and his eyes widened.

"Yes, it's always more effective when the one deciding on who shall live and who shall die realizes the consequences of his decision."

"These are my grandchildren!"

"Taken yesterday. If I don't make a certain phone call in the next ten minutes they all die. And if within an hour after that call, I don't make it to a place that I'll be directing your driver to take me, they all die."

The father slouched back in his chair. "What do you want from me?"

"Your son has to die. An example must be made."

"I'll never tell you where Tank is. Never."

He shrugged again. "That's okay, we'll kill your other son. The choice is up to you."

"What kind of people are you, to kill the innocent?"

"Frankly, I think we're pretty much the same as Tank."

"He's not a killer of innocents."

"Really? He did let your daughter's killer walk away free. That's what gave him his second chance. I'd say that makes him at least complicit in her death."

"I don't believe you."

"I don't care whether you do or not. But if you really want to know, ask the people who were with him when it happened. But press them to tell you the truth, not the lies Tank had them tell the cops and press." The man leaned back and stretched. "I have a phone call to make, so make up your mind which son gets it. Or would you prefer both sons plus the grandchildren?"

The father ran his fingers through his thin, long, gray hair. "I'm sure we can work something out. All we need is time."

"I don't have time, just orders."

"Well, goddamn it, *get* time!" He raised his hands as would a supplicant. "Sorry, sorry, I didn't mean to yell. All I meant was I think we should find some time to see what sort of money your boss wants to drop everything."

"Everything?"

"Yes, everything," said the father.

He shook his head. "That's going to be costly."

"*Just call!*" He raised his hands as if apologizing again for shouting.

"Okay. But I'll need a bit of privacy. You don't mind if I walk over to the pool do you?"

The father looked at his bodyguards. "Did you check the phone?"

"Yes, it's clean."

He stood up and walked toward a pool that seemed to run off into the sea, calling back over his shoulder, "You're so distrusting."

The father and his men watched him pace back and forth on the far side of the pool, as if walking on water in animated, inaudible conversation. After five minutes he shut the phone, came back, and sat across from the father.

"You're in luck. My boss will take cash instead of your son's life."

"How much?"

"Fifty million euros."

"That's preposterous, ridiculous, out of the question."

"Yes, I know. Imagine how tough it is working for someone like that. But that's the terms, take it or leave it."

"How do I know you're who you say you are? This could all be a hustle. A set-up."

"Yes, it could. KGB guys are like that. But ask Tank, and I'm sure he'll convince you it's all true." He handed the father a card containing a Greek cell phone number. "Call me by tomorrow or else we'll assume you said no."

"It's far too much money."

"Then I suggest you spend the next twenty-four hours raising the cash. Or tell Tank to immerse himself in *prayer* that another of his siblings gets to die in his place."

The father's right eye twitched at the reference to prayer.

The man nodded knowingly. "Like I said, my boss knows everything. And be sure to tell Tank that my boss sends her regards." He stood. "It's been a pleasant chat, but I really must run." He extended his hand across the table toward the father. "I hear Delphi is lovely this time of year. And Tank's such a party guy. He must be going out of his mind cooped up in Monastery Hosios Loukas."

The father stared at Kharon's hand. He did not take it.

◇◇◇

Eleven centuries ago, twenty miles east of Delphi, a holy and pious hermit (*osios* in Greek) found his way into a valley of awe-inspiring natural beauty. In that pastoral haunt of antiquity's Muses, Hosios Loukas began construction of the only church built on mainland Greece in the tenth century, the Church of Panaghia (the Virgin Mary). That church still stood today within the walls of Greece's largest extant monastery of Byzantium's second golden age, and adjacent to Greece's oldest existing dome octagon church, the Katholikon (big church) of Hosios Loukas.

In keeping with the teachings of Greece's ancient temple builders, the monastery sat in harmony with its natural surroundings. Terra cotta roof tiles, above classical Byzantine cloisonné-style masonry walls of marble, brick, and limestone, enclosed frescos and mosaic masterpieces set upon backgrounds of gold. But only a fraction of the monastery's legendary lavish decoration remained, the balance of the place's precious gold and silver plate, murals, icons, and furnishings lost to time and plunderers.

Though remembered for his gift of prophecy, Hosios Loukas also possessed great skill at cultivating relationships with the generals in control of nearby Thebes. He relied upon their generosity and that of powerful others of his time—much as did subsequent shepherds of his vision with their respective secular powers that be—to create and maintain an isolated sanctuary of tranquility that remained today, a thousand years later, as one of the Mediterranean's most impressive monuments and a World Heritage Site.

And the perfect hideaway for a scion of one of the monastery's wealthiest, most powerful benefactors.

◇◇◇

Tank's father's driver made it in thirty minutes to a highway intersection that normally took forty-five, dropped Kharon off at a bus stop, and sped away in the direction from which he'd come.

Kharon started walking the two hundred yards to where he'd hidden a stolen motorcycle. He'd left it there very early that morning before catching a bus to the airport in time to be met there by that same driver.

He had to admit he was in awe of Teacher's intelligence network. The father's neighbor who'd started asking questions about Tank's business partners found that his inquiries had quickly gotten back to Teacher, and once he knew of Teacher's interest the neighbor told her whatever she wanted to know and agreed to do precisely as she instructed him. Those old-time KGBers certainly knew how to survive.

Kharon shook his head. Crazy how otherwise intelligent people thought they could trust total strangers to do dangerous things for them. Spouses trying to find someone to kill their mates were just the tip of the iceberg on that score. The lucky ones ended up being stung by an undercover cop, the others milked by blackmailers for life.

Teacher had pegged the old man right. She knew he'd offer money in exchange for his son's life. It was just a matter of setting him up for it. She'd left those details to Kharon. He liked that sort of improvisational freedom.

He knew his gambit about having to make two phone calls within an hour of each other wouldn't work without the photographs. That's why he'd spent the day before taking candid shots of the grandchildren. Preparation always paid off.

Kharon pondered whether he actually could have killed those children. He'd never killed a child. Then again, the choice would not have been his, as he'd only threatened their death should Tank's father kill him first. To Kharon, that order of events made serious soul-searching on the subject a meaningless waste of time.

Besides, it was all a bluff. Kharon had been out there on a tightrope, performing without a net, the entire scenario made up, including the telephone call to his "boss." He'd dialed the number for the weather and recited song lyrics until he sensed he'd softened Tank's father up enough to hit him with Teacher's demand: an amount she'd told him the day before.

He found the bike right where he'd left it. It would be a long ride home in traffic. He'd be lucky to make it in six hours; depending on how much time it took to get to where he'd left the BMW. He couldn't wait to ditch this piece of crap. He should have known better than to steal a rental motorbike. Then again, he had no reason to rush home to Delphi. Or to Hosios Loukas.

What a stroke of luck for Tank to end up in a monastery Kharon knew so well and so close to his home.

Once again, he had to credit Teacher and her connections for finding Tank. She'd guessed he'd hidden out on a church property.

"Greeks always flee to churches. It's tradition," she'd told him.

It took a little more than a day of working her banking connections to come up with a list of religious institutions enjoying Tank's family's generosity. But after hearing Hosios Loukas Monastery had made the list, it took Kharon only two bottles of wine and a fine dinner with a talkative fellow who worked maintenance at the monastery to learn that the newest member of the community was a "celebrity" from Thessaloniki.

Kharon started the bike and eased out onto the road. The early afternoon was hot, but the wind would keep him cool.

Kharon wondered if, for his part, Tank's father would keep things cool…or heat them up. The next play was up to him.

◇◇◇

"Are you calling with more good news?" asked Teacher.

"I'm beginning to worry I might be spoiling you."

"To the contrary. You're building up a rather large credit balance for the day you inevitably fail."

"Here's hoping that day never comes."

"Why? Failure is reality. We all do at some point. It forms us, makes us stronger."

"Considering what I do for you, failure is likely to mean I am no more."

"Hmm. Perhaps you're right."

"I'd have preferred if you'd disagreed with me on that point."

Teacher laughed. "Touché."

"Tank's father just called me."

"That was quick. It's not even dinner time."

"He said he's trying to see what sort of package he can put together, but because he knew whatever number we agreed upon would be 'a very large one'—those were his words—he couldn't possibly get back to me by tomorrow. He said he needed a week and since his son had just told him you were involved, he didn't want to raise a question with you over his '*bona fides*' waiting until tomorrow to make that request."

"Anything else?"

"Yes, he apologized for speaking to me as he did. Said he'd never have done that had he known I was your emissary."

"What did you say?"

"Thank you, but that your number was non-negotiable. He said he understood that, but all he could do was promise to give us what he could raise and if that wasn't enough there wasn't a thing in the world he could do about it."

"Did you mention the three hundred million his family made in ripping off the Greek government of its tax dollars in that electricity bill scam?"

"Yes. He said the actual amount was far less and he only got to keep a small part of even that."

"Interesting that he didn't deny his involvement. The father knows how to negotiate. I respect that. Even if not a word of what else he said is true. I should have been in business with him rather than the son."

"What should I tell him?"

"What he expects. Give him two days and tell him if we don't have an answer with an acceptable number *and* the money in hand by then, he'd best start making funeral arrangements."

"And just what is that number?"

"I'll let you decide. Just make sure it's big enough to be painful, but not so much that he decides to sacrifice his son."

"If Tank were my kid, fifty euros would be too much."

Teacher chuckled. "You're not a parent."

"Okay, I'll figure something out."

"Just be careful and don't take chances. After all, by now the father knows you're the one who killed his daughter."

"No doubt about it. My picture must have been taken a thousand times with all the surveillance cameras around his house. Anyone in the *cafenion* that day with Tank could identify me. But that cuts two ways…it lets him know I'm serious."

"True, but like I said, Kharon, be careful. Just because you live in Delphi doesn't mean you can always rely upon your Fates to protect you."

"Thanks, I'll keep that in mind."

They exchanged good-byes and Teacher hung up the phone. *This one has great promise.* He was a bit of good news in her life. Now if only her health remained stable.

She picked up a file on her desk bearing Tank's father's name across the front and opened it to a financial summary prepared by her banking sources. She studied it for a moment and looked up at the photograph on her desk.

"The man asked for a week to raise less than fifty million when he has four times that amount sitting in Swiss and Luxembourg banks, every cent capable of being wired to me instantly. Is he just negotiating for a better price or does he have something else in mind?"

Teacher put down the file. She had wondered whether to tell Kharon about it when he called, and decided not. She'd reconsidered for a moment, but again decided no. It would be a good learning experience for him.

Chapter Twenty-two

Maggie and Kouros came bursting into Andreas' office.

"What the hell's with you two? Is there a fire?"

"We identified the shooter," said Maggie.

"Kharon?"

"Yes, but only because of her." Kouros bowed to Maggie. "If Maggie had made copies of the drawing of the killer instead of my doing it myself, we'd have known who he was the day of the murder."

Andreas looked at Maggie. "I'll take that to mean I should have shown you the photographs Rolex emailed me."

Maggie shrugged. "What can I say? I can't expect you two hotshots to show me every piece of paper that passes through this office." She smiled. "But it wasn't all that hard to figure out who he was."

"Yeah, sure," said Kouros. "I spent a day plowing through mug shots, and days more showing cops the drawing and photos without getting so much as a guess at an ID. Maggie gets just a glimpse of the drawing on my desk and—*bingo*—she nails him."

Maggie fake punched Kouros in the shoulder. "And don't forget the part about the drawing being upside down when I first saw it."

"When the two of you are done with the love-in part of your routine, would one of you mind telling me who our mystery killer is?"

"The kid who killed two boys in that orphanage about a dozen years back," said Maggie.

Andreas' face held a blank stare.

"I can understand Yianni not recalling, he was a kid, but you must remember. It was in every magazine, every newspaper, on every television channel. The twelve-year-old who escaped conviction and a record because of his age."

Andreas began to nod. "Yes, it's coming back. The papers vilified him. But how could you recognize him from the drawing? He was only a boy then."

"From the eyes. I'd looked at them a thousand times, wondering how a child could kill so brutally."

"He wasn't exactly a child," said Kouros.

"Yes, he was," snapped Maggie. "And what I saw in those eyes then, I saw in *his* eyes in the drawing."

"And what did you see?" said Andreas.

"Something not from this earth." Maggie crossed herself.

"From heaven or hell?" said Andreas.

"Not sure."

"But you're sure it's him?"

"Positive," said Kouros. "We ran his name through our national database and came up with a military service record and photo. It's definitely him."

"Any arrest record?"

"Clean as a whistle."

"What about his military history?"

"Two years, no trouble, made it through advanced special forces training, but left after two years."

"Do you have an address for him?"

Kouros smiled. "It's Jacobi's place in Exarchia."

"I guess we have our man. What's his name?"

"Fred Raucous."

"What kind of Greek name is that?"

Maggie laughed. "Your education obviously did not include the source of all knowledge in Greece. The tabloids. Everything about him came out in those rags after the murders. He'd arrived at the orphanage an anonymous newborn. No father, no mother, no name. The nurse in charge of naming new admissions once lived in America and, being a big fan of the American dancer

Fred Astaire, called him Fred. She told reporters that when she jokingly asked the baby 'What should I name you that goes with Fred?' he let out such a bloodcurdling scream she took it as a sign to use the Greek sounding English word meaning 'a disturbing harsh or loud noise.' *Voila*, Fred Raucous."

"I don't know about his dancing, but he's sure lived up to the bloodcurdling part," said Andreas.

Maggie rolled her eyes.

"So, now what do we do?" said Kouros.

"It doesn't really change anything. We still have no solid evidence of his guilt, whether we call him Kharon or Fred." Andreas shook his head. "But dropping his real name as the sister's possible killer into the already massive media shit storm raging out there raises mind-blowing ramifications I can't even begin to comprehend at this moment."

Andreas stood up and walked around his desk. "So, I think I'll just sleep on it. And to do that I must first go home. Which is precisely what the two of you should do. You both did great work. Take the rest of the day off."

"It's almost eight," said Maggie.

"At night," added Kouros.

"Well, it's the thought that counts. See you tomorrow."

Andreas ignored the diverse collection of hand gestures that followed him out the door.

◇◇◇

The National Gardens served as a source of great pride to Athenians and, in summer, a respite from the intense heat. Cool evenings drew locals out in hordes, and for those who could afford it, dinner in the Garden's chicest restaurant close by the nineteenth-century neoclassical Zappeion Megaron, a sunshine-yellow and white masterpiece, constructed as part of a plan for reviving the modern Olympic Games.

Lila and Andreas lived only a few hundred yards away, just across the street from the Gardens, and like many of the restaurant's regular customers, chose to sit outside. Their table offered a spectacular view of the Zappeion's Corinthian portico, but much like museum guards surrounded by familiar treasures, most regulars would only have taken full notice of the sight if it vanished.

"It's a beautiful night to be eating at the Aigle," said Lila, adjusting the light blanket over her son in his stroller.

"It was a great idea you had to come here." Andreas looked at his son's sleeping face. "And to bring Tassaki with us."

"Why not? It's the Greek way. Bring your kids along to sleep while you party. Besides, I'd promised Marietta the night off."

"Were the Gardens like this when you grew up?"

"Pretty much so, though I haven't checked recently to see if the flashers are still hanging out in the bushes."

"Flashers? You mean like the kind that, uh…" Andreas pointed at his groin.

Lila nodded. "Yep, raincoats, and all."

"I never noticed them."

"I doubt you're their type."

"I better start teaching Tassaki self-defense."

Lila smiled. "I've a better idea. Let's teach him how to push a stroller. That way he can earn his keep for hanging out with us at night."

Andreas took Lila's hand and kissed it. "Soon enough he'll want to be alone. Figuring things out for himself."

"Darling, he's only four."

Andreas turned and fixed his eyes in the direction of the Zappeion.

"What's on your mind?"

Andreas shook his head and looked back at Lila. "Nothing."

She stared at him.

"Well, just thinking about my father, and how differently things likely would have turned out had he lived."

"I think you turned out rather nicely."

Andreas smiled. "I'm not complaining. In fact, I'm feeling a bit guilty about my thoughts."

"How's that?"

"My father died when I was eight, and if he'd lived I'm sure he'd have tried to steer my life."

"He was a cop and you're a cop. Where else would he have steered you?"

"No, I mean in my personal life. He'd have wanted me to marry and have a family with someone known to our family."

"Leaving me out of the running for the spot."

Andreas nodded. "Precisely. My mother tried before we met, but it's not the same thing as when your father's pressing you."

Lila smiled. "Are you complaining?"

"Nope, just trying to remember to keep that in mind whenever I think I have all the answers for our kids."

"Meaning?"

"The right person may not be from your own clan."

"I get it. It's the person, not the packaging that matters."

"Yep," said Andreas.

"If I recall correctly, you most enjoyed the unwrapping."

Andreas reached down and squeezed her thigh with his hand. "Still do."

She pressed his hand. "Me too."

"I've changed. I know it."

"No you haven't. You're still the same lovable iconoclast I married."

"Yes I have." Andreas smiled. "Just knowing what 'iconoclast' means proves it. All this is part of the life we lead." He waved his arms around him. "Not in my wildest dreams did I ever think I'd be sitting in a place like this, exchanging nods and smiles with our country's movers and shakers as if we're old friends."

"We are."

"No, you are, but I've come to accept that I'm now part of it. It comes with the territory of being your husband."

"Okay, you met them because of me, but you're liked because of what you are as a man."

"I'm not complaining. Just telling you all this has me thinking of my responsibilities as a father." He paused. "A father has the bottom line duty of leading his children to appreciate a world without limits both in terms of what they can achieve in their careers and personal relationships, provided, of course, their choices are of good character."

"And that your children are raised to be of good character."

"For sure. Sitting all around us are examples of fathers and mothers with money and power who believe that entitles their children to do whatever they want to themselves and anyone else."

"Why do I sense you're getting off the subject of our children?"

"I see you're wired into my thoughts."

"Yep, like all good wives."

"Scary."

"And don't you forget it. So what's on your mind?"

"Just thinking about how Tank ended up like he did. And what part his father played in all of that."

"A lot," said Lila. "The father is a white-collar political crook. Smart and self-important to an extreme. He let his children run their lives any way they wanted without regard to right or wrong, always bailing them out whenever they got in trouble. But the mother's no prize either. She did little more than bear the children, leaving the rest to nursemaids and nannies while she spent most of her time in their Athens apartment playing around in Athens society. She and her husband haven't lived together for years."

"Some parents."

Lila nodded. "Sort of like letting your dogs run wild on fenced-in property you control, thinking no harm can possibly come to them while they're under your protection."

"Until one day little puppy Tank opened a gate and let the Teacher-wolf in."

"And?"

Andreas shrugged. "No idea. Not a word on anything from anyone anywhere."

"Quiet as a graveyard, huh?"

"I like that analogy a lot better than the one that's been running through my mind."

"Which is?"

"The calm before the storm."

Chapter Twenty-three

Andreas had purposely left his police mobile at home while they were out for dinner. No way he'd allow some bureaucrat with a brilliant idea or a politician with a complaint that couldn't wait until morning to wreck his first night out alone with his family in weeks. Besides, if anyone in his unit had to reach him they knew his personal mobile number.

He forgot to check his police mobile when he got home, distracted first by busying himself putting Tassaki to bed, and later by enjoying himself putting Lila to bed.

He lay next to his wife, breathing deeply.

"Did I wear you out?" said Lila, turning on her side and running the finger nails of one hand down along his bare belly.

"I'll never tell."

She pinched his stomach. "You don't have to."

"Hey, are you suggesting I've gained weight?"

"Nope, just appreciating your love handles."

"That's it, no more bread or wine for me."

"Or chocolate."

"Hey, let's not go overboard."

"No, problem. In fact, I'm touched by your consideration. After all, how many husbands would be willing to share in a wife's pregnancy by making sure his belly keeps up with hers?"

Andreas frowned. "Okay, no chocolate."

"But pickles and nonfat yoghurt are okay."

"Enough, I got the point." He jumped out of bed headed toward the bathroom, but stopped when he noticed the blinking message light on his police mobile. "Now what?" He picked it up off the top of the dresser and pressed a button to listen to his messages, pacing as he waited for them to play.

"Are you trying to get me worked up again by prancing around the room like a naked Adonis? You're not fooling me by making me think you're concentrating on listening to—"

Andreas held up his hand, then sat on Lila's side of the bed and listened.

"*Andreas, it's Ted. Okay, Rolex. Call me as soon as you get this message. Doesn't matter what time and do it from a secure phone. I'll be waiting for your call.*"

Andreas checked the time of Rolex's call. Three hours ago. "Dammit. I've got to make a call from the phone in the study."

"One of your girlfriends?"

"No, it's two in the morning, they're all asleep by now. They have school tomorrow."

"Ha, ha, ha."

He kissed her on her forehead, stood up, and walked toward the door.

"Uh, darling, put something on please, just in case Marietta decides to come home tonight. We wouldn't want to shock the poor woman."

"I doubt she'd be shocked." He reached for his pants. "After all, she's used to nude statues of Greek gods."

"Yes. But not of Buddha."

◇◇◇

Andreas sat at Lila's desk in her study and dialed Rolex's number.

"Hello," answered a sleepy voice.

"Ted, it's Andreas. Sorry to call so late but I was out with the family."

"And you conveniently forgot your official phone. Yep, I've done that too."

"I really didn't expect you to answer at this hour."

"No problem. I can't sleep anyway," said a yawning voice.

"Is it the reason you called me?" Andreas fiddled with the desk lamp, trying to dim it.

"I'm afraid I have to say yes. We've got a *very* serious situation."

"What's up?" Andreas leaned back in the chair and looked off through the window behind him toward the lights on Likavitos.

"There's a heavy-duty player out there offering big money for someone to take out a very important person."

"Translation please." Andreas stretched out his arms.

"Bottom line?"

"Yes," said Andreas, suppressing a yawn.

"It looks like Tank's father is shopping for an assassin to take out Spiros."

Andreas bolted forward in the chair. "Our minister, Spiros?"

"Yes."

"How the hell did you come up with that?"

"The father went to somebody he used many years before for a similar purpose."

"Are you serious?" said a no longer drowsy Andreas.

"I wish I weren't," coughed Rolex. "Do you recall about fifteen years ago a well-known politician was murdered? He'd been crusading against Tank's father. We all knew who was behind it and even caught the killer, but the killer wouldn't talk. Instead, he chose a very long prison sentence."

"I remember the case. But didn't he get out?"

"Yes, he served only three years before his friends in government arranged for his release. And they repaid him for his service with a license to open a club. Today it's one of the most successful in Athens."

Andreas thought to curse the corrupt bastards, but he'd be preaching to the choir in Rolex. "How'd you find out about their happy reunion?"

"The club guy came to see me."

"You gotta be kidding me."

"Nope. He'd gotten older and richer. He likes his new life and doesn't want to revisit his younger years. At least that's what he said he told Tank's father. But the old man wouldn't take no for an answer. Said he'd destroy the guy and his business if he didn't do what Tank's father wanted him to do."

"So Club Guy decided to come to you?"

"He knew me from his other case. Said he could 'trust me.'"

Andreas rubbed at his forehead. "I see he's gotten wiser too."

"Tank's father made a big mistake in pushing him. He's lucky the guy didn't take him out on the spot. He still has that killer instinct, just no longer for hire."

"What did Club Guy have to say that made you think Spiros is the target?"

"He said Tank's father is very angry, very tense. He'd never seen him that crazed. The father kept ranting on about someone threatening to destroy his whole family, and how he'd 'kill the bastard' before he'd let that happen."

"Did he name 'the bastard'?"

"No, just described him as someone arrogant enough to believe he was untouchable because of his position."

"Untouchable because of his position?" Andreas picked up a pencil and began tapping the eraser end on the desktop.

"That's what Club Guy said. The father offered no name or title. He told him he didn't have to know any of that, because the father would arrange for the target to be in a certain place at a certain time and all Club Guy had to do was kill him."

Andreas shook his head and tapped faster. "Don't you just love guys who think murder is so simple? How could the father think he'd get a professional to kill someone blindly?"

"Because he offered Club Guy a half-million euros to do it."

Andreas dropped the pencil. "And he turned it down?"

"Tells you something about how much money clubs make these days."

"But what makes you think the target's Spiros? I get it that the arrogance and untouchable allusions fit him, but it's still a hell of a jump from there to him being the target."

"We know Tank's father is going after Spiros big-time in the press for what he did to his son's business. Now he's trying to line up a guy he'd used before to kill a politician to take out some anonymous target he's really pissed at. To me that adds up to Spiros as the likely target."

"But why not go after me, too?"

Rolex chuckled. "The thought did cross my mind, but you don't fit the 'arrogant' profile. Pain in the ass, yes. Arrogant, no."

"How nice of you to say, but I still don't see the percentages in the father going after Spiros. After all, he's not the big man applying the pressure. That's the prime minister."

"Precisely. And that's what has me worried for Spiros. I think he's being targeted in order to send a message to the prime minister."

"I don't follow you."

"Club Guy said that Tank's father was obsessed with killing the target, but that he wanted it done in a way that sent a message to the target's master."

"Master? You're saying Tank's father considers the prime minister to be Spiros' master."

"Well, Club Guy didn't actually use the word *master*. But it describes what he meant."

"Do you remember his exact words?"

"I figured you'd ask that. Let me check my notes."

Andreas closed his eyes, not to sleep but to concentrate, as he waited for Rolex to get back on the line.

"What he said was, 'The old man wants me to take out the target in a way that will get a message back to his teacher.'"

Andreas froze. "Teacher?"

"Yes, he wanted the target killed in a manner that would get 'back to his teacher.'"

"And you're absolutely certain he said *teacher?*"

"Andreas, I may be tired but I can still read. Yes, 'teacher.' It's not how I'd describe the relationship between Spiros and the prime minister, but considering the father's obsession with all Spiros has done to his family, it makes sense to me he's the likely target."

"Thanks, Rol—I mean Ted. I'll get right on it."

"Let me know if you need any more help from me. Good night."

"Will do. Sleep tight."

Andreas put down the phone and shook his head. *Even NATO won't be able to help Tank's father if he's nuts enough to go after Teacher.*

◇◇◇

"The Turks better be invading and at my front door for you to be calling at this hour."

"That we could handle. Apologize to Maggie for me, then shut up and listen."

He heard Tassos say, "Andreas says he's sorry. If you care to believe him."

Andreas spoke quickly. "I just got off the phone with my buddy Rolex from antiterrorism. Looks like Tank's father is shopping for an assassin and my friend thinks the target is Spiros."

"Our Spiros? Is the father mad? That makes no sense."

"Apparently he's made that sort of thing happen before, but I have to agree with you. I think it's Kharon he's after."

"The one who killed Tank's sister?"

"Yes. The guy that Tank's father tried to hire told Rolex that the father's angry at someone threatening his family, and he wants the target killed to send a message to the target's 'teacher.'"

"Damn."

"I don't want to even think of the Humpty Dumpty mess we'll have on our hands if the old man starts a war with Teacher."

"But why would he want to do that?" said Tassos. "The media hasn't picked up yet on Tank being as big a crook as any of those he'd put on his list."

"Who knows what bad blood has passed between them since our raids shut down Tank's business. Or maybe the father found out Kharon killed his daughter and he simply wants revenge. All that we do know is Tank's disappeared off the face of the earth. Not a sight, sound, peep or even wink for the TV cameras."

"Maybe Teacher took out Tank and that's what this is all about?" said Tassos.

"I think we'd have heard about that. Teacher seems to like those sorts of hits broadcast to the world as examples to others."

"I wonder if the father realizes whom he's about to seriously piss off? You'd think his son would tell him, if just to warn him."

"Tank's so used to his father bailing him out of jams he probably thinks his father's invincible. And the old man's just arrogant enough to believe that he is."

Tassos snickered. "Or Tank's too afraid to tell his father how seriously he fucked up this time."

"Either way, going after Kharon is bad news for Tank's family and any innocents who happen to be in the general vicinity when the world as we know it comes to an end by Teacher's hand."

"You make her sound like a god," said Tassos.

"I was trying for devil."

"I see a bit of middle of the night humor. But let me jump to another possibility. What if Spiros really is the target?"

"I told Yianni to get over to the guard booth outside Spiros' house and alert the two cops stationed there that they and the minister may be targets. He's also arranging for a couple of blue and whites to stay parked outside the house all night."

"What about telling Spiros?"

"It would just mess up his head waking him in the middle of the night with this kind of news. I'll wait until the morning."

"How's that going to make what's happening any easier for him to take?"

"Because by then, dear friend, you and I may have something better to tell him."

"What's this 'you and I' bullshit?"

"Just get dressed. I'll pick you up in thirty minutes. And don't end up looking like a cop unless you want us to get killed."

"This sounds like a very inviting proposition. Stay in a warm bed with my beloved or race off into the night to indulge a crazy man with a death wish."

"Thirty minutes."

"Bye."

◇◇◇

Andreas pulled up to the curb in front of Maggie's apartment building. Not a soul anywhere to be seen. A rarity in the normally bustling Athens middle class neighborhood of Pangrati.

Andreas sat watching the front door of Maggie's first-floor apartment. He glanced at his watch. It wasn't like Tassos to be late. Out the corner of one eye he caught a stocky man in a black Greek fisherman's hat, dark woolen pants, and a blue denim work shirt step out of the shadows at the far end of the building and head toward his car.

"Who the hell are you supposed be?" said Andreas as Tassos opened the passenger side door.

"You said not to look like a cop."

"Yeah, but we're not going to a masquerade party. You look like a Russian revolutionary straight out of 1917."

"Look who's talking," said Tassos dropping onto the seat. "You're dressed like a preppy out of Kolonaki trying to look like a hippie. Jeans, boat shoes, and a Grateful Dead tee shirt. And what's with this shit box of a beat-up old Atos you're driving?"

Andreas steered the dark blue Hyundai away from the curb. "I borrowed it from my building's night-elevator operator."

"But why?"

"I don't want to be conspicuous."

"Where are we headed?"

"Exarchia."

Tassos slammed his right hand on the top of the dashboard. "Damn. She's right again."

"Who's right?"

"Maggie. I told her what you said and she told me to dress like an old anarchist."

"Am I that obvious?"

"You and me both. We're crystal clear to her."

"How'd she know?"

"She said if you're looking into something having to do with Teacher and Kharon, the only link you have to them is that taverna owner in Exarchia, Jacobi."

"I wonder if she'd be interested in picking horses for us at the track."

"She doesn't gamble."

"So you tried."

"Uh-huh," nodded Tassos drumming his fingers on the dash. "So what's the plan?"

"You should know better than to think I have one."

"That's what I thought. It's also why I'm carrying two guns."

"Wise decision."

"As opposed to the one I made that has me in this car with you at three in the morning."

"Stop complaining, I know you love a good time."

"Yeah, this should be real fun, a hippie and a Bolshevik arriving in anarchist party central at just about the time of the night when antiestablishment types are drunk, high, and angry at their lot in life that has them sweltering in Athens summer heat while capitalist lackeys are off enjoying the sea, islands, and mountains."

"Hey, man, it's the price we gotta pay for the revolution."

"Somehow that fails to comfort me."

"Stop with the sarcasm and let me concentrate. It's almost show time."

"Great. I always wondered what it would be like to die on stage."

Chapter Twenty-four

Tassos walked into the taverna alone and headed straight for the bar. Customers, mostly young men, huddled over drinks at four tables, a young woman in bring-on-the-revolution garb with complementing facial piercings and tattoos sat next to a fat man at the bar. Every eye in the place fixed on Tassos as he sat on a barstool three stools down from the fat man and ordered a beer from a Heracles size bartender sporting a King Leonidas-style beard.

As Tassos patiently waited for his beer, he glanced into the mirror running behind the bar, making eye contact with no one. He nodded thanks to the bartender, lifted the bottle to his lips, doing a quick scan of the room in the mirror as he did. He noticed only one table, possibly two, still paying him any attention.

He reached for a copy of the newspaper *Avriani* on the bar and began reading it. As he turned the page he glanced in the mirror again. No one was looking at him now.

Ten minutes later, Andreas strolled in. He looked at the faces at each table as he made his way toward the bar. He stopped a few paces away from the fat man sitting by Tassos and waved. "Jacobi, how are you, my friend?"

Jacobi studied Andreas' face until a look of recognition came across his own. "I am definitely not your friend."

"Of course you are, you just don't realize it yet."

Jacobi glared. "I'm tired of being pushed around by you fascist fucking cops."

"Easy now, or your friends here might not realize just how buddy-buddy we are."

"*Malaka*," said the girl, spitting at Andreas but not quite reaching him.

"Honey, you need some practice with the spitting. But don't do it in front of your boyfriend here, because he might get jealous at how freely you share your bodily fluids with total strangers."

She lunged off the stool at him, but tangled her feet together, tripping, and falling at Jacobi's feet.

"But first you ought to learn to walk." Andreas pointed at the girl and said to Jacobi, "I think you ought to help your girlfriend up off the floor."

Jacobi smiled. "She's not my girlfriend. She's his." He nodded toward the bartender coming up behind Andreas, a lead pipe in his right hand.

Andreas' raised his hands in front of his face. "Whoa there, big fellow. Not a good idea."

The bartender paused but Jacobi growled, "Break the asshole up bad."

The bartender lifted the pipe above his head and drove it diagonally across his body toward Andreas' head, but in the instant it took to bring the pipe down, Andreas slid off to his left and the bartender stumbled forward, tripping over his girlfriend.

"You two should produce wonderfully coordinated children together," said Andreas.

The bartender regained his balance with the help of the bar stool next to Tassos, lead pipe still in hand, and came up facing Tassos.

Tassos smiled, his semiautomatic service pistol pointed squarely at the middle of the bartender's forehead. "Uh-uh, play nice."

The bartender turned his head to look at Jacobi.

"What are you looking at him for? I'm the one who's going to put a bullet in your head if you don't drop the fucking pipe." Tassos jammed the barrel of the gun against the side of the bartender's head. "*Now*."

All heard the distinct clunk of a lead pipe hitting the floor.

"Good decision. Now pick up your girlfriend and take her over to that table against the wall. And don't either of you dare move from there until I tell you to."

Tassos watched the bartender carry his girlfriend to the table. "Terrific. I love young people who listen."

Tassos reached down to his ankle, pulled out a second gun, and waved it at the people still at the other tables. "As for the rest of you folks, two choices. Leave now with whatever bill you've run up on the house, courtesy of your host." He pointed the first gun in Jacobi's direction. "Or stay put and be a part of whatever additional unpleasantries are yet to come. Ten seconds to decide."

He looked at his watch. "Nine, eight..."

The place was empty by three.

"So, with that, back to you, maestro."

Andreas nodded. "Thank you." He bent down and picked the lead pipe up off the floor.

Holding it in his right hand and slapping it against his left he fixed his eyes on Jacobi's. "'Break the asshole up bad.' So, that's what you think of our relationship, huh?"

Andreas smiled, Jacobi forced a grin, and Andreas drove a butt end of the pipe hard enough into Jacobi's solar plexus to take him off the stool and double him over on the floor, struggling to breathe.

"That's just so you remember there are consequences for ordering someone to attack a police officer. But that's not why I'm here in the middle of the night. I came to give you the opportunity of choosing between living and dying."

Jacobi wheezed for air. "You're not going to kill me. No way."

Andreas lifted Jacobi's chin up off the floor with the pipe. "I never said I'd be the one to kill you. But how I decide to play what I'm about to tell you will definitely determine whether you live or die. So, are you ready to listen?"

"Can I sit down?"

"Sure, pick a table, any table, the place is yours."

Jacobi crawled to the nearest table and pulled himself up onto a chair facing the door.

"Nope, other side. I face the door."

Jacobi struggled to stand and move to the other side of the table. "You hurt me bad."

"File a complaint." Andreas sat down, putting the pipe on the tabletop.

Jacobi coughed and leaned forward, head down. "What do you want from me now?"

"The last time we met, you mentioned the name of a certain lady."

Jacobi lifted his head. "Go ahead, beat me to death with that pipe. That'll be nothing compared to what she'll do to me if she finds out I talked to cops about her."

"Good, I'm glad we understand each other, because that's precisely what she's going to do to you if you don't pass along what I'm here to tell you, and she learns that the bad stuff about to happen to her only went down because you didn't warn her when you had the chance."

"You do know you're fucking crazy."

"Yep," nodded Andreas.

"I don't even know how to begin to get a message to her, let alone convince her I have a warning from cops trying to help her."

"That falls into the category of not my problem."

Jacobi dropped his head and banged it lightly on the table. "So, what is it you want me to pass along?"

"All we know is that somebody is setting up a hit intended to send a message to Teacher."

Jacobi lifted his head and smirked. "Someone put out a hit on Teacher? Say good-bye to whatever idiot did that and all his nearest and dearest."

"I didn't say 'a hit on Teacher.' It's on someone in Greece close enough to Teacher to get her attention."

Jacobi's eyes widened. "Do you have a name on the target?"

"No, nor on the person placing the hit. If we did we wouldn't be here asking you for answers."

"I'm afraid I can't help you."

"What about your friend? Maybe he could help you."

"What friend?"

Andreas cocked his head. "Jacobi *mou*. Are we going to play that game again?"

"Oh, *that* friend."

"That's right. Kharon."

"No, he wouldn't know."

"Are you sure, because if somebody close to Teacher dies who would have lived had you cooperated, I can assure you that message will get out there too."

"You made that point before."

Andreas shrugged. "Repetition is good."

"So, why are Greek cops so interested in preventing someone close to Teacher from getting whacked?"

"You already know why. If she gets angry, a lot of innocents are going to die on Greek soil. And we Greek cops don't want that happening here."

Jacobi stared at Andreas. "How about I say I'll see what I can do? When's this maybe hit supposed to take place?"

Andreas looked at his watch. "Anytime from five minutes ago to who-the-fuck-knows. I'm here at four fucking o'clock in the morning dodging lead pipes, and you're asking me for an appointment time on a hit." Andreas shook his head. "If I were you, I'd be on the phone the moment you see me waving good-bye."

Andreas stood, nodded to Tassos, and the two cops headed toward the front door. Andreas stopped at the doorway, waited until he caught Jacobi's eye in the mirror, and waved.

◇◇◇

The pain where the bastard cop hit him with the pipe still throbbed, but at least he could breathe. Jacobi stared in the mirror at the spot where the asshole had stood and waved to him.

"*Malaka*," he said aloud, still looking in the mirror. He noticed the bartender and his girlfriend hunched over the table against the wall. *There's a real* malaka. *Can't even swing a lead pipe.*

"Close up the place and get the hell out of here," shouted Jacobi. He bent his head over the table and shut his eyes.

How can I get to Teacher?

She didn't know him from Adam. And if he figured out how to reach her, it wasn't likely to end well for him, no matter how important she found the cop's message. The odds were she'd assume him an informant carrying messages for cops, an informant who knew how to find her. What reason would someone like Teacher have for keeping someone like him breathing?

No, he'd go directly to Kharon and warn him. The idiot cops didn't realize Kharon was the likely target. It all must tie into that job he did for Teacher up in Thessaloniki. No doubt in his mind Kharon had done it. And probably Tank's family had ordered the hit. Stupid cops. They couldn't find their dicks in the dark. All they knew was their hardball, beat-the-proletariat-with-lead-pipes routine. No brains in those fascists.

Yes, he'd call Kharon and avoid the whole Teacher play.

He opened his eyes. But what would he say if Kharon asked how the cops knew to come to him to get to Teacher? Not *if* he asked that question, *when* he asked it.

Jacobi shuddered so hard he had to shake the table to steady himself. He could hear the cold, flat tone of Kharon's voice as he asked that question. Like a hangman inquiring of the soon to be deceased's weight as he tied the noose around the subject's throat.

If he told Kharon the truth, that the cops came to Jacobi already knowing both Kharon's name and that he'd killed Tank's sister, and that he gave the cops Teacher's name to take the heat off himself, Kharon would say, "Why didn't you tell me that before?"

Or maybe he'd say nothing at all, for once Kharon doubted his loyalty, Jacobi knew he'd be just as dead as if Teacher wanted him that way.

I'm boxed in.

He saw three choices. Reach out to Teacher as the cops wanted, warn Kharon, or simply ignore everything and pray nothing happened. The first two choices put him in direct, immediate grave danger. The third presented the least risk to his life, but the greatest to his childhood friend's.

Fuck.

◇◇◇

Too wound up to go back to sleep, and too wired to jump straight into an evaluation of their confrontation with Jacobi, Andreas and Tassos stopped at an all-night bar close to Maggie's apartment. It had the sort of subdued, working class crowd feel perfect for bringing adrenaline levels back down to normal.

Each man ordered a beer and a shot of vodka. They clinked shot glasses and chugged their *sfinakis,* and slowly sipped their beers.

"I was worried when I saw the gorilla bartender coming at you with the pipe," said Tassos.

"So was I."

"You had to know things might get rough, so why didn't you yank one of your young tough guys out of bed in the middle of the night instead of me?"

"I thought of that, but Jacobi would recognize Yianni and Petro, and I needed someone he didn't know who could slip in ahead of me to watch my back."

"I thought of shooting the gorilla with the lead pipe but figured your head was hard enough to take the hit."

Andreas lifted his bottle and clinked it against Tassos' glass. "Good thing he was about as coordinated as Tassaki's Slinky."

"Slinky?"

"It's a toy. Hard to find in Greece, but a friend of Lila's sent us one for Tassaki from America. It's a flexible spring you can get to walk down steps, all in *very predictable movements.*" He took a chug of his beer. "Thank God."

Tassos laughed. "It really was a funny scene. I mean Little Miss Spitter and her boyfriend made quite a team."

Andreas grinned. "Yeah, they did."

The two men clinked again.

"So, do you think he'll run to Kharon?" said Tassos.

"That's a better bet for him than getting Teacher's attention. But who knows? He might decide to do nothing."

"That's probably his safest play."

"Is that how you'd play it if I were the target?" said Andreas

"You mean not tell you? Hell, I've done that a hundred times already. Maggie threatens to kill you almost every day." Tassos took a sip of his beer.

Andreas smiled. "Jacobi not telling Kharon could most definitely get Kharon killed."

"Who cares? They're all bad guys."

Andreas drained his bottle and placed ten euros on the bar. "Let's go, I'm exhausted."

Tassos finished his beer, tipped his hat to the barman, and said to Andreas as they slid off their bar stools. "It's always nice to know what's waiting for you at home."

"Yeah, but I'd sure like to know what's out there waiting for Kharon."

Tassos patted him on the shoulder. "Soon, my friend, soon."

◇◇◇

Kharon's phone rang. "Hello."

"I have the money."

"All of it?"

"Yes."

"Good, because your two days end today. Do you have a pencil?"

"For what?"

"The wire transfer instructions."

"No way," said Tank's father.

"Excuse me?"

"You can't expect me to simply wire transfer fifty million euros."

"That much in cash would amount to one hell of a heavy suitcase, even in five-hundred euro notes."

"I'm not talking about giving you cash."

"Then precisely what are you talking about?"

"My son is worried."

"He should be."

"This money is his inheritance."

"Either way, by the end of today it will be someone else's inheritance. But with my alternative he'll at least have the chance to build up a new one."

"He's not concerned about the money, just that you may not be telling him the truth. He trusts Teacher, but doesn't know you. He's afraid the money will never get to Teacher, or that Teacher hasn't agreed to let him live even if he pays."

"Are you suggesting—?"

"That he needs the personal assurance of Teacher that payment of the money will end this once and for all."

Kharon paused. "You want a meeting between your son and Teacher?"

"No, Tank realizes she'd never agree to that. He just wants to call her in your presence so she can vouch for you and tell him that all is forgiven once he pays."

Kharon paused again. "And when will the payment be made?"

"The moment Teacher gives him those assurances, the funds will be transferred into her account."

"Where are you proposing that we hold this meeting?"

"I thought the monastery would be an appropriate neutral venue."

Kharon paused for a third time. "Do you have that pencil yet?"

"Why?"

"For the same reason I said before, to mark down the wire transfer instructions."

"So we have a deal?"

"Yes."

"Terrific. Okay, give me the instructions."

Kharon gave them.

"So, when should I tell my son to expect you?"

"Just say 'anytime.' I assume his schedule is open."

The father paused. "Yes, certainly. I'll just tell him to expect you sometime today." He told Kharon where Tank would be in the monastery.

"For sure. And one more thing."

"Yes?"

"I do not like being surprised."

"I don't understand."

"You will, if I am." He hung up the phone.

It all sounded reasonable, yet something about the conversation bothered Kharon. Tank's father agreed to the fifty million far too quickly, without so much as a hint of negotiation. That didn't sound like the father's business style. Then again, it might have been Tank's call if it truly were his inheritance. And Tank was probably literally scared to death at the possibility of losing this opportunity to save his life.

Yes, that sounded like something Tank would do. Kharon could hear him now: *Daddy, save me!*

Those were words Kharon never had the opportunity to utter in his life. Nor had most of his friends. Which reminded him, *I better call Jacobi.*

He hadn't heard from Jacobi in days, not since he asked him to make some decision about what Kharon should do about the motorcycle he'd borrowed from him. With all the heat connected to that bike, Kharon suggested he make it disappear. Jacobi hemmed and hawed about wasting such a beautiful BMW.

In their last conversation Kharon told him to make a simple yes or no decision. That was three days ago and still no word from him. He'd call him tomorrow, after he'd finished up this thing with Tank. It would be one glorious, fifty-million-euro, final run for the BMW, no matter what Jacobi decided.

"Just like him," Kharon said aloud. "The poor guy can't make a decision to save his life."

He shook his head. "Sure glad mine isn't in his hands."

Chapter Twenty-five

"It's Spiros, Chief."

Andreas looked at the intercom. "My God, Maggie, that's the third time he's called today and it's not even noon. What's with him?"

"Do I really have to tell you?"

"No."

"Did I detect a sigh?"

"Just put him through."

Andreas forced himself to laugh before picking up the phone. It was Lila's trick for making herself sound absolutely cheery whenever she had to speak with someone she dreaded.

"Spiros, how are you? Long time no talkie."

"Why are you so happy? I'm being crucified in the press, you have me in constant fear for my life, my home's a virtual prison, and you sound like you just won the lottery."

"Look, I've told you twice already today that we don't think you're the target, but we also don't want to take any chances."

"Well, the press is killing me in any case. That damned father of Tank's won't let up. He's making up stories about me tied into international crime rings, and demanding a Parliamentary investigation of me *and* the prime minister. I thought the son was bad. The father's worse. And all you ever say to the press as my spokesman is, 'Sorry, but we can't comment on an ongoing investigation, no matter how unfounded the allegations you raise for comment.' You're just tightening the noose around my neck."

"Let's not lose sight of where this is headed. Media wounds heal; bullet wounds in the middle of the forehead do not."

"How's that supposed to comfort me? I thought you said I'm not a target."

"I'm talking about the risks to Tank and his father."

"And how are we going to know if your plan works?"

Good question, thought Andreas. "When Tank turns up, dead or alive."

"Alive won't help me. Neither will dead as long as the father is still breathing."

"Uh, Spiros, I know you didn't mean what you just seemed to have said."

"What?"

"That you wanted Tank and his father dead."

"Are you nuts? Of course not. Do you think someone's recording this call? Great, more anxieties! Now I have to worry that everything I say in my own office will be playing on the evening news."

"Get a grip. This is going to come to a head in a matter of days, not weeks. Trust me on that."

"Why should I?"

"Because I'm the only one you can."

Silence.

"Now, just relax. I can't guarantee the outcome, but I can guarantee we're trying our best."

Spiros cleared his throat and spoke softly, just above a whisper. "I really can't take much more of this. Honestly, Andreas, I can't."

"I know. Just try your best to hold on a bit longer. Something's going to break. I just feel it."

"Okay. But you'll let me know as soon as something happens, right?"

"Absolutely."

"Thank you. Bye."

Andreas blew through his lips as he hung up the phone. What he didn't tell Spiros was how really bad things would get for him if Tank's father succeeded in getting to Kharon. If he killed him, both the father and the son would think themselves invincible and do whatever it took to destroy Spiros and resurrect Tank's public image.

Andreas had no doubt that Teacher ultimately would find some way to end both their lives, but by then Spiros would be long gone.

Andreas winced at his thought. He'd meant Spiros would be driven from office, but he'd had the more morbid thought, and couldn't unthink it.

Andreas crossed himself. *Poor soul.*

◇◇◇

Eight miles east of Arachova, Kharon turned south off the main road out of Delphi toward the village of Distomo, where he would turn east toward the neighboring village of Steiri.

Distomo, thought Kharon. A place of execution, of massacre, where for two hours on June 10, 1944, Nazi SS troops went door-to-door, murdering two hundred fourteen civilians, bayonetting babies in their cribs, beheading the local priest. Slaughter haunted this place to its very bones.

A mile beyond Steiri, the road took a sharp left, but Kharon continued straight onto a well-paved two-lane road. The BMW wound along hillsides covered in fir, cedar, myrtle, arbutus, and pine, high above a broad green valley filled with cultivated olives, almonds, and patches of grape, all running off toward distant limestone mountain slopes. It was a far different world from the struggling, melancholy farm communities he'd just passed through. Here, not a hint of modern times was to be seen anywhere along the mile-and-a-half run up to Monastery Hosios Loukas' hillside perch on a western slope of Mount Helicon.

Kharon loved coming here at sunset as just another anonymous pilgrim, when shadows were long and light practiced its magic upon the monastery's rusty earth tone architectural jags and juts, contours and edges. Out here, at this time of day, he'd lose track not only of time, but of centuries.

But not this sunset. This was not a time for dreaming. The great beauty of hallowed places such as this did not cleanse them of their haunting secret intrigues, betrayals, and bloodshed; accommodations to the times through which they passed that allowed them to flourish while others vanished from the earth. He would not allow himself to become part of that history. At least not tonight. Or so he hoped.

◇◇◇

Tank sat alone beneath the Katholicon in the Crypt of Saint Barbara, the monastery's oldest church, a place of peace, quiet, and massive stone pillars supporting the dome of the Katholikon above it. The tomb of Saint Loukas lay against the crypt's northern wall beneath an oil lamp kept burning for ten centuries by monks devoted to his memory. Soon the lamp's faint glimmer would be Tank's only light, but he'd find no comfort in the remains of Saint Loukas. They were removed in 1011 and now resided beneath their own perpetually burning oil lamp in a glass-enclosed casket off the passageway between the church and Katholikon.

The monastery had closed at six to tourists and no monks would be coming down to the crypt tonight. His father had made sure of that. Nor would Kharon expect to find Tank there. It was the perfect place to wait out the next step in his father's plan, safely away from what was about to happen. Tank smiled as he crossed himself.

His father was right. The plan depended on Kharon dying before Tank spoke to Teacher. Tank could not ask for Teacher's word, then betray her by killing her messenger. That would dishonor her in a way she would never forgive. No, Kharon must die before the call.

Then it would be Tank's turn to get in the game. He'd call her, being sure to sound mournful and sad over what just happened. He'd explain how her messenger turned into a raging madman, demanding more than they'd agreed to pay, drawing a weapon in a place of God, and forcing Tank's people to defend his life in self-defense.

Tank thought the story a bit weak, but his father assured him a hard-headed businesswoman like Teacher need not be convinced, only sufficiently appeased to justify taking the money they'd offer her to allow them to go in peace. Of course, the money would now be substantially less, but that was only fair, seeing as her messenger had just tried to kill the very basis of their bargain.

Yes, his father had no doubt that once Kharon was eliminated, and a face-saving excuse offered to Teacher, all would be resolved through a simple, straightforward financial negotiation for a far less costly sum than what the bitch had been demanding.

◇◇◇

Kharon faced a path he'd walked many times before, one leading down from the visitors' parking lot to the monastery's south entrance. He'd always found purpose in his few minutes' stroll along the broad, terraced steps of marble blocks set as randomly as tiles, gazing out upon the peaceful valley and hillsides, and inhaling scents of wild lavender, clematis, and daffodils. It served as a passage from the isolated reality of his life to a place of tranquility shared with souls from a thousand years past.

But this evening Kharon's thoughts focused on another sort of passage: One that involved negotiating two hundred yards of wide open space safe from those who might possess less tranquil intentions in their minds and perhaps a sniper rifle or more in their hands. And he had good reason to think someone might be out there.

So he did not park, but raced his motorcycle down one hundred yards of thirty terraced marble steps, spun into a switchback turn for another fifty-yard run of steps, and raced the final fifty yards across an open terrace to a skidding stop by a stone domed pylon close by the entrance to the church and Katholikon. He'd apologize to the monks later.

No one within earshot could have missed the distinctive roar of the big BMW's dual exhausts reverberating off the walls. Nor the eerie sudden absence of sound the moment he'd turned off the engine. Yet he heard no shouts or running footsteps, only the wind through the trees, and he saw no more than a cat cowering off in a corner away from the unexpected intruder.

Where is everyone?

The instructions from Tank's father had been for Kharon to meet Tank in the old cells up above the west facing entrance to the church. Kharon scanned every window, doorway, and roof he could see. No one. The courtyard surrounded him with hiding places: On the ground stood doorways, latticed windows, and walls dropping down and rising up; turrets, a dome, and the roofs on which they sat loomed above him; and in between rose four to five stories of windows, nooks, and crannies, each offering a different clear angle on him for a marksman.

I am the proverbial sitting duck, he thought. So he did just that: he sat. But around the back, in the shadows, on a block of stone protruding from the rear wall of the Katholikon, in a tiny cove-like spot a few feet from where the church and Katholikon abutted each other. Dirt ground, a view of what could be coming from the north entrance of the monastery fifty yards away, and a bit of cover from the sides offered him options for dealing with what might be out there. He put his backpack down beside him, stretched, and focused on the hunt—but as the hunted, not the hunter. They would have to come to him.

After all, it was Tank who'd invited him.

Two hours passed without the sight or sound of a human soul. He sat quietly in total darkness, calmly identifying each sound as friendly, waiting for the first one he'd know meant something else.

Two more hours passed. Still nothing. Kharon appreciated patience as a great virtue in the hunter. But in the hunted it accounted for far more; it meant the difference between living and dying. And so he sat, with his back flat against the east wall of the Crypt of Saint Barbara.

◇◇◇

What is taking so long? Why has no one come for me? Tank knew hours had passed, but not how many. The monks did not allow him a phone or a watch. *Damn them.* He'd paced the floor a thousand times. *Quiet as a tomb* kept running through his mind. He wanted to get out. He wanted to know what was happening. The only window in the crypt sat in the rear, east wall of the

Katholicon, beyond the altar, covered in grillwork, and draped over with a dark curtain. He'd listened for a sound at the window but heard nothing. It seemed as soundproof as the walls.

No wonder. He'd heard that the crypt had once been used to house psychopaths. The monks would chain them to its stone pillars until cured of their madness.

I'll go just as mad if someone doesn't show up soon.

Tank thought to look out the window in case someone might be out there. Maybe his father's men had forgotten about him? He shook his head. He knew his curiosity was getting the better of him. He'd do better to relax. If he drew back the curtain to look out, dim as the light from the oil lamp might be, it would draw the immediate attention of anyone out there. If seen by one of his father's men, he'd have hell to pay to his father for not sitting tight as ordered. If seen by the only other possible person out there interested in him, it could mean a bullet in his head.

He toyed with putting out the lamp, but decided ending a thousand years of light just to peek out a window risked too much bad karma, even for him. So, he resigned himself to playing it safe and waiting for someone to come for him.

Then he paced some more.

Chapter Twenty-six

Tank's father looked at his watch. He'd told his son to stay put and not move until the men he'd hired came for him. That would be when Tank would make his call to Teacher, after the killer of his daughter had been quietly disposed of without a trace, and long before the monks emerged from their solitary, dusk-to-dawn prayer vigil and fasting for his daughter's soul. Their unique commitment to remain confined to their cells in all-night individual prayer came in exchange for a generous donation from Tank's father toward refurbishing the monastery's most endangered treasures.

He looked at his watch again. The assassins he'd hired told him they'd found the perfect place along the corridor leading to the old cells. Sooner or later their target must pass that way, and when he did, they'd be waiting for him. With but a faint pop from their silenced weapons, he'd be dead. They'd told the father to relax, mentioned again how many times they'd done this sort of thing before, and assured him it would all be over soon.

That was six hours ago.

He poured himself a scotch and stared at his reflection in the sliding glass door leading from his office out to the pool. He'd decided to wait out the night's events in Chalkidiki. He felt more secure there. At least he had before that asshole killer had shown up.

He looked at the telephone number on the piece of paper on his desk. It came with clear instructions: "Only call during

the operation to abort or inform us that our lives are in danger."
He wondered whether Alexander the Great ever received similar
instructions from those he'd delegated to execute his plans.

He put the scotch down on the desktop, muttered, "Enough
of this macho, special operations bullshit," picked up the phone,
and dialed the number.

It rang five times. On the sixth ring he heard a whispering,
obviously annoyed man. "I told you not to call during the
operation."

"Let me explain who's calling. It's the man who's paying you
a shitload of money to do something you repeatedly tell me
you've done many times before."

"This is not the time—"

The father's voice rose. "Shut up and let me finish. The whole
purpose of your 'operation' is evaporating. If my son doesn't
make a call soon telling someone that your target's dead, either
my son is dead or we're out a hell of a lot of money. Neither one
will keep you in my good graces."

Pause.

"Did you hear me?"

"This guy's good—"

"I know he is. That's why I hired you."

"We heard him arrive four and a half hours ago."

"He's there?"

"The bike is, so we assume he is."

"Assume. As in you don't know?"

"Affirmative on the bike."

"I don't care about the bike. What about the target?"

"We haven't seen him."

"Have you looked?"

"Sir, you don't understand—"

"*Have you looked for him?* Just answer yes or no."

"No, but it's not that easy. It's dangerous to hunt someone
like him in a place like this."

"Dangerous? You say 'it's dangerous?' Of course it's dangerous. If it wasn't I'd have sent a *ya-ya* with an umbrella to beat

him to death. Fuck, man! A grandmother would have more balls than you."

"If worse comes to worst we'll get him at sunrise."

The father's voice dropped to calm and flat. "That's the first thing you've said in this conversation that I agree with completely."

"Yes, at sunrise—"

"No the part about it being the very worst thing that could happen."

The father's voice remained perfectly measured and even. "At sunrise, many tired and very hungry monks will be running all over the place. Each one a potential witness to a murder no one is ever supposed to know happened. Though to be honest with you, from your current performance, I think that come sunrise, you're the ones who'll most likely be dead."

The father cleared his throat. "Let me put it to you this way. Get off your asses and use your vaunted special operations military backgrounds and equipment to find this killer of my daughter on your terms, or wait until morning and be dead on his. End of story."

Pause.

"Do you understand?"

A whispered, "Yes."

"Good. Now get to work."

The father hung up the phone and stared back out toward the pool. *Men like that need firm leadership*, he thought. He picked up his scotch, put his feet up on his desk, and leaned back in his chair. *They're damn lucky I'm here for them.*

◇◇◇

Kharon originally assumed they'd come dressed as monks, an obvious cover for assassins working in a monastery. But not now. Too much time had passed for that ploy to work, and whoever held this monastery under wraps had to know that. He'd not seen or heard a single monk since he arrived. If the monks were being held by force, he likely faced a lot of armed men. If by guile, not so many.

His eyes long ago adjusted to the dark, and he smiled at a cat dozing fifteen yards away, straight ahead to his left, at the southeast corner of the church atop a nearly seven-foot high wall. *Maybe they'll come disguised as cats.*

He stretched. He hadn't done that in a while. He'd done isometrics to keep his muscles from cramping up, but not stretching. Stretching required noticeable movement that might give away his position. He wondered how people could possibly sit at desks all day without moving. Kharon shook his head. *I'm losing concentration, I'd better—*

He heard a sound. The cat had leaped off the wall onto the open ground in front of Kharon and disappeared up a stone pathway to Kharon's right running along the south side of the Katholikon. He slid his right hand into the backpack and came out with a Heckler & Koch MP5K submachine gun, cocked and ready to fire. With his left he reached in for a grenade and crept carefully toward the corner of the church.

He stood two paces away from the corner when the same cat shot out of the same narrow pathway to Kharon's right, racing straight away from the church, the Katholikon, and Kharon. Kharon paused only long enough to arm the grenade and, with his left hand, toss it up into the pathway vacated by the cat.

On the sound of the grenade hitting stone Kharon dropped to the ground, tightly shut his eyes, covered his ears, and waited for the flash and near stun-level noise. At the explosion, Kharon sprang to his feet and brought the muzzle of his submachine gun up over the edge of the wall, close by the corner of the church. Two men in body armor and dressed for nighttime military combat stood swinging Kalishnikov AK-74Ms in wild sprays of automatic fire, each blinded by their own night vision goggles from the flash grenade explosion.

Hugging close to the edge of the church, Kharon took careful aim and dropped each man with a shot to the head. The instant the second man fell, Kharon raced across the open ground to the southeast corner of the Katholikon. He listened. He heard nothing. Someone had to be out there. The grenade startled, not killed.

His choice of grenades had nothing to do with sparing life; Kharon simply wasn't willing to chance harming the monastery unless left with no choice. He had frag grenades, but they risked driving shrapnel and shock waves into walls and windows, doing potentially serious harm to the place and its treasures. Nazi planes had failed at trying to destroy the monastery in 1943, and he wasn't about to inadvertently accomplish what Hitler's bombs had not.

The roar of a motorcycle thundered down the path at him, but not the bike. Whoever had been on the path must be fleeing on Kharon's BMW. But there could be more.

He heard the clamor of running feet and voices shouting, all headed his way.

He hurried to his backpack and managed to put the MP5K away just as the first monk came upon him, flashlight in hand.

"Who are you?"

Kharon stood facing the monk, hands clenched and held tightly to his chest, his body shaking. "A very frightened pilgrim. I came here in search of a place to stay for the night and, finding no one, I came to sleep over there." He pointed at the backpack on the wall.

Other monks now joined the first.

"What happened?" asked another.

"I don't know," said Kharon speaking rapidly, as if terrified. "I awoke to an explosion and a bright flash of light, then men dressed like soldiers," he pointed toward the rear of the church, "started shooting at someone over there," he pointed at the south side of the Katholikon, "who shot back and then must have run up that path," he pointed again to the south side of the Katholikon, "because the next thing I heard was a motorcycle roaring away." Kharon hadn't stopped shaking.

"Yes, I heard the motorcycle, too. The defiler must have fled on it," said an older monk, holding a candle. He put his arm around Kharon. "Relax, my son. Your ordeal is over."

Kharon put his head on the monk's shoulder and wept.

Another monk with a flashlight edged his way up onto the wall behind the church. "Oh, my Lord. There are two men back here. I think they are dead." He crossed himself and said a prayer. The other monks did the same.

Kharon backed away from the older monk and sat on the wall next to his backpack.

"Who would dare commit such a sacrilege in our holy place?" said the older monk

"Yes, who?" asked the others.

Kharon was about to offer a suggestion, but wasn't quite sure how to raise it.

"There can be only one answer," said the monk with the flashlight. "The newcomer. It was his father who paid the abbot for all of us to remain in our cells in prayer through the night."

Bingo, thought Kharon.

A murmur of agreement came from the other monks.

"We must find the abbot, tell him what has happened, and have him deal with this heretic tonight."

"Yes, tonight!" said another.

"Let us find this man of the devil and bring him to the abbot. His face will show his guilt."

At that, the monks dispersed as quickly as they'd appeared. Kharon gathered up his backpack and quietly but quickly moved toward the northern gate fifty yards away. There was still the chance of an assassin hiding somewhere inside, or more likely outside, though at this point Kharon saw both risks as minimal. Still, he wanted to get away from here as fast as possible. So far, no one had suggested calling the police, and he did not want to be there when someone did.

He stopped by the gate and looked back at the church and Katholikon. He knew he couldn't return. He wasn't religious, and crossing himself meant nothing to him, but this place had been special to him for a very long time, and tonight it sheltered and saved him. He owed it a sign of respect.

Kharon drew in and let out a deep breath, lifted his right hand to his forehead, "Thank you, Hosios Loukas," saluted, and left.

Chapter Twenty-seven

Every monk in the monastery somehow found a way to pack into the abbot's study. No one was going to miss this.

A broad-shouldered man with a salt and pepper beard and dressed in formal abbot's garb sat in a tall back, Byzantine era chair, behind a Byzantine era desk, surrounded by Byzantine mosaic and icon masterpieces. Purposeful or not, the setting made clear the seminal importance of that time to this place, and the absolute power of the occupier of the abbot's chair over the monastery's affairs.

Tank sat directly across the desk from the abbot. Two monks stood beside Tank, one on either side.

"Do you know why you're here?" asked the abbot in a soft voice.

"No. I was brought here in the middle of my all-night vigil praying for the soul of my sister by these two." He pointed at the monks beside him.

"Did you ask them why?"

Tank hesitated. "No."

The abbot nodded.

"I assumed it had something to do with the loud noises."

The abbot nodded again. "And what led you to that conclusion?"

Tank shrugged. "It's the only explanation I could think of."

"And why were you in the crypt instead of in your cell as instructed?"

"In such a holy place I felt I could be closer to God than alone in my cell."

The abbot's eyes narrowed slightly. "Would you like to know about the loud noises?"

Tank shrugged. "Why not?"

The abbot leaned back. "Two men were murdered tonight inside our walls."

Tank blinked. "Two?"

"Were you expecting more?"

"No."

"Less?"

"No, no, I'm just surprised. Here, in a place of God—"

The abbot raised his hand. "Please, no more of that. Do you know who died?"

Tank crossed his legs. "How would I?"

"Perhaps you've seen them before?"

"I doubt it. I wouldn't know such men."

"Such men?"

"Yes."

"How do you know the dead are not from among our own?"

Tank blanched. "You mean they killed monks?"

"Did you expect *them* to kill someone else?"

Tank uncrossed his legs. "I don't know what you're talking about."

"I'm talking about two men, in full combat dress, equipped with night vision goggles and Kalashnikovs, each killed with a single shot *to the head.*" The abbot leaned forward and said in a firm, commanding voice, "Does that method of death sound familiar to you, sir?"

Tank crossed his arms over his chest. "I really don't know what you mean by that. Why would I know? How would I know?"

"My brothers and I spent the night praying for the soul of your departed sister, killed by a bullet to her forehead, and you don't know what I'm talking about?"

"I swear to—"

"Stop! You have lied to me at least three times since you sat in that chair, and invoked our Lord's name twice in your subterfuge. *Do not* do it again."

"I don't have to sit here and take these accusations."

The abbot nodded. "Brother Ilias," he said to a monk by the door, "bring us his things."

"You have no right to go through my property."

The abbot waved for the monk to go. "I have no intention of going through your things. That is the sort of thing police do."

"I have nothing to say to the police. I was in prayer when those men were killed."

"Yes, I'm sure. Though I dread ever learning the object of your prayers."

The abbot pushed back from his desk and rose up from his chair. He stood nearly six and a half feet tall. "Before finding my way to the Lord, men such as you sent me off to fight their battles. I swore I would never do service for their like again, only the Lord's. And yet here I am, tricked into doing your and your father's bidding, while you sat cowering in a corner by the tomb of our beloved Hosios Loukas, even as the two who now stand beside you came for you."

The abbot came around the desk and stood directly in front of Tank. "You brought murder into the house of the Lord and for that you shall be punished."

Tank tried to stand but the monks next to him held him down.

"Have no fear of us," said the abbot. "We shall not judge or punish you. Yours and your father's punishment awaits you outside our walls."

Brother Ilias returned with a bag and held it out to the abbot.

"Thank you, Brother," said the abbot, taking the bag and turning to Tank.

"Here is your property. Now leave."

"What? I don't want to leave."

"But you are, and now." He pushed the bag into Tank's arms.

"My father paid you a lot of money."

"And we said a lot of prayers."

Tank looked from the abbot to the others, then back again. "I require sanctuary. I'll be killed out there!"

The abbot placed hands the size of hams on Tank's shoulders. "And I shall pray for your soul. Now *leave*."

◇◇◇

"Fuck, fuck, fuck, fuck, fuck," muttered Tank to himself as he stumbled in the dark along the path toward the service area parking lot outside the north wall. "How could they have blown it? And so fucking badly. I'm a dead man."

The explosion had scared him shitless. Nothing like that was supposed to happen. He knew it had to be Teacher's man, the one who'd killed his sister in cold blood. And when he heard the pounding on the door of the crypt he'd tried to hide, certain he was about to die.

Maybe Teacher's man was out there waiting for him? He spun around looking, but even though his eyes had adjusted to the dark, with only a sliver of moon in the sky and sunrise still hours away, he could barely see ten yards in front of his face.

No, he's long gone by now. Tank's mind kept looping through alternatives as he moved toward the gravel parking area. No way Teacher's guy would be hanging around waiting for the police to show up. Besides, he'd want to make a big show of taking out the son and the father at the same time. Messages like that were Teacher's trademark. *Dramatic bitch.*

He wished he could get a message to his father about what had happened, but that would have to wait until he reached his SUV. The damn monks wouldn't let him bring his mobile phone into the monastery. It had been a real pain in the ass coming up with excuses to get back to the SUV every time he wanted to use the phone. And they'd searched him for it each time he came back. *Bastards.*

Tank saw his black Range Rover off to the right.

"Finally, civilization." He'd almost yelled the words.

Tank held the keys in his right hand and squeezed the unlock button on the remote. He heard a chirp and saw the interior lights go on inside. He paused. The lights would make him an easy target anywhere within ten yards of the vehicle.

He waited for the lights to go off before creeping toward the vehicle, scanning all around him as he did. He saw nothing. He heard nothing. He put down the bag he'd held in his left hand, gripped the driver side front door handle in that hand, yanked open the door, and leaped inside to turn off the interior lights just as they went on.

Once all was dark again, he leaned out to pick up the bag, tossed it on the floor in front of the dashboard on the passenger side, closed the door, started the engine, and sped away.

Tank's mind raced as fast as the engine, but scattered, unfocused. Maybe the third mercenary hired by his father had actually killed Teacher's man, and the reason the monks never found his body was because the mercenary had disposed of the body before they could find it. After all, that was the mission, and ex-military types were trained to put the mission ahead of everything else. At least that's what he knew from the movies. He'd better call his father. He'd know.

Tank reached down and felt around in the compartment between the front seats for his phone. It wasn't there. He glanced away from the road to look in the compartment and on the passenger seat. Nothing.

With his eyes still on the road, he leaned over to open the glove compartment in front of the passenger seat, in the process unintentionally turning the steering wheel clockwise enough for the right front wheel to strike a soccer ball size boulder at the edge of the road. The impact sent the car careening toward a steep hillside drop-off on the left. Tank struggled to maintain control, swerving the car back and forth until finally coming to a stop inches before tumbling off the road.

"Whew," said Tank to himself aloud. He rested his right elbow on the steering wheel, and put his head in his hand.

"To spare us any more of that, is this what you're looking for?" A hand holding Tank's phone reached out to him from the backseat.

Instinctively, Tank drove his right elbow back in the direction of the voice. But the top of his arm hit the headrest before the elbow could find its mark, and when Tank swung around to carry the fight on into the backseat he faced a nine-millimeter pistol pointed at the middle of his forehead.

Tank froze, and stared into the eyes of his sister's killer.

"You do know that I have absolutely no compunction about pulling this trigger. Though I must admit I'm not looking forward to the pain to my eardrums that comes with doing so in such a confined space. But, of course, you'll never get to feel that pain."

"Are you going to kill me like you did my sister?"

"If you make me."

"I'll pay you the money we were going to pay the three others."

"If you mean the two I killed and one who ran away, I don't think that could possibly be enough to cover all the trouble you've caused."

"Give me the phone to call my father. He'll make it worth your while."

Kharon nodded. "You know, you just might be right about that."

"Good, give me the phone." Tank reached out his hand.

"No, no, no. I think this is the sort of discussion we must have face-to-face."

"My father's not anywhere around here."

"So start driving."

"I don't know where he is. I need to call him to find out. Give me the phone."

Kharon smiled. "If that's the case, I suggest you pick up where you left off in the monastery."

"What do you mean?"

"Praying, but in these prayers, ask for guidance on finding your way to your father here on earth, because if he isn't where you're taking me...." Kharon shrugged. "I'm sure that with all the time you recently spent in a monastery praying to your Lord in heaven, there's no need for me to finish my thought."

Kharon slid over on the backseat to just behind the driver seat. "I've always wondered what it would be like to be chauffeured around in one of these."

Tank didn't move, just kept staring at the barrel of the gun in Kharon's hand.

Kharon leaned forward and pressed the gun barrel to Tank's temple with his right hand. With his left hand he slid an ear plug into his own left ear, put his left forefinger into his right ear, and said, "Drive or die. Five seconds to decide…four…three…"

Chapter Twenty-eight

He dreamed of flowers, streams, and hillside walks with his father. Of his sister tagging along far enough behind to slow them down continually with running descriptions of every plant and bug along the way. Of his mother smiling at their five-year-old unofficial tour guide in golden braids and her impatient, seven-year-old brother pressing his sister to hurry on to wherever their hike might take them. One year later, the father was gone. No more walks, no more smiles from Mother, no more chattering sister. *Poof.* In an instant, all gone.

He tried to drive his dream to a different place. One where the little boy and little girl continued on together in happiness. He saw his son but no little girl yet among the flowers, though he could hear the faint buzz of the bees. The children best be careful of their stings. The buzzing wouldn't end. He charged forward, waving them away, protecting the children, chasing—

"*Andreas!* Wake up, you're swatting at me."

"What? Huh?" Andreas sat up in bed and looked at Lila. In the light from the clock on her nightstand he saw his wife clutching a pillow in front of her. "I was what?"

"Waving, pushing something away."

"Sorry about that. My dream was so real." He shook his head, blinking away the remnants of the dream-turned-nightmare. "I could hear the bees buzzing around our children."

"*Our* children? Any vision of the new one's gender?"

"As a matter of fact I saw a—"

BUZZ, BUZZ, BUZZ.

"There it goes again. It's my phone. I had it on vibrate." He looked at the clock. "It's five in the morning."

"Middle of the night telephone calls are starting to become a habit around here."

"Tell me about it." He swung off the bed and picked up his mobile phone from his nightstand. "It's Spiros. I'll take it in the other room."

"Don't you dare. Since you batted me awake I want to hear the good stuff firsthand. Turn up the volume so I can hear what he says."

Andreas smiled, sat on the edge of the bed, and pressed TALK. "Hi, Spiros. Sorry I missed you before, but my phone was on vib—"

"There've been two murders in Hosios Loukas Monastery outside of Arachova."

Andreas felt a chill run down his spine. "Of monks?" He crossed himself as he said the words.

Lila sat up in bed and turned on the light.

"No, thank God. Two men dressed as combat soldiers. No ID on them yet."

"What the hell were they doing in a monastery?"

"Precisely what I asked the local police chief when he called me."

"What did he have to say?"

"No idea, but I think we might."

Andreas detected a tone of relief in Spiros' voice. "What are you saying?"

"The police chief spoke with the abbot. I understand the abbot's quite a character. Highly distinguished military career until he decided he preferred saving souls to dispatching them. Anyway, he told the police chief they'd had a guest staying in the monastery who might be able to answer those questions for him."

"The guest being?"

"Tank."

"So that's where he's been hiding."

"Yep."

"Have the police spoken to him yet?"

"He's not there," said Spiros. "The abbot told Tank to leave and threw him out in the middle of the night."

"Why'd he do that? He should have held him until the police got there."

"That's what the police chief told him. The abbot replied that they're monks not cops, and besides, the police shouldn't have any trouble finding him, since no other monastery will likely take him in after word of this gets around. Those were the abbot's words."

"Sounds like he wanted Tank out of there before the monastery's publicity nightmare got fully underway."

"I see you're getting the hang of this political game. Tying Tank's name into this would turn the monastery into the center ring attraction of a major media circus."

"It's still going to be hard to avoid that, if Tank was the target."

"I don't think he was."

"Why's that?" said Andreas.

"The abbot said there was an explosion, likely some sort of grenade, and right after that some monks came across a man in the middle of the mess, shaking like a leaf. He said he was a pilgrim looking for a place to stay for the night and had been awakened by the explosion. In the confusion after finding the bodies he slipped away. The police found remains of a grenade on a path just beyond where the monks found the bodies and the pilgrim. The path led up to the gate where some of the monks heard a motorcycle drive off less than a minute after the explosion."

"The pilgrim could be our boy Kharon," said Andreas.

"Especially since the two dead weren't carrying grenades and each died from a bullet to the head."

"Sounds like a Tank family setup to take out Kharon that went very wrong for someone. Make that two someones."

"Yeah, ain't that a shame," said Spiros.

"We ought to get a photo of Kharon up there for the local police to show the monks."

"Not sure that will help much. The local chief told me it was so dark and the monks so rattled they've already given him three very different descriptions of the same guy."

"Damn." Andreas shook his head. "I hate to say this, but don't you think we should warn Tank's father?"

"You just said it sounded like an ambush for Kharon set up by Tank's family. Don't you think the father will know by now what happened?"

"I'd like to think his son would have told him, but that's not the point. The man's life's in danger and, as big an asshole as he is, we're cops and have a duty to warn him. It's what separates us from the bad guys."

"Sometimes I can't figure you out, Andreas. Okay, I'll call him right after breakfast. It's not the sort of conversation I can have on an empty stomach."

"Thanks for the update."

"You're welcome and…ah…thanks for counseling me to hang in there. Good night, and apologies to Lila for waking her up."

"It's okay," said Lila from her side of the bed.

Andreas shot her a glance as she covered her mouth with her hands.

"What was that?"

"Lila, she talks in her sleep."

Lila flashed him the thumbs-up sign.

"And snores."

The thumbs-up morphed into a middle finger.

"I never would have thought that. Good night."

"Night."

"Kaldis, you are in such trouble," said Lila.

Andreas rolled over and slid his hand up under the covers to rest on her bare breasts. "Not as much as I plan to be in momentarily."

◇◇◇

At this time of the morning, the drive from the monastery to Tank's father's home in Chalkidiki should take a little over six hours. That would get them there around breakfast time, Kharon thought, unless Tank tried something foolish.

He studied Tank's eyes in the rearview mirror. They darted left and right just as you'd expect from a man desperate for a way to escape.

"Please don't try ramming the car into a tree or something silly like that. Your air bag won't save you. That only works in movies. You'll be dead from a bullet before you hit the tree. Besides, I'm snug in the backseat of this behemoth SUV wearing a seat belt and watching every move you make." Kharon grinned as Tank bit at his lip.

"How much will it take for you to let us go?"

"Don't worry, we'll talk about all that with Teacher."

"She's meeting us there?"

"Like I said, we'll talk about it."

Kharon had called Teacher shortly after he'd fled the monastery. She wasn't surprised about the assassins and congratulated him on his resourcefulness. He told her he'd found Tank's Range Rover in the parking lot and about his idea of reuniting Tank with his father. Teacher liked it. She told him to text her once he'd collected Tank and they were on their way to Chalkidiki.

Kharon almost asked her if she saw his night spent under the stars as some sort of test or trial, but he decided it was probably best not to let her know he'd picked up on some of her ways. Instead he added it to the list of things he'd decided to keep from her.

Like his conversation with Jacobi.

A high anxiety Jacobi had called him yesterday afternoon to say that a cop had pressed him for information on a hit put out "on someone in Greece close enough to Teacher to get her attention." From what the cop said, Jacobi worried Kharon might be the target.

When Kharon asked why the cop came to Jacobi, he said, "I asked the cop the same question and he told me to go fuck myself. I have no idea how he knew, but he did."

Kharon knew. The cops probably picked something up off a phone tap or microphone planted in Jacobi's place. Telling Jacobi to be careful about running off at the mouth was like telling the sun to stop rising. Who knew what the cops had found out about Teacher from Jacobi? *Or about me.*

That's when Kharon decided to check the BMW and found the tracking device. The question was, who put it there? And when? Based on his conversation with Jacobi, police were the likely suspects. But he couldn't rule out Tank and his father. Whoever it was, he didn't want them to know when he moved again. So he left the device in a rosemary bush near where he parked the bike by his home in Delphi.

Kharon hadn't mentioned anything about his conversation with Jacobi to Teacher. Not out of concern that if she knew he'd been warned she might think him less of a magician in neutralizing his assassins, but he had a nagging suspicion that if she thought Jacobi had talked to cops, she'd want his friend dead. Maybe even order Kharon to do it as another of her tests.

Kharon knew that would be the sensible thing to do. Jacobi wasn't the sharpest blade in the drawer and that, coupled with his loose lips, made him a risk. Then again, if Jacobi hadn't done something to attract the cops, they wouldn't have known to come to Jacobi with information that helped save Kharon's life. As Kharon scored it, one canceled out the other. Teacher wouldn't see it that way. She always favored elimination.

Besides, Jacobi was the closest thing Kharon had to anything resembling family, and when it came down to family, one must learn to live with their faults.

Perhaps my moral center isn't yet lost?

He watched Tank's frantic face looking back at him in the mirror.

For sure he hopes not.

Kharon kept his gun aimed at Tank's head with his right hand as he pecked out a message with his left on his phone, ON OUR WAY, and hit send.

Thirty seconds later came the reply announced by a ping: GOOD. IT IS TIME TO SEND THE OTHER MESSAGE. And so he did.

◇◇◇

Tank's father loved his early mornings in Sithonia. The birds sounded more alive, the sky a bit rosier, the sea air fresher. His home didn't offer a good view of the sun rising out of the Aegean, gilding sapphire blue in gold, but that never mattered much to him for he thought of early mornings as more like nine o'clock anyway.

And this was a fine morning. Word from his son had put his mind at ease after a most restless night.

Now he sat on his bougainvillea-covered veranda, staring out above the pines and olive trees across the bright blue bay toward Mount Athos fifteen miles away. Artists and architects had struggled for centuries to capture the essence of the Church's spiritual power in temporal expression. For him, only Mount Athos achieved that goal, perhaps because it represented God's own handiwork on earth, his gift to the Virgin Mary as her Garden of the Mother of God, a place forbidden to any other woman. Or so went the legend.

Living so close to a place of such reverential holy power, Tank's father thought of himself as the first to touch the same sea as edged upon that holy land, the first to breathe the same air as passed over from that blessed place, the first to see eagles, kestrels and gulls stray across the sky from their holy mountain roosts, the first to hear what sounds might carry from so far across the sea. He built a little church down by the edge of the water in honor of the Virgin Mary to honor the spiritual markings of such holy power on earth.

To his way of thinking, all of that could not but help cleanse him of his sins, bring redemption to his soul. A lot of his neighbors along the shoreline must have thought the same way if the prices they'd paid for the opportunity of such proximity were any measure.

The father was on his second cup of coffee when the phone rang inside the house. He yelled for his assistant to answer it.

"It's the minister of public order calling, sir."

The malaka *must be calling to beg me to let up on him.* "Tell him to go fuck himself."

"Sir?"

"You heard what I said, tell him precisely that." He smiled and went back to staring at Mount Athos.

"Sir."

The father jumped slightly in his chair. He hadn't noticed his assistant coming up behind him. "What is it?"

"The minister told me to give you a message."

"What? Did he threaten me? Did he beg for me to call him back?"

"No, as a matter of fact he laughed."

"Laughed?"

"Yes, and said to please tell you, 'Don't say I didn't try to warn you.'"

"Warn me? Warn me of what?"

"He didn't say."

He waved his assistant away and went back to sipping his coffee.

A few minutes later he heard the sound of a helicopter coming in from the east. For a country supposedly in crisis, an awful lot of people had their own helicopters. This one was a two-engine job, though. Very fast, very expensive. It hovered out to sea about two hundred yards from shore, then made toward his Russian neighbor's helicopter pad. *Just what we need, more Russian visitors.*

He looked at his watch. It was after ten. His son should be here any minute. Things hadn't gone quite as planned, what with two of the assassins getting killed and the third fleeing from the police, but their goal was achieved. The killer of his daughter had been eliminated and Teacher had agreed to accept twenty million euros as compensation.

He'd tried calling Tank for more details but he didn't answer. At least his son had the presence of mind to send that text message telling him what happened and that he was on his way here.

He's finally showing indications of not being a total fuckup.

His mobile rang. It was the front gate. "Why aren't you using the walkie-talkie?"

"Sorry, sir, your son is here and told me to call you at this number. He has guests with him."

"Guests."

"Yes, a lady and three men."

"Who are they?"

"They said you know them."

"Put my son on the phone."

Pause.

"Father."

"What the hell is going on?"

"Sorry, but he was going to kill me."

The father's heart skipped three beats. "He?"

"Yes, the one sent by Teacher to meet me at the monastery."

"You fool! You—"

Another voice came on the phone. A female voice. "I have no more time for games. Tell your man to open the gate and let us in or that helicopter you saw hovering above your property will give you a demonstration of its military capabilities."

"You don't frighten me."

"Watch me."

He heard the crackle of a communicator through the phone and her voice saying something in an Eastern European language. Next he heard the roar of twin turboshaft engines coming to life and saw a modified Russian-made Mi-24 attack helicopter swing around to within thirty yards of his property, camouflage on either side of the cockpit removed to reveal twin Yakushev-Borzov 12.7x108mm caliber four-barrel Gatling guns capable of delivering up to 1,470 rounds each—aimed straight at him.

"Okay!" he cried into the phone. "Okay, okay! Let them in!"

"Thank you, but could you please say that slightly louder and more clearly so that your man on the gate understands you?" said the woman.

"*LET THEM IN,*" he screamed.

Chapter Twenty-nine

The road from the gate passed through a hundred yards of pine trees and offered random glimpses of the sea. But Kharon's eyes stayed focused on the men in the woods. He'd counted six, plus the one now tied up at the gate, and if his last visit served as any indication, at least two more in the house. "Figure on eight armed men, plus another six cooks, housekeepers, gardeners, and assistants."

The two men next to him in the backseat of Tank's Range Rover nodded.

"Your father must be a very nervous man," said Teacher from her seat up front next to Tank.

Tank didn't speak, just kept glancing in the rearview mirror at the two men behind him wearing ballistic vests, carrying Russian-made A-91 assault rifles, and wired for sound with combat-style headsets.

"I guess you're a bit anxious too, *partner*. How are your grand political plans holding up? You remember them, don't you? All the big ones you told me about. The ones you said justified doing business your way instead of mine?" Teacher looked out the side window next to her. "You do remember what I told you back then?"

Silence.

"Don't you?"

Kharon nudged the back of Tank's head with a pistol barrel.

"No, I don't."

Teacher shook her head without looking at him. "What can I say? You're incorrigible. You'll never learn. I'll never be able to work with you."

She turned to face Tank and leaned in close to his right ear. "I said, 'My bottom line is simple: I don't care what sort of little masturbation games you want to play with yourself, but if you ever even *think* of screwing with me or our arrangement again, I promise to cut your balls off. Literally. Slowly. Painfully.'"

Tank's body trembled and he bit fiercely at his lower lip.

Teacher patted Tank's shoulder. "It's okay if you want to cry, Tank. It beats shitting your pants." She took her hand away. "That will come later."

By the time Tank reached the front of his father's house, he looked less like the proverbial deer caught in the headlights and more like one laid out in the taillights of the truck that had pancaked it.

"Nice house your father has here. I particularly like how the terra cotta roof tiles, and all those marble inlays around the windows add a nice touch to the white stucco. Sure hope this isn't the last time you guys get to see it."

Tank stopped the car. Teacher reached across and took the keys. "Just in case you think of trying to run off again."

Teacher's two men in headsets jumped out of the backseat and opened her door while the chopper hovered overhead. Tank's father stood by the front door of his house.

Teacher stepped out carrying a black crocodile Hermes Birkin bag. She pulled a headset out of the bag and fitted it on her head as she walked over to the father. Kharon remained inside the car with Tank.

"Thank you for inviting us to your lovely home," she said, not extending her hand.

The father stood with one eye twitching uncontrollably and both fists tightly clenched. Still, his voice stayed flat. "Welcome. Please, let us go inside where we can talk in peace and quiet." He turned toward the front door.

"No, thank you," Teacher said. "I prefer to conduct our meeting here, where my friends above can keep an eye on me," she nodded up to the sky, "even from a distance of, say, three hundred yards."

Instantly the helicopter moved up and away to what seemed three hundred yards.

She smiled. "Don't you just love it when you have employees who do precisely what you want the moment you ask them to do it?"

She reached out and touched the father's arm. "Oh, forgive me. I forgot. You're not used to working with those sorts of people."

The father forced a smile. He motioned for Teacher to follow him around the side of the house and waved for his men in the woods to do the same.

"Yes, that's a very good idea," she said. "Let's have all your armed men and all my armed men together in one spot. That way they can keep an eye on each other and not become nervous while we talk."

The father's face tightened. That obviously had not been his intention, but he nodded. "Yes." He yelled to his men, "Stay here all together in front."

"And the ones inside?" she said.

He exhaled and yelled, "And get the ones in the house out here with you."

Teacher nodded to the two men with her, and they moved over to stand by the father's men.

Teacher waved to Kharon.

"Okay, Tank, it's time to move," said Kharon opening the rear door behind Tank still sitting in the driver seat.

"That guy stays here with the rest of your men," said the father.

Teacher gestured no. "Not possible. He's the equivalent of your son for purposes of these negotiations. You need Tank, I need him."

It was hard to hear the father through his clenched teeth. "Okay, as long as he doesn't have a gun."

"Of course," smiled Teacher. "Leave your gun in the car," she told Kharon. "I'm sure you won't need it." She nodded toward the rear of the house. "After you."

Kharon left his gun and backpack in the car, pushing Tank ahead of him as the father led them along a marble walkway lined with palm and fig trees to the patio abutting the infinity pool. He pointed to the table where he'd been sitting. "Is that acceptable?"

Teacher nodded. "Yes, and no need to offer us any refreshment. We won't be staying long."

The father stood while Teacher, Tank, and Kharon chose where to sit. They left him the chair in front of his coffee cup and mobile phone. Tank sat to his father's right, and Kharon sat between Tank and Teacher.

The father sat, picked up the cup, and took a sip of what now had to be cold coffee. "Since there's no reason for me to make on as if I don't know why you're here, I guess you should begin."

Teacher nodded. "I admire your candor. It doesn't forgive your treachery, but I admire it nonetheless."

The father nodded and put down the cup.

"So, permit me to tell you exactly what I want. I'm prepared to forgive the past for a price, a very steep price. Consider it a 'buyout' of all my past, present, and future interests in the wine and spirits industry in Greece, one that will allow you to live and carry on your business here in peace."

"I created the business, not you," said Tank.

The father wheeled around and slapped Tank hard across the face. "Shut up and don't open your mouth again unless I tell you to."

Teacher nodded. "An appropriate reaction and sage advice. Too bad it took you until now to render it."

"Just tell me what you want." The father's anger at his son still tinged his voice.

"Two hundred million euros."

"You must be crazy?"

"Crazy, no. Angry, yes."

"I don't have that sort of money."

Teacher shook her head. "Tsk, tsk. Now you're shaking my confidence in you. I'm starting to see the son in the father."

The father banged his hands on the table. "Look, if you want to make a deal, I'll make a deal. But I can't make a deal with money I don't have. Period. End of story."

"Not quite 'end of story.'" Teacher reached into her bag, pulled out a sheet of paper, and slid it across the table. "On this you'll see a list of your Swiss and Luxembourg Bank accounts containing more than the amount I've just asked for. Additionally you'll find instructions for wiring the requested sums into the indicated accounts using that phone in front of you."

The father's face turned bright red. Veins popped out in his neck.

"Don't have a stroke over this. It would be a shame to pay my price, then die. That would defeat the purpose, no?"

Tank's father clenched his fists and rubbed them on his thighs.

"After all," she said, "it's not as if I'm asking you to turn over money you earned. It's all tax money stolen from the Greek people."

"Fuck you."

Teacher sighed. "God, so many have tried."

He pounded his fists on the table and shouted, "I don't care what you do to this poor excuse for a son. He's been nothing but a fuckup his entire life, living off my name and reputation and protection, never standing on his own two feet. And now he's cost my daughter her life to protect his own. I'm through with him. Do with him as you wish." The father sat back in his chair and threw up his hands.

"You can't mean that," said Tank, reaching across the table and grabbing his father's forearm.

The father sat grim-faced in his chair, staring off toward Mount Athos.

Teacher clapped. "Nice performance. I'm sure it will lead to some wonderful family reunion moments, assuming of course there's any family left to get together."

The father shifted his stare to Teacher. "What are you saying?"

"You raised him, you tolerated his bad behavior, you enabled him. But I'm not blaming you for how he's turned out." She leaned forward. "Then you decided to protect him, to go after my people. *To go after me.* You chose to be your son's savior and failed. That's why you're responsible for his obligations to me. All two hundred million of them."

He glared. "You think killing me will get you your money?"

Teacher turned to Kharon. "Do you still have the photos?"

"Not with me."

"No matter, I'm certain he remembers what his grandchildren and children—make that *surviving* children, sorry for your loss—look like." Teacher turned to Kharon. "Why don't you explain to the gentleman the alternative to not making this deal on these terms, on this day, at this moment."

"It's simple," said Kharon. "Everyone dies. In random order. I shuffle the photographs and whomever's photo come up dies. The next shuffle determines the next one to die, and so on. Until only one remains alive." He pointed his finger at the father. "You."

"You're a sick bastard." Spittle came out of his mouth as he trembled with rage. "You're both sick bastards."

Kharon shrugged. "And if you're not permanently crippled in mind from witnessing all your progeny disappear off the face of the earth, one funeral at a time, once the last of your seed dies, you'll suffer a beating so crippling to your body that you'll never again know a moment of joy." Kharon reached over and tapped on the father's phone. "Or."

The father stared at the phone.

Teacher said, "To quote your son's eloquent speech at your daughter's memorial service, 'Give us what we want or watch your family die.'"

Tank's father shut his eyes and drew in a breath. "Damn you. *Damn you all to hell!*" he yelled. He opened his eyes and glared at his son. "Most of all, *you.*"

"I understand what a great disappointment your son has been to you. And, frankly, from the way you've raised him I can only see him continuing on unchecked in all aspects of his life. So, if that curse is your heartfelt wish and desire…" Teacher cocked her head toward the father.

He jutted out his chin and stared straight ahead. Teacher nodded to Kharon.

Kharon did not move, but sat with his hands in his lap until the father's eyes met his. Then he smiled, brought his right hand up from his lap, and pointed toward Mount Athos.

"What are you pointing at?" said Tank, leaning in to look.

"Ask your father," said Kharon. As Tank turned to face his father, Kharon drew a stiletto up from his lap in his left hand and sliced through Tank's carotid artery, straight across his throat. Tank gurgled as he grabbed at his neck and tumbled forward toward his father, spinning wildly and spewing blood over them both before falling on the ground at his father's feet, dead.

The father's mouth fell open in a scream, but not a sound escaped. His eyes fixed on the blood on his clothes. He lifted his hands and stared at the blood there too.

Teacher sighed. "I trust you now understand how very serious we are."

The father looked at the faces around the table, then down at his son's body. He reached out as if to touch it, but paused. He sat up, stared off at Mount Athos for a moment, and picked up his phone.

◇◇◇

Kharon and Teacher spoke through headphones as the helicopter sped southwest toward Delphi.

"You did well, Kharon. Very well, indeed."

"Thank you."

"I have some good news for you."

Kharon turned to face her, eyebrows raised.

"The olive oil processing facility and owners of the other groves you wanted agreed to sell. Everything you asked for is now yours."

"That isn't good news, it's great news."

"And there's more."

"More?"

"Yes. A tiny part of those wire transfers Tank's father put through went into your Swiss bank account."

"I don't have a Swiss bank account."

"You do now. Funded by a one percent finder's fee."

Kharon's jaw dropped slightly. "That's two million euros."

"Yes, I know."

"But why?"

"Because you earned it."

Kharon shook his head. "You kept your word to me on the olives. That was our deal, and that's all I want."

"Consider it my way of thanking you for doing what you did without questioning my motives, even though you had to know I wasn't telling you everything."

Kharon didn't acknowledge her comment.

She smiled. "Even now I see you're keeping your thoughts to yourself. I like that. It shows caution, not disloyalty."

She paused. "Okay, there's another reason. A selfish one. I don't want you thinking I don't appreciate your efforts. It might lead you to look elsewhere. Not today, not tomorrow, but someday. I'll also try not to keep things from you in the future. It's a pesky habit left over from too many years among too many betrayers."

"I'd appreciate it if you just told me the sort of things that might get me killed," said Kharon.

Teacher laughed. "I'll try."

She paused. "In fact, I'll start now. With those two you killed in the monastery."

"What about them?"

"They were brothers."

"Too bad."

"And the one who escaped was the oldest brother."

"Yes?"

"I just thought you should know."

"Thanks."

"Aren't you worried?"

"Not really. They went down in action trying to take me out. I don't think the survivor's going to blame me for fighting back."

"Interesting thinking."

"With professionals, the time to worry is if you're the one who gave an order they didn't want to carry out and it got somebody killed."

"You mean like Tank's father?"

Kharon shrugged. "If he made the brothers do something that got two of them killed, I'd say he damn well better worry."

Teacher nodded. "Thanks, I'll try keeping that advice in mind."

"What advice?"

"Only tell you what to do, not how to do it."

Make a pledge and mischief is nigh came to mind, straight off the carvings on the Temple of Apollo, but Kharon smiled. "Works for me."

The helicopter swung around Mount Parnassos, headed south toward the Phaedriades cliffs above sacred Delphi, the Pleistos River Valley, and the Gulf of Corinth beyond. Teacher pointed ahead. "You're almost home."

Kharon nodded.

Teacher smiled. "Just one more thing."

"What's that?"

"A loose end."

"Loose end?"

"Yes, your friend, Jacobi."

Kharon's heart jumped. "What about him?"

"He knows too much about us."

"He's like my only family. He would never say a word."

Teacher shrugged. "We can't take the risk. Our future together has too much at stake. You know that even without my telling you."

Kharon stared out the window at the olive groves below.

"But I want to make this easy on him," she said.

Kharon did not look at her.

"So, you should do it."

He whipped his head around to face her. "Me?"

She nodded. "Yes, if you do it, you'll be merciful. If I have to send someone else, they may not be as kind. You owe him at least that."

Kharon picked up his backpack and clutched it tightly to his chest.

"You do it, or someone else does. It is his fate."

Kharon squeezed the backpack harder and turned away from Teacher to face out the window.

"But you don't have to decide now. I'll give you until noon tomorrow to choose."

A minute later the helicopter touched down, Kharon was out the door, and the chopper was back in the air.

He'd nodded a hasty good-bye and she'd nodded back.

He'll come around, she thought. *He only has two choices. It will be instructive to see which one he picks.*

She looked across to where Kharon had been sitting and said to herself, "Don't worry, you now have me as your family." That's when she noticed he'd left his backpack on the floor.

She wondered what might be in it. Secrets perhaps? She loved secrets. Especially another's deepest, darkest ones.

She leaned across the seat and lifted the backpack onto her lap. She studied it for a moment before opening it. As she lifted the flap she heard a pop, looked inside, drew a quick breath, and smiled. *So, you found a third way.*

Teacher shut her eyes and thought of her children.

◇◇◇

Kharon stood among the olives—now his olives—and watched the helicopter head north across the valley. No doubt she was right about Jacobi, but this wasn't about Jacobi. She wanted Jacobi to die to prove a point: that Kharon was like her, no longer caring who he slaughtered. It was a test he could not pass. If he killed Jacobi, a man as close as a brother, she'd see Kharon to be just as capable of betraying her. If he refused, she'd see him as disloyal. Either way, one day she'd likely see him dead.

Despite what Teacher had said about Jacobi's fate, she no more believed in trusting to the Fates than did the Delphic Oracle. Each demanded absolute obedience to their pronouncements.

Kharon believed in leaving decisions on who should live and who should die to the Fates. Perhaps that's why he saw another choice. A risky one, for if Teacher lived she'd know it was Kharon who'd acted, and he'd be dead by sundown.

He'd clutched his backpack to his chest as he'd turned away from her in the helicopter, reached inside, removed the safety pin from one of the frag grenades he'd brought with him to his battle at Hosios Loukas, and wedged the safety lever into a loop on the inside of the backflap. If someone lifted the flap, the lever would pop off, and—the Fates willing—seconds later it would be over.

But if she never noticed the bag on the floor in front of his seat, or wasn't curious enough to open it, or....

He saw the flash in the sky above Delphi before he heard the explosion.

Chapter Thirty

"So, any news?" said Tassos dropping onto Andreas' couch. He nodded a greeting at Kouros, who sat on one of Andreas' office chairs.

"About what?" asked Andreas, looking at his watch.

"Anything. I'm just looking for someone to talk to until my girlfriend's boss lets her take off early from work. We've tickets for the Spanoudakis concert tonight at the Herodeon."

"It doesn't start until nine and besides, we both know you're going to use your badge to get good seats."

"What's the matter, you don't want me to feed her first?"

Andreas shot him an open hand.

Tassos dismissed it with a wave. "So, like I said, any news?"

"Tank's disappeared. No one's seen or heard from him since the abbot booted him out of Hosios Loukas."

"Sounds like it could be terminal."

Andreas shrugged. "Only time will tell. We thought he might have been in a helicopter that exploded over Delphi. It sounded like something Teacher would have planned for him, and the timing was right. Plus, Delphi is her boy Kharon's backyard. But our foreign ministry said it was a hush-hush diplomatic mission out of the Ukraine and no one but Ukrainian diplomats were allowed to see the wreckage. All they told us were that no Greeks were among the dead."

"And the old man?"

"Not a peep from him either. Word is he's holed up in his place in Chalkidiki."

"Is he still gunning for Spiros?"

"Doesn't look to be. Seems more like he's hiding out."

"What about the business?"

Kouros answered, "If you mean Tank's counterfeit booze business, all kinds of *bomba* crap is streaming in through places like Bulgaria, Albania, Turkey, and Cyprus trying to jump in on our tourist season action."

"You know what they say about nature abhorring a vacuum," said Tassos.

"Especially when it comes to champagne in the summertime," said Kouros.

Andreas looked at his watch.

Tassos nodded. "Amazing how many jerk-offs with more money than taste or brains get their kicks out of spraying the most expensive champagne they can afford on the bustiest women they can find."

"For sure," said Kouros. "Just slap a high-priced phony label on anything that will fizz and you can sell two euros' worth of packaging and bubbles for a hundred to a thousand times its cost."

Tassos shrugged. "I guess that works so long as they don't taste the stuff, just spray it."

Andreas waved a hand in the air. "How about we look at the bright side, guys? We've closed down a hell of a lot of illegal manufacturing and distribution operations in Greece. Sure, the customers are still out there, but we're talking about cheap booze. There will always be a market for that. For what it's worth, I've passed on to Europol what we learned about Teacher's operations, along with a request that they do something about shutting down alcohol smugglers coming into Greece through EU member states."

"And the chances of that happening?" said Kouros.

Andreas shrugged. "From past experience, I'd say it depends on whether big-time legitimate wine and liquor companies who want to shut them down have more juice with enforcement authorities than the bad guys."

"Good luck to them," said Tassos. "Hasn't worked very well for the designer watch, hand bag, and sunglasses crowd."

Andreas looked at his watch.

"That's the third time you've looked at your watch since I came in here," said Tassos. "What has you so antsy? It can't be any of this bullshit. Let the victims and the folks who make money off the real stuff fight it out."

Andreas pointed his right forefinger at Tassos. "Aha, the typical government response to just about any time-consuming problem confronting our country today, ignore it, pass it on, anything but address it. With Tank out of business, if not dead, his father muzzled, and no one willing to point a finger at Kharon for so much as a speeding ticket, Teacher seems to have faded away, and our government is perfectly content to leave it at that."

Andreas slammed the palm of his right hand on top of his desk. "I'd like to think we could do better."

Now Tassos pointed his finger at Andreas. "I don't give a damn about our government's mess over *bomba* or how those fools in the ministry underestimate Teacher. I'm talking about you. Just tell me what has your balls in a sling?"

Andreas drew in and let out a deep breath. "Lila's at the doctor."

"Is everything okay?"

"It's just a regular checkup."

"Then why are you so anxious?" said Tassos.

"I'm not anxious, just...concerned."

"Someday you'll explain the difference to me."

"When I feel this way, it's concerned. If anyone else does, it's anxious."

Kouros laughed.

"Thank you for clearing that up," said Tassos.

"Any time," nodded Andreas.

Andreas' phone rang on his direct line. He snatched it up immediately. "Hi, honey, is everything all right?"

"Honey?"

"Whoops, sorry, Spiros, I thought it was Lila." Andreas tried to ignore the silent hoots and hollers of Tassos and Kouros.

"That's a relief," said his boss.

"Anything new on Tank?"

"Nothing. That's not why I'm calling. There's something I need to talk to you about."

"Sure, what's up?"

"It's a conversation to have with you face-to-face."

Andreas cleared his throat. "Okay, when's good for you?"

"How about in an hour, in my office?"

"Fine, see you then."

"Bye, honey."

Andreas stared at the phone.

"What's wrong?" asked Kouros.

"Nothing…I think Spiros just made a joke."

"Miracle of miracles."

"It also sounds like he wants to talk to me about his health."

"I hope it's not bad news," said Tassos.

Andreas rubbed at his forehead with his left hand. "Me, too." He looked at his watch.

◇◇◇

Andreas had just pulled into the Public Order Ministry's parking area off Kanellopoulou Street when his phone rang.

"Hi, my love, what did the doctor have to say?"

"Everything's fine. We're on the road to having a very healthy baby something-or-other. Still too soon to tell more than that."

Andreas crossed himself as he muttered, "Puh, puh, puh."

"I thought you weren't superstitious?"

"I figured it couldn't hurt to be careful."

Lila laughed. "Since I'm out and about, what do you think of catching an early dinner somewhere?"

"Like when?"

"Like now."

"I wish I could, but I'm just about to go inside the ministry to meet with Spiros. He called an hour ago to say he wanted to talk to me face-to-face about something that sounds serious."

"Ouch, like his health?"

"My thought exactly."

"Just be supportive and listen. Take all the time you need. Don't worry about dinner."

"I really don't want to be doing this."

"But he does, and that's what matters. Besides, it's the right thing."

Andreas blew through his lips. "I don't know anything about this sort of grief counseling."

"Of course you do. Just go with your instincts and you'll do fine. You can achieve anything you set your mind to."

"You're a pretty good cheering section."

"Of course I am. I'm your biggest fan."

Andreas smiled. "Love you. *Filakia.*"

"Kisses to you, too, my hero."

Andreas' smile stayed with him until he stepped inside the ministry building. He'd been to the ministry hundreds of times before, but he never felt as he did at that moment. Melancholy might have been the word. His thoughts drifted from his day-to-day hassles and battles with its bureaucracy. The influence peddlers, the hustlers, the corrupters, the incessant politics.

The adage, "a fish rots from the head," came to mind. It was up to the minister to set an example, and though Spiros wasn't corrupt, nor had he ever been diligent or confident enough to take on the interests that were. He'd never been a cop, only a bureaucrat, bouncing around between ministries until he'd ended up here.

No matter, all that's in the past. *Poor bastard.*

The moment Andreas walked into the minister's anteroom, the secretary waved him straight though into his office.

"The minister is waiting for you."

Spiros stood in front of his desk between two chairs. He gestured at one of the chairs and sat in the other.

Of all the times Andreas had been in this office, this was the very first time Spiros hadn't taken a seat behind his desk.

Spiros nibbled at his bottom lip, and his skin looked as if he'd not seen the sun in a lifetime, but what Andreas noted most was that his once carefully dyed, jet black hair showed a full quarter-inch of gray roots. He looked like a man who no longer cared.

Andreas shifted in his chair and clasped his hands together on his lap.

Spiros sat staring at his portrait hanging behind his desk. "My wife had that done. Then insisted I hang it here rather than in the house. I think so she wouldn't be reminded of me."

Andreas looked down at his hands.

"We never had children. There are no photographs of us together, or even alone. Just ones of her with her family or friends."

Andreas kept looking down.

Spiros turned his head to face Andreas.

Andreas looked up.

"Do you know who's going to miss me when I'm gone? Who's going to know I even existed?"

Andreas prayed that was a rhetorical question.

"Not a soul. At least not a soul outside of this building."

Andreas didn't move.

"And I want the people in this building who do remember me to say I was someone who did his job in a way that mattered."

Andreas nodded as emphatically as he could.

"You saved my reputation. I don't want to know how you did it, but you got the media, Tank, and his father off my back."

"You're the one who gave us the time we needed by your political maneuvering with the prime minister," said Andreas.

"Only because you told me how to handle him. Listen, Andreas, this is not meant to be a mutual backslapping session." He smiled. "Or a love-in, *honey*."

He's really playing that one-liner for all it's worth.

"So there's no reason for us to speak other than honestly. I've been virtually AWOL here, leaving you to bring the ball up the field all on your own."

Andreas didn't move.

"I'd like to tell you I'm giving you a raise, but I can't. Perhaps you'll find your reward in my successor."

"Successor? You're resigning?"

Spiros nodded. "I've been thinking about it for weeks. I can't take the stress anymore. Physically or mentally. And things will only get worse. It makes no sense to go on kidding myself that I can do this job while I'm battling for my life."

"Of course it does," said Andreas.

Spiros gestured no. "It doesn't. Besides, perhaps it will give me time to find another way to live." He looked Andreas straight in the eye. "We're all going to die sooner or later." Spiros looked up at his portrait. "I've decided to move to a place I have near Tripoli, in my father's village." He looked back at Andreas. "I still have family there and thought it might be nice to spend time getting to know them better."

Andreas drew in and let out a breath. "As much as I hate to say it, I think you're right."

"Why do you 'hate to say it'?"

"Because you're the devil I know, and now I'll have to break in an entirely new *malaka* boss."

Spiros smiled. "That's about the nicest way you've ever described me."

Andreas grinned. "You caught me in a weak moment."

Spiros patted Andreas on the thigh. "I've already spoken to the prime minister. I told him that whoever he chooses must be someone who'll work well with you."

Andreas did a double take. "Wow, that's quite flattering. Thank you."

"He's agreed, and so I'm here to tell you who he's chosen to replace me."

By law it has to be a member of Parliament. A long list of potential assholes raced through Andreas mind.

"You."

"Yu? A non-Greek? Who the hell's Yu?"

Spiros laughed. "No, *YOU*," and he pointed at Andreas' chest.

"Now you're playing games with me. I'm not a member of Parliament, so I can't be a minister."

Spiros gestured no and smiled. "It's taken years, but I've finally proven you wrong. As a result of the financial crisis the law's been changed to allow professionals, not just politicians, to be appointed to run ministries. Granted it doesn't happen often, but it's the new law. Besides, your appointment is only until the upcoming elections, and with the leftists likely to win, who knows who will be in that seat then." He nodded toward his desk chair.

Andreas slid down in his chair and shook his head. "I can't do that. I wouldn't know where to begin."

"Of course you do. There's a laundry list of problems out there, and you know them at least as well as I do. Problems I ignored." He looked at his hands. "Because I didn't have the balls." Spiros looked up. "But I want to be remembered as the minister who had the mega-balls to bring you on as my successor."

"I think the word for how you'll be remembered in this ministry if you brought me on as your successor is despised."

"Then so be it."

"I've got to think about this."

"Sure. Take all the time you need. Just let me know by tomorrow at noon. The prime minister wants to make the announcement in time for the evening news."

Andreas rubbed his eyes with his fingertips and dropped his hands back into his lap. "I've got to speak to Lila."

Spiros shrugged. "If that's the only bridge to cross, then let me be the first to say, Minister Kaldis, welcome to your new digs."

"How can you possibly say that?"

"It's simple, Andreas. Lila is your biggest fan."

To receive a free catalog of Poisoned Pen Press titles, please provide your name, address, and email address in one of the following ways:

Phone: 1-800-421-3976
Facsimile: 1-480-949-1707
Email: info@poisonedpenpress.com
Website: www.poisonedpenpress.com

Poisoned Pen Press
6962 E. First Ave. Ste 103
Scottsdale, AZ 85251